THE TENTH PLAGUE

A NOVEL

Alan N. Levy

ISBN 978-1-7329139-2-9

Front cover illustration and book design by Fiona Jayde

Chickadee Prince Logo by Garrett Gilchrist

Visit us at www.ChickadeePrince. com

First Printing

"A white-knuckle thriller of sweaty paranoia…. In today's insane world, it's outlandishly and sadly feasible."
— Alon Preiss, author, *A Flash of Blue Sky*

ALAN N. LEVY

The Tenth Plague

Alan N. Levy was born and raised in Chicago. His degrees are in Engineering Physics, Mathematics, and Applied Statistics. He writes regularly on politics for *The Times of Israel* and *Audere Magazine*. He lives in Florida with his wife, Helene, and Max the Chihuahua.

THE TENTH PLAGUE

A Novel

Chickadee Prince Books
New York

This novel is dedicated to the

memory of Jeffrey A. Solomon

(June 24, 1943 to August 3, 2016)

No one could ever have a better friend

AND MOSES SAID

So said the Lord: At the dividing point of the night, I will go into the midst of Egypt, and every firstborn in the land of Egypt will die, from the firstborn of Pharaoh, who sits on his throne, to the firstborn of the slave woman who is behind the mill stones and every firstborn animal. And there will be a great cry throughout the entire land of Egypt, such as there never has been and such as there shall never be again. But to all the children of Israel, not one dog will whet its tongue against either man or beast, in order that you shall know that the Lord will separate between the Egyptians and the Israelites.

— Exodus 11:4-7

INTRODUCTION

"I know not with which weapons World War III will be fought, but World War IV will be fought with sticks and stones."

— Albert Einstein

In November of 1998, The *Sunday Times* in London reported that Israel was attempting to perfect a biological "Ethno-Bomb." In theory, this biological weapon could specifically target genetic traits present in those of Arab descent.

The article was immediately denounced as a hoax perpetuated by an Israeli science fiction writer. Microbiologists and geneticists throughout the world were skeptical about the feasibility of designing a weapon of this type, and the article was dismissed as rubbish.

It was not a hoax.

CHAPTER 1

January 1, 2028 ... Tabriz, Iran, 0100 Hours

They departed from the Iranian's modest home near Tabriz shortly after 1:00 AM.

The highway was virtually deserted, and the Israeli felt a sense of relief until their Zamyad Z24 pickup truck stalled and died just north of Avaciq, sixty miles short of their planned destination. It had been sputtering and lurching for the past hour, and finally the rusty Nissan, a relic by any standards, succumbed to old age and exhaustion.

It was 5:22 AM.

To the east, the morning sky was a subtle pink.

The two men exited the truck.

"I told you it was a bad idea to take my truck on this journey! We should have stolen a car. What the hell are we going to do now?" yelled the Iranian.

The Israeli shrugged off the remarks. He removed a small screw driver and a pen light from his pouch and bent down behind the truck.

"What are you doing?" Another question from the Iranian.

"I'm removing the license plates, and then I'll pry off the VIN plates from the dash and driver's door. That should delay them, for a while, from realizing this truck belongs to you."

"And then what?"

"We walk."

"Are you out of your mind?"

The Israeli stood slowly. He stretched his back and grimaced. Sleeping on a wooden floor for the past three nights hadn't agreed with the screws and rods in his back, and he replied harshly. He jabbed a finger to the west.

"Turkey is about four miles that way. Or, if you prefer, we can simply sit in the truck and wait for your friends at VEVAK to locate us. I'm sure you've been witness to their handiwork at Evin Prison."

He finished removing the VIN plates.

"You do realize those snow-capped things in the distance are mountains," replied the Iranian. He sounded defeated.

The Israeli laughed and started walking.

Colonel Arshad Sassani shook his head briefly in resignation and followed. Their pace quickened, and the only sound in the wilderness they entered was the repetitive crunch of their boots on the impacted snow and its layer of thin ice.

An hour later that morning, at Vezarat-e Ettela'at va Amniyat-e Keshvar, the Iranian Ministry of Intelligence Agency, or "VEVAK," it was noted that the Colonel had failed to respond to a phone call from his superior officer late the evening before. But since Colonel Sassani was a privileged and respected member of Oghab 2, Iran's counter-espionage agency chartered to protect the nation's nuclear facilities from threats, he was given some latitude by those currently on duty at VEVAK. His continued failure to respond to a second telephone call, placed to his residence at 7:10 AM, caused growing concern and immediate action. VEVAK agents were soon dispatched, and they reported the Colonel and his truck were missing.

Arshad Sassani was a career military man with twenty-six years of service, second in command at Ogbad 2. He was also an agent of Mossad and Israel's most highly-placed informant in Iran. For the past seven-plus years, Colonel Sassani had dutifully fed the Israelis a stream of useful information about Iran's nuclear and missile launch technology. But Sassani's latest revelations stunned the Mossad and Israel's Prime Minister, Joshua Ben-Gurion, into a highly perilous decision to extract Sassani from Iran and grant him eventual asylum in Israel or the United States. First, of course, Israel's Mossad would interrogate the Colonel in person.

The two men trudged on. One mile slowly approached two.

They were in the mountains now, and there were ice-covered walls of granite and dense pine forests in all directions. The Israeli activated his sat-phone and a rapid exchange in Hebrew took place. The wait seemed an eternity, but the light on his phone came on and began flashing. He listened as directions were given.

Tel Aviv would steer them and guide them through the seemingly impassable terrain. The chip imbedded in the Israeli's left shoulder was all they needed, as he could be pinpointed anywhere on the planet to within a distance of four feet. An ancient goat herder's path became their precious yellow brick road, and a lone operator at a terminal deep in a bunker at Mossad's headquarters became their eyes.

Directions were given in periodic, deliberately clipped sentences into the Israeli's headset, and the two men moved slowly forward, sometimes a bit north, sometimes to the south, but inevitably in a westerly direction.

Their path was a perfect Kipniss landscape, barren and snow-encased. If not for the fear that clutched relentlessly at his heart, the Colonel might have considered it beautiful. But appreciation of their surroundings instead gave way to exhausting footsteps, and the Israeli and the Iranian concentrated on their feet, neither of them hardly ever looking up or around.

The Colonel's thick black beard became a tangle of icicles.

It was 10:48 AM.

An observant Revolutionary Guard Lieutenant stopped and reported an old Nissan truck parked at the eastern side of Highway 32, between Avaciq and Beyk Kandi to the north. It matched the description of the missing vehicle, and when his second radio report mentioned there were no license plates on the vehicle, concern at VEVAK gave way to panic. Three helicopters with more than thirty VEVAK agents were in the air within minutes, and a Revolutionary Guard contingent was ordered to leave Tabriz shortly thereafter. Their column consisted of ten armored personnel carriers, filled to capacity with a hundred and twenty heavily-armed troops.

At 12:03 PM the helicopters arrived. A brief inspection of the pickup truck revealed the engine was seized up, a result of a massive coolant leak. First, the VEVAK agents correctly surmised there had been no pre-planned exodus from the vehicle on this desolate road. Then they discovered two fresh sets of footprints in the snow.

"Rahim to base. Rahim to base. Over."

"Go ahead, Rahim."

The agent named Rahim continued, excitedly.

"We've located the vehicle owned by Colonel Sassani, at least we believe this is his truck. The engine has failed, and the truck has been abandoned. We surmise there were just two occupants, because there are two sets of fresh footprints, heading west."

"What do you mean, Rahim, when you say you *believe* this vehicle is the one owned by Colonel Sassani? Did you not already trace the registration numbers?"

"We cannot do that, sir. In addition to the license plates being gone, the metal registration number tags have also been removed from the vehicle. But I've seen the Colonel stubbornly drive in and out of headquarters for more than three years in his grandfather's dilapidated old truck, and I can assure you this is the same vehicle."

"So what do you think is going on, Rahim?"

"I can think of only two possibilities, sir. Either he has been kidnapped, or he is attempting to defect. I'm also assuming that since his truck unexpectedly broke down, those two sets of footprints in the snow give a strong statement that he and his accomplice or his abductor had planned all along to head toward our border with Turkey."

"He cannot possibly be trying to defect, Rahim. He's traveled at least a dozen times with our delegations to the U.N. and Switzerland, and it would have been a much simpler matter to seek asylum during any of those visits rather than to now trek over icy mountains toward the Turkish border. So I dismiss one of your two stated scenarios. We must conclude that the Americans or Israelis are attempting to kidnap a man who has extensive knowledge of our weaponry and our plans, and we must prevent him from crossing our border into Turkey."

"Yes, I understand, sir."

"Rahim," the voice added, if you are incorrect, and if this vehicle turns out not to be our faithful Colonel's ancient Nissan truck and we create an incident with the sovereign nation of Turkey, you do understand this will not go well for you."

"Yes, General, I understand."

Twelve minutes later, the General issued orders.

"Rahim, your helicopters are to take up positions at the border and wait for Colonel Sassani and his kidnapper to emerge from the mountains. There is an old goat herder's path in that area, and our analysts believe that is the only way they can wind their way through the forests and mountain passes. And Rahim, if, somehow, these two men get through the gauntlet we're preparing and appear to be escaping into Turkey, you have my permission to pursue and kill them. Even, that is, if that means you must violate Turkish air space."

"Kill Colonel Sassani?"

"His head is filled with our secrets, Rahim. It must be severed from his body to protect our great nation."

It was 6:40 PM.

All was still. Precise instructions had been given by Tel Aviv for the two men to hide at the edge of the tree line and wait for darkness to engulf the area.

They could hear occasional distant sounds from the forested slopes behind them. The contingent of Revolutionary Guard troops was getting ever nearer, closing in.

There were now eight helicopters at rest ahead, which had landed to disperse more than a hundred VEVAK agents. These agents now formed a well-established skirmish line, and effectively blocked the path to the border.

Directly in front of the two men in hiding was a broad clearing, a perfect killing field. It extended for perhaps three hundred or four hundred yards.

The Israeli mumbled something.

Theirs not to make reply,
Theirs not to reason why,
Theirs but to do and die:
Into the Valley of Death
Rode the six hundred.

"What was that you whispered?" asked the Iranian.

"Tennyson."

Colonel Sassani shrugged at the insufficient reply. This Israeli agent of Mossad was a strange character. He seemed tireless, driven by some unknown force. But "Tennyson," here and now?

"Absurd," he mumbled.

An Iranian helicopter suddenly exploded. Then another, and another in quick succession. The night sky was immediately engulfed in bright light, as a wing of American AH-64D Apache Guardian helicopters swooped in from the Turkish side of the border. Their infrared sensors easily pinpointed the Revolutionary Guard troops less than three hundred yards into the forest, and four well-placed AGM-114 Hellfire missiles killed more than half of them instantly, and halted their advance.

The four Apaches circled as avenging angels, and in less than three minutes all eight Iranian helicopters were ablaze. In the bright torch light that emanated from their burning transports, the VEVAK agents became simple target practice for the Apaches. KMK-42 laser weapons on swivel mounts in both side doors of the Apaches were arced back and forth by their gunners, cutting and slicing through the helpless men and leaving them to bleed out on the frozen ground.

The Israeli spoke rapidly into his headset and nodded, as though the man in Tel Aviv stood directly in front of him.

A CH-47 Chinook, illuminated by the flaming carnage below, appeared overhead and landed in the clearing near the two men.

Eight well-equipped Navy SEALs exited the helicopter and moved toward them. A sat-com message was received and obeyed, and the Israeli tapped the Colonel on his shoulder.

"Time to go."

They raced toward the SEALs and the Israeli shouted the word, "Terrapin" to indicate they were the package to be delivered.

Safely aboard the Chinook and well within Turkish air space, the Iranian Colonel looked at the Israeli and asked a question.

"What is this 'terrapin' you shouted at the Americans?"

"It's a turtle, sir," replied the SEAL team leader.

"You're a lot slower moving than your Israeli pal," added one of the other SEALs, "so your code name for this mission was terrapin."

The Seals all laughed at that, and for the first time in four days, the Israeli smiled. He then said something, softly.

Half a league,
Half a league,
Half a league onward,
All in the Valley of Death
Rode the six hundred.

"More Tennyson, my friend?" asked the Colonel.

"Yes, sir, that's correct," replied the Israeli.

Exhausted, Yaakov slowly closed his eyes and nodded off.

The Iranian studied his savior. The Israeli was perhaps thirty-five and had the chiseled, no-nonsense features of a boxer. At one point in their perilous journey through the mountains, Sassani slipped and fell. The Israeli simply reached down, secured the Iranian under one arm, and dead-lifted him to his feet. Strength, endurance, and dedication were to be respected, thought the Colonel.

He also glanced around at the Navy SEALs. They clearly were all of that same mold.

Less than an hour later, the Israeli and the Iranian arrived at a Turkish military airfield near the city of Çetenli.

They promptly boarded an unmarked Gulfstream G650, were greeted professionally by three agents of the CIA, and the plane immediately taxied toward the runway.

"Happy New Year," remarked one of the agents to the two men. The aircraft then streaked toward Tel Aviv.

CHAPTER 2

"Even if we are forced to stand alone against Iran, we will not fear. In every circumstance we will preserve our right and our ability to defend ourselves."

Benjamin Netanyahu, Prime Minister of Israel
Holocaust Remembrance Day
August 15, 2015

January 4, 2028 ... Tel Aviv, Israel, 0800 Hours

At the head of the conference table at Mossad's headquarters was Joshua Ben-Gurion, Israel's Prime Minister. His great-grandfather, David Ben-Gurion, was the legendary founding father of the State of Israel, and Joshua consistently performed his duties with the diligence one would expect of a man with his ancestry. To his immediate right was Lt. General Gadi Eizenkot, Chief of the General Staff of the Israel Defense Force, and to Prime Minister's Ben-Gurion's left was Shlomo Mizrahi, Director of Mossad. Also at the table were Rabbi David Blumenthal, holder of a Ph.D. from the 'Technion,' the Israel Institute of Technology, and two senior research scientists.

"Gentlemen," said the Prime Minister, "we've all studied the statements made by Colonel Sassani in his debriefing two days ago, and I find it astounding that, once again, we must deal with Nazis, even though it's simply their lethal technology that's now the cause for our concern."

He looked down and began to read aloud a brief excerpt from Colonel Sassani's testimony. The steely tone of his voice was ominous and filled with determination.

"In 1944, once the V2 rocket had been developed, the Nazis began work on 'Project Prufstand XII.' They designed a container large enough for two V2 rockets, with the intention of having a U-boat tow that container across the Atlantic. Upon the submarine's arrival off the Eastern Seaboard of the United States, the container was to be flooded, and the rockets would rotate toward a vertical position. The V2s would then be launched at New York City from a distance of roughly one-hundred and fifty miles out to sea. The Nazis realized they could do little damage to the continental United States herself, and the real purpose of this project was to do psychological damage, to dampen the Americans' spirit by bringing the war directly to their home soil.

"Gentlemen, the Islamic Republic of Iran has taken this Nazi concept and their Prufstand XII project to an entirely new level.

"It is my government's intention to have several of these 'Rocket U-boats' leave our naval base at Bandar Abbas in May of this year. Each will tow a container similar to that which was designed by the Nazis in 1944, but each one will be equipped with two missiles armed with nuclear warheads.

"It is our belief that our submarines can quietly slip through the American SOSUS network undetected, but if that's not the case, all that's needed is just one of them to get through. Their targets are to be New York City and Washington D.C., and we intend to launch from one hundred miles out to sea at noon on the Fourth of July. The Americans will have no time to react, and the golden part of this plan is that they will not know who has attacked them. Our submarines will then release the towed containers and simply slip away into the ocean depths, without the Americans identifying them.

"Eleven days later, at dawn on the fifteenth of July, we intend to launch twenty nuclear tipped missiles at Tel Aviv and Israeli military targets, on the morning of your weekly Sabbath.

"It is my nation's sworn commitment to carry the sword into the midst of the Jews, and to kill every last one of you.

"Gentlemen, I am vehemently opposed to all this continuing madness in Tehran, and that's why I have agreed to assist you and the Americans for the past several years. It is my fervent hope that the United States and Israel will inform Tehran that you know of their plans, and you will warn them that nuclear aggression will be met with nuclear retaliation. Mutually Assured Destruction is not a game, but a certainty. I can only pray that sanity will prevail in Tehran, and this holocaust can be avoided."

Rabbi Blumenthal was the first to comment.

"Our dear Colonel views himself as an Iranian patriot, and he clearly believes there is a path toward changing the minds of those in Tehran, if the Americans know in advance who is about to blow up their capitol and New York City. But 'Mutually Assured Destruction' is only viable if both sides are truly fearful of the consequences of their actions."

"That's precisely my concern," added the Director of Mossad.

"We have no substantive reason to believe Tehran is concerned about nuclear penalties in retaliation for their actions. These men are prepared to die 'glorious' deaths. We've never been able to have dialogue with terrorists, nor can we expect them to think and reason the way rational people do. A reasonable man can be forewarned; an unreasonable one can't be dissuaded from a highly perilous path."

"Colonel Sassani is a reasonable Iranian, gentlemen, and that alone gives me hope," added the Prime Minister reflectively. He ran a hand through his mass of dark hair and scratched the back of his neck, a nervous habit since childhood that made him a rather poor poker player. "Perhaps there are others in Iran who can still think logically and reason, and obviously the Colonel believes that's the case, as he's argued passionately and somewhat convincingly."

"What if Colonel Sassani is the only sane official in the Iranian government or armed forces, Joshua?" asked General Eisenkot. "I seriously doubt, if I picked up the phone and called the commanding general of the Revolutionary Guard to say, 'We all know when and where you're going to attack Israel and the U.S.,' that they'd begin disassembling their weapons. These men are fanatics, and our dear Colonel's dream of sharing information with us to make Iran a better place is truly the desperate prayer of a fool. They cannot be dissuaded from sending their submarines on that mission, nor can they be dissuaded from their plan to launch against us."

"Gadi, is it not somehow feasible for us to locate and destroy Iran's missile inventory before those weapons are unleashed?" asked the Prime Minister.

The IDF General responded.

"No, Joshua, we've often discussed this problem, and we cannot. The intelligence provided by Colonel Sassani and our other lesser agents in Iran indicates each of their nuclear missiles is mounted on a transport truck, and those trucks are in bunkers beneath mountains. I must assume those vehicles will be called upon to roll from their bunkers just a few minutes before a scheduled launch time. The exposure time, when they're in the open and therefore vulnerable, will be well under an hour. Prior to the time those transports are exposed and vulnerable, conventional weapons would be useless against bunkers deep within mountains. Our neutron weapons, should you elect to authorize their use in a preemptive strike, would *also* be ineffectual. A neutron explosion might kill most or all of the Iranian personnel working deep inside a mountain, but their nuclear weapons and transports would remain intact. The Iranians could immediately bring forth other people and launch against us in less than a week."

"So, Gadi, you're saying it will be impossible for us to stop Iran's scheduled launch of missiles, even though we now know the date and precise time of day they propose to attack us?"

"Not impossible, Joshua," added the Director of Mossad.

He was the oldest of the men in attendance. At seventy-two, he always appeared to be exhausted, with deep, dark circles beneath his eyes. But no one ever questioned his skill at planning operations down to the last detail. He always worked out contingency plans, which gave the operatives options. Mossad's agents called him, "Zayde," the affectionate Yiddish term for "Grandpa."

He continued.

"We could conceivably mount an operation that has our people on the ground to greet the trucks just before the scheduled launch time of 6:00 AM on the fifteenth of July. We would need help from the Americans, but such an operation is possible."

General Eisenkot's voice strained a bit.

"What if they change the launch date between now and then?" he asked. "Now that Colonel Sassani is here in Israel, we would have no way of knowing they've done so. And what if everything goes as planned, and we're in position when these trucks come out of their hiding places? What if just one of those mobile missile carriers is still able to launch its nuclear weapon, while our people are in combat with Revolutionary Guard troops? I'll answer that question for all of you, gentlemen. Tel Aviv will become a sheet of glass for a thousand years! No, we cannot assume that we can get our people into Iran and take out twenty trucks without a single thing going wrong. The risks are far too great. Will any of you be satisfied if our commandos place a call to Mossad's headquarters to report they have destroyed nineteen of twenty trucks and missiles? Of course not, because there will be no one alive to take the call!"

"What do you suggest, then, Gadi?" asked the Prime Minister.

"There must be no one available to drive the trucks, Joshua."

"What do you mean, Gadi?"

"Deuteronomy 20:7. It is time for us to enforce our Torah!"

Before the Prime Minister could react, Rabbi Blumenthal looked from face to face as he recited the verse.

"… the LORD thy God shall bring thee into the land whither thou goest to possess it … And when the LORD thy God shall deliver them before thee, ***thou shalt smite them, and utterly destroy them***; thou shall make no covenant with them, nor show mercy unto them."

"That's correct, Rabbi, and thank you," added the General. "We must utterly destroy them, nor show mercy unto them. In other words, gentlemen, it is time to kill them all."

Prime Minister Ben-Gurion sat in the silent room, thinking.

He ran a hand through his hair and scratched the back of his neck for a moment. "What are you suggesting, Gadi?"

"Plague Ten."

Shlomo Mizrahi of Mossad shook his head in resignation.

"Any plan I might conceive would have a small probability of failure, leading to the consequence that Tel Aviv would be destroyed by an Iranian nuclear missile if anything goes wrong. And all this doesn't even take into account the fact that Iran supposedly has at least fifty nuclear weapons at the moment. I'm convinced that within a week of successfully halting their scheduled launch against us on the fifteenth of July, they would launch another array, then another, and another. Gentlemen, I unfortunately agree with General Eizenkot. The only way to protect ourselves from these madmen in Tehran is to kill them. That's what's done to a rabid dog, after all, isn't it?"

The Prime Minister looked toward the two research scientists, who had been silent thus far.

"Tell me about the current developmental status of Plague Ten, gentlemen."

The older of the two men, Israel's most prominent biochemist, cleared his throat.

"Mr. Prime Minister," he began, "first, let me provide all of you background information. Bear with me, please.

"A 'somatic' cell is any cell in the human body, other than sperm and egg cells, and all somatic cells are 'diploid,' which means they carry two unique sets of chromosomes, one from each parent. Human cells have twenty-three pairs of chromosomes, and which specific chromosome from each of these twenty-three pairs that's inherited from the mother and father is purely a matter of chance. That means there are precisely 8,324,608 possible combinations of the twenty-three chromosome pairs.

"But it's far more complicated than that, I'm afraid. An 'allele' is a variant form of a gene, and each human chromosome can contain literally hundreds of possible different genes. So the actual number of allele combinations in humans is significantly more than seventy trillion. That's what makes us all unique and different."

Gadi Eisenkot was becoming impatient.

"What's the bottom line then, Dr. Bachman? I've been led to believe that you've perfected a viable biological weapon."

"The bottom line here, General, is that with over seventy trillion possible unique genetic characteristics, we have been unable to sufficiently isolate all specific traits of those of Arab ethnicity. After thirty years of research and experimentation, this is where we are. Our latest laboratory viruses can be tweaked to kill those possessing certain genes that match whatever genetic combinations we dial into the composition of the virus. And, in fact, we can dial in hundreds, perhaps thousands, of different genetic combinations. But in reality, with more than seventy trillion combinations from which to choose, we cannot even scratch the surface of the problem at hand. Our scientific conclusion, therefore, is that a genetic-based weapon of this type will yield at least a sixty-three percent survival rate, if utilized. And if a weaponized virus is to be efficient, it must successfully destroy *all* residents of any nation we attack. The concept that we can create a plague that uniquely kills all those who surround us, sadly, is folly. Furthermore, we have been equally unable to assure ourselves that citizens of our own nation, who have a similar genetic structure, would not also be attacked and killed by the specific genetic components which we've dialed into the weaponized virus."

"Then how can we consider this a viable weapon, Doctor, if it will possibly kill our own citizens?" The Prime Minister was becoming highly annoyed and frustrated.

The scientist noticed, as did the others at the conference table, the pursed lips and cold stare of the Prime Minister. "It *is* most certainly a viable weapon, gentlemen," assured Dr. Bachman in a loud and convincing voice. He stood, slapped the table sharply with an open palm, and walked slowly around the conference table. He began to lecture them.

"What has evolved through our research and gives credence to adopting the label and term, 'Plague Ten,' is that the current form of this virus we've developed kills everyone in its path, Mr. Prime Minister, including not just the firstborn, but every man, woman, and child in the infected area. It is absolutely indiscriminate and completely lethal. And just as importantly, we have also developed the antidote.

"When our laboratory stumbled upon the perfect virus, one that kills every living creature without exception, my colleagues and I at Technion and the IDF research laboratories finally realized we have been going in the wrong direction for more than three decades. And the revelation was so simple that I'm astounded we didn't pursue this logical avenue many years ago. You see, with several trillions of possible genetic traits from which to choose, in retrospect it seems foolhardy that we embarked upon a project that sought to kill an Arab in Iran, for example, and yet spare a distant relative of his, one who possesses a quite similar genetic structure, who was born in Israel and is a model citizen. And there are more than two million similar scenarios, since that's the number of those of Arab descent who are currently Israeli citizens.

"Admittedly, while we've been going in the wrong direction for years, we now have seen the light. Gentlemen, the Plague Ten virus is the most deadly ever to be studied, and all we have to do is first inoculate all our citizens and then release it at key points along our borders. The winds of war, so to speak, shall do the rest. The virus is airborne and rabidly contagious. In the specific case in point, if a few canisters of Plague Ten are released at our border with Jordan, the winds that blow constantly eastward there will carry this highly lethal virus into Jordan, then Iraq, and within a week, Iran will be infected as well. There is one other feature of the Plague Ten virus that I find to be rather elegant, for lack of a better word. In addition to infecting and killing its host, the virus attacks and devours bone as well as other tissue. There will be no sign it has ever been there, nor will we have the tedious problem of disposing of millions of corpses or skeletons in some monumental cleanup program. Perhaps they'll be articles of clothing on the ground, but that's all. Within three weeks or four at the most, the nations of Jordan, Iraq and Iran will simply be empty, as though no human being has ever resided there.

"And I believe it would be highly appropriate to release Plague Ten on the morning of Passover this year, the eleventh day of April, to honor our heritage. The inoculation of our citizens prior to that date is akin to painting lamb's blood on the lintels and door posts of our homes during the time of Moses, so that our firstborn would be spared by the Angel of Death. But, as I have said, in the scenario I imagine, not only shall the firstborn sons of our enemies be annihilated, but every man, woman, and child in the nations who have threatened our right to exist for the past eighty-plus years. Gentlemen, Plague Ten is truly the incarnate Angel of Death."

"This is madness," said the Director of Mossad. "How can it be controlled? It seems obvious to me that so virulent a disease won't necessarily stop at borders. There are no 'lines in the sand' here. Commercial aircraft will deliver this plague to London and other major cities around the globe, for example, and what you're proposing will be a worldwide pandemic."

"I concur," added the Prime Minister. "But I want all of you to stop and realize what we're contemplating here this morning. We're calmly talking about the 'Angel of Death' as though he's some soccer star and we're playing for the World Cup.

"Applying a cute biblical name to this virus cannot hide the ugly truth. This is *genocide* we're discussing today, gentlemen, and releasing Plague Ten will be a more thorough 'Final Solution' than all the Nazis with all their weapons and concentration camps accomplished during their disgusting reign in Europe. Dr. Bachman, with all due respect for your genius, how can Jews, of all people, sit here and discuss the application of a far more heinous weapon than anything Adolph Hitler and his ruthless henchmen ever imagined or conceived?

"My great-grandfather was David Ben-Gurion, as you all know, and he and thousands of concentration camp survivors carved out this nation, so that never again would we Jews be victims. Now, we will be the aggressor, and we are poised to become all that we so deeply despise. We are the new Nazis, gentlemen, and this is a most shameful discussion."

Gadi Eisenkot, however, was unmoved by Joshua Ben-Gurion's remarks and was thinking purely along logistical lines.

"How long to produce ample vaccine and inoculate our people, Doctor?" inquired the General.

"Forty days, Gadi," was the confident reply.

"And to alleviate the concerns you all must feel, let me assure you that we CAN control it, Mr. Prime Minister," the scientist added confidently.

"How?" Three voices asked the question as one.

"The virus lives as a virulent strain for precisely twenty-eight days, and not a day more. After that, it mutates into something milder than the common cold, gentlemen."

Joshua Ben-Gurion leaned forward in his chair, acutely aware he had the weight of his nation's survival on his shoulders.

"So let me ask you a key question, Doctor," he said. "We're now talking about killing every person in Jordan and Iraq, as Plague Ten marches toward Iran. And if I read you correctly, Dr. Bachman, I believe you are suggesting an even broader use of this virus. But something puzzles me. Let's say that one single strand of the Plague Ten virus lives its twenty-eight-day term, and on the twenty-seventh day of its existence it reproduces. Would that newborn strand of virus not also then live twenty-eight days, Doctor? And so on and so on, as generation upon generation of this deadly virus is created? If your answer to that immensely pivotal question is, 'Yes,' then we are truly talking about releasing a weapon that will kill every soul on the planet, except our own previously inoculated citizens."

"Mr. Prime Minister," said the biochemist very softly, "the most direct answer to your incredibly astute question is, 'No.' "

The General also leaned forward in his chair.

"Explain, please, Doctor."

"Twenty-eight days is it, gentlemen," explained the second of the two scientists, excitedly. "The initial Plague Ten virus strand lives in its current state for only twenty-eight days, as Dr. Bachman indicated. But when it reproduces after its first two days of existence, the new strand lives only twenty-six days, and so on. Mr. Prime Minister, to address your concern, sir, most recent developments in our field of study now enable us to precisely program cell death and mutation as never before. If one of the initial virus strands reproduces after it has existed for twenty-seven days, the new strand will live just one day before it also mutates into something as mundanely harmless as the common flu virus, and a mild one, at that. With Dr. Bachman's guidance and genius, we have perfected an extraordinary virus and weapon."

"So we won't have to control the virus, Mr. Prime Minister," added Dr. Bachman with a slight smile of satisfaction. "The virus quite efficiently controls itself. Gentlemen, let me offer an opinion, please. Earlier, I alluded to the concept that we could release the Plague Ten virus into Jordan, and it would work its way into Iraq and then Iran. As Prime Minister Ben-Gurion has mentioned, life in all three of those nations would be extinguished, and I view that as completely necessary. It is my humble opinion that we must take a quite broad approach when we deal with these hostile Arab nations. We cannot leave ourselves exposed to the ire of the Saudis with their formidable arsenal, which Mossad believes also includes nuclear weaponry, nor to the Egyptians and other Arab nations when they realize what we've done to Iran and two other nations in the path of Plague Ten. This is our moment in history, gentlemen. The only path that guarantees success and our survival is to expand the release of this viral weapon into several other Arab nations, and in doing so, we must kill all who reside there. And yes, Mr. Prime Minister, we are quite indeed talking about genocide. But, of course, that is Iran's plan for us, as well. In this sad circumstance, we must be the first to attack."

Director Mizrahi sat silently for a moment and contemplated this unique, albeit horrific, method to end the generations of conflict that had become a way of life for Israel and her enemies.

"I understand your logic, Doctor," he said slowly, "but as the Prime Minister mentioned, we're contemplating an act that is genocidal, and I agree that Israel, among all other nations, should be the last to condone what we're discussing today. On the other hand, it's my opinion that we must do this fully, or not at all. If those in the remaining Arab world awaken one morning and realize the State of Israel has terminated all life in Iran, Jordan, and Iraq, there will be a rapid escalation into a massive conflict with unpredictable consequences. Let's say, for a moment, that we adopt your thesis that a dozen Arab nations must be wiped off the face of the Earth. While Plague Ten has commenced its twenty-eight-day journey of death, what of commercial flights that are leaving Tehran and Cairo and at least a hundred other airports on the days immediately after we release the virus? Twenty-seven days of exposure to the residents of Paris or London is ample time for this virus to kill everyone in each of those cities."

"Our allies must be convinced to assist us, and aircraft that leave the targeted Arab nations during that twenty-eight-day period must simply be blown out of the sky," replied Dr. Bachman, quite matter-of-factly. "We should be able to bribe any nation to cooperate with us, with the antidote to Plague Ten as our bargaining chip."

"Ships, trains, cars?" asked the Prime Minister.

"Ships and trains are extremely simple issues compared to cars, trucks, and aircraft," commented General Eizenkot, his mind now in full swing. "Ships travel tediously, and trains along a quite specific path. They can be stopped with ease. It's really the people trying to escape a pandemic in a dying city by car or on foot who concern me the most."

"It must be the responsibility of the nations adjacent to those we attack to effectively seal their borders," added the General.

"I've prepared for this aspect of our discussion, gentlemen," announced Dr. Bachman. He typed for a moment on his laptop, and a large map appeared on the wall at the far end of the conference table. "It is my suggestion, in addition to our allowing the prevailing winds to carry the virus eastward, that we embark on an ambitious program to release the virus in the following nations, and going from left to right on the map displayed here, they are Libya, Egypt, Jordan, Lebanon, Syria, Saudi Arabia, Yemen, Oman, The UAE, Iraq, Kuwait, Bahrain, Qatar, and Iran. Wind speed, of course, is a variable, but if our mathematical model is correct, and we are absolutely confident it is, twenty-eight days of exposure to Plague Ten is sufficient to kill virtually every person in these fourteen nations without residual contamination of neighboring sovereign states. And just as we cannot conceivably control wind direct nor its speed, we have to be prepared to shrug off collateral damage to any neighboring countries. When we use the Winds of War in so graphic a manner, the price of a massive victory will be a certain level of unpredictability. How we manage to deliver this virus and release it in these various locations is more a challenge for Mossad, I assume."

"We can accomplish that," added Director Mizrahi, "but that's far easier than the containment issue we'll face."

"Gadi," began Prime Minister Ben-Gurion, "the map displayed here indicates the nations surrounding our proposed kill zone are Tunisia, Algeria, Niger, Chad, and Sudan in Africa, and six other nations are to the north and east of Iran. It seems preposterous to believe all these nations can prevent those exposed to Plague Ten from fleeing and that this won't immediately become a worldwide pandemic."

"I agree with you, Joshua," added the General after a moment of contemplation. "But this is the question I must ask of all of us."

Gadi Eizenkot stood and looked into each somber face.

"What other choice do we have, gentlemen?

"Perhaps, if we share Iran's timetable with the Americans, they'll sink the Iranian submarines somewhere in the Atlantic, before New York City and Washington disintegrate on the Fourth of July. Or perhaps they'll orchestrate and execute a preemptive attack on the Iranian naval base and destroy the submarines long before they sail. But what of us, gentlemen? What of us?

"Our motto, the IDF's battle cry, is the phrase, 'Never Again,' and we sit here today, knowing the precise moment in time at which a second Jewish Holocaust is about to occur. A porous decision to do nothing is far too reminiscent of our ancestors silently shuffling into cattle cars in 1943, like lambs preparing to visit the mass slaughterhouses that were Dachau and Auschwitz."

Gadi Eizenkot pounded his fist on the table with such force and venom that one of the research scientists was so startled by the sudden erupting violence that he tipped precariously on his chair and had to grab the table for support. The General's eyes were ablaze, and he was once again the vibrant warrior of his younger days, the legendary commander of Israel's Bashan Armored Division.

Defeat had never been an option for the General, and it was not an option at that moment.

"Never Again!" he demanded viciously. His voice reverberated off the walls with incredible passion, and he pointed a finger at each of them, daring them to disagree.

"We have the means to save this nation and prevent scheduled nuclear genocide. We must deploy and utilize this heinous weapon, perhaps warn the innocent and our allies at the appropriate time, and to hell with any collateral damage. It is time for us to be made of steel, gentlemen, and I for one will not tolerate any plan that puts our families and this nation in harm's way. If the worst-case scenario occurs, and Plague Ten spreads throughout the world, then so be it. Israel will survive, and that's all that really matters, isn't it?"

The debate continued for another hour, but ultimately they all agreed. The Plague Ten virus would be produced in sufficient quantities to attack and kill all in the fourteen targeted nations hostile to the State of Israel, and the attack would be on Passover morning, in keeping with history and tradition.

The Angel of Death would necessarily be called upon to knock on doors once again.

The next task at hand for the State of Israel, as a prelude to war, would be to produce sufficient quantities of vaccine to inoculate more than ten million Israelis within the next forty days.

"May God forgive us," commented Prime Minister Ben-Gurion as the meeting concluded.

Rabbi Blumenthal echoed the same sentiment, in prayer.

The meeting was at an end. They rose, shook hands, and repeated the same word in farewell.

"Shalom," they each said, somberly.

It means, "Hello." It means, "Goodbye."

And it also means, "Peace."

CHAPTER 3

February 1, 2028 … Washington, D.C., 1000 Hours

"They've threatened us?"

The President was furious.

"Mr. President," began General Joseph Dunford, Jr., Chairman of the Joint Chiefs of Staff, "the Israelis and their Mossad are skilled chess players, sir. We've been unable to dissuade them from the course of action to which they're committed. This 'Plague Ten' virus they've developed is off their drawing boards and will be released soon after Israel's population is fully inoculated, and they realize the only way we can prevent that act of aggression is to intervene against them militarily. The Pentagon has already drafted a plan to take out Iran and Israel in preemptive strikes, and clearly Mossad anticipated that as a distinct possibility. If we elect not to attack Israel in order to prevent this madness, then they desperately need our cooperation to carry out this plan, and they're playing this poker hand very, very well.

"They are one step ahead of us, Mr. President, and that's why, while they've been busily inoculating their citizens for the past few weeks, they've also informed us that there are at least a dozen Mossad operatives scattered around the U.S., each armed with a container of the Plague Ten virus. If we decide to attack Israel, those agents will release the virus in retaliation for our strike against their nation. I frankly have a dim view of the FBI's capacity to locate and arrest closet Israeli agents, especially within the time frame we have at hand. The statement that those agents exist may not even be true. But the threat alone is sufficient cause for us to consider assisting them."

The President's voice rose an octave higher than normal.

"They want us to 'assist,' General, is *that* what we're calling it, should commercial aircraft leave any of these fourteen nations on or after the eleventh of April?" he asked. "It is sheer madness for these United States, the world's leading democracy, to commit to downing dozens, or even hundreds, of civilian aircraft in the name of containing a virus. And I sure as hell don't like being blackmailed into doing so, by some pipsqueak nation like Israel. I want the FBI to ferret out these Mossad agents and arrest them! You got that, Morgan? And you have thirty days to do that, period."

"Mr. President," began Morgan Wallace, Director of the FBI, "we will do that, sir. However, logic dictates that as we arrest their agents, they will simply send others, perhaps via our porous border with Canada. If they sense we are doing this in preparation for a strike against Israel, I feel the *threat* of releasing this virus somewhere within the continental United States will become a *reality*."

The Director of the Central Intelligence Agency put down his coffee cup.

"Morgan is correct, sir," he said. "With all due respect, let's put aside for a moment our disdain for Israeli threats and blackmail attempts. We are allies, sir, and may I remind you of all the lives we've lost in the Middle East. Or of the incredible cost of preventing and fighting terrorism for the past thirty years? The first nine-eleven attack still haunts us all, and the second such attack, on the twentieth anniversary of the first one, has put an even deeper scar on the American psyche. When that airplane was hijacked and flown into the Capitol Building while the Senate was in session debating, of all things, aid to displaced citizens of Arab nations, we lost four hundred and ninety-two fine Americans that day, including thirty-nine Senators, sir. This Iranian Colonel Sassani has given us a timetable for a nuclear attack against this nation and, in addition, a nuclear conflagration that will wipe Israel off the face of the Earth. If I were Director of their Mossad, I'd immediately plan a preemptive strike against Iran, just as they've done. And I also concur with the logic that a conventional attack on Iran's bases, or a neutron bomb attack on those facilities, would be ineffectual, because their nuclear missiles would not be destroyed in the process. I concur with their logic sir, that the only viable course of action is to attack Iran, and somehow kill all the inhabitants of that nation. As the Israelis have explained, if there is no one left to drive those missile-launching trucks, there will be no launch against their nation."

The President thought for a moment.

"John, we're not simply talking about a biological attack against Iran, now are we? There are fourteen nations on their proposed hit list, for Christ's sake! Fourteen!"

Now, the aging John Brennan spoke, who had served as Director of the CIA for nearly fifteen years. Though the incredible complexity of his position usually showed in his every movement, at the moment, he was clearly energized.

"Mr. President," he said, "We have not been given an outlandish plan by the Israelis. We have been given a reprieve! What better way to ensure there are no further attacks against this nation than to eliminate all who may plan and execute future attacks from Middle Eastern nations? Yes, we must agree to cooperate with Tel Aviv and shoot down any aircraft that attempt to leave those fourteen nations for a period of roughly thirty days. But look at the proverbial end of the rainbow, please. We will have no treaties with Arab nations that they may then violate. We will have no nuclear arms race between Arab nations and the Israelis. We will have no hidden network of massive contributions to terrorist causes, and most importantly of all, we will have no future terrorist attacks on this nation mounted from the Middle East."

"Are you telling me you condone the destruction of all life in fourteen sovereign nations? We're talking about a plot to indiscriminately kill millions of men, women, and children here, gentlemen," commented the President. "This is not war; this is genocide."

"There is at least a precedent, sir," added General Dunford.

"What possible precedent?"

"President Harry S. Truman, sir," stated the General.

"General," commented the President with a trace of sarcasm in his voice, "as we all know, President Truman elected to use a nuclear option in the war against the Japanese in order to avoid a distasteful alternative, the estimated eight hundred thousand Allied casualties had we elected to invade the Japanese homeland. That's hardly the same as extinguishing all life in fourteen Arab nations."

"What I meant, Mr. President, is that President Truman did, in fact, make the difficult decision to use nuclear weapons with the knowledge that all citizens of those two cities, including the innocent, would be killed. That's the precedent to which I refer."

"Gentlemen," added CIA Director Brennan, "there is a hidden silver lining in this event. First of all, we need not agonize too long about what's to occur. It's the Israelis who will release their Plague Ten virus in April, not us. So we are not the ones who will technically have blood on our hands. Our discussion must be either to move against Israel, in order to prevent what they intend to do, or to cooperate and deal with the aftermath of their actions, as we anticipate the future shape of the Middle East. I, for one, feel it's imperative to focus on one simple fact. Fourteen Arab nations, most of which are wealthy oil-producing states, will summarily be there for the taking. Empty and uninhabited. We must focus on taking over those assets, for if we do not, surely the Russians or the Chinese will."

"This is a great opportunity, Mr. President," added the General. "We must assume that once Plague Ten has wiped out all life in those nations and eliminated Jihadist threats to this nation, we'll need to maintain the flow of crude oil out of the Middle East. If Israel attempted to take over those oil fields, there would be, in my opinion, a third World War. But if we, the United States, did that, no nation would dare attack us. I agree with Director Brennan, sir. We should not agonize over the loss of life as a result of an Israeli operation, regardless of how massive and destructive it may be. We must also agree to cooperate with them, and down any and all aircraft that attempt to leave those fourteen nations for the proposed month after the virus is released."

"You agree that it's permissible to down unarmed commercial aircraft and kill innocent civilians, General?" asked the President.

"Jihadists killed thirty-nine Senators and many other innocent Americans on September 11, 2021, sir," said the CIA director.

FBI Director Wallace cleared his throat. He was a quiet man, not one to engage in lengthy debates.

"Mr. President, I agree that we need not ponder the efficacy of an action instituted by the Israelis. I also agree that we should not attempt to stop that action militarily. It makes no sense to attack our one ally in that region and then be faced with ongoing Jihadist threats for decades to come. If we are to participate in this event by shooting down commercial aircraft for a finite period of roughly four weeks, we should view that action as purely defensive in nature. We cannot allow this virus to spread throughout Europe, Asia, or possibly enter the United States. We must, therefore, unilaterally view casualties as will assuredly occur when we engage planes leaving those nations in one way, and in one way only."

"Go on, Morgan," said the President.

"They will be 'collateral damage,' sir."

"There is absolutely no difference, Mr. President," added CIA Director Brennan, "in downing a plane hell-bent on destroying the Capitol Building and downing an aircraft containing people who carry a lethal virus. The body count at the Capitol that heinous day was miniscule, compared to what might occur if that Plague Ten virus is unleashed in this nation."

The General nodded in approval.

"Collateral damage," he repeated.

The President understood.

"May God help us," he said, as he stood to indicate the meeting was at an end.

February 2, 2028 ... Tel Aviv, 1100 Hours

"Good morning, Yaakov. I trust you've enjoyed your holiday and the last few weeks with your family," began Director Mizrahi of Mossad. They were seated in his office.

"Yes, thank you, sir. Riva and I took the girls to the beach," replied Yaakov.

"A bit chilly for that, wasn't it? asked Director Mizrahi.

Yaakov flashed a broad smile.

"Not as cold as those mountain passes in Iran, sir," he said.

"How's your back?" asked Director Mizrahi.

"Always hurts like hell. Thanks for asking, sir." said Yaakov.

It was time for business.

"That was fine work, by the way," added the Director as Colonel Sassani was ushered into the office and sat down.

"Gentlemen," said Director Mizrahi, "I am an old man."

"You're not that old, 'Zayde,' " added Yaakov.

"Sir, what is your surname?" asked Colonel Sassani.

"Rafaeli, Major Yaakov Rafaeli," replied the Mossad agent.

"Thank you, Major Rafaeli," said Sassani. "I've never had the opportunity to formally tell you how much I appreciate the way you were able to get us safely out of Iran."

"Colonel, the three of us are speaking English today, since that's the common language we share. So let me please explain something to you. My name, as you know, is Yaakov, and in English that would translate to 'Jacob.' So you may call me 'Yaakov,' or 'Jacob,' or 'Jake,' sir. And you are welcome. I was simply doing my job."

"And you may call me 'Arshad,' Yaakov."

The Mossad agent smiled again.

"Now that your little mating dance has been concluded," said Director Mizrahi, "let me explain why you're both here today. As I mentioned, I'm the old man around here and having been with Mossad for decades, the one thing I've learned is to trust my instincts. Colonel, just as Yaakov and I are Israeli patriots and would give our lives to protect this nation, you have pledged an equally deep commitment to the Islamic Republic of Iran.

"While we assuredly disagree fundamentally about many things, it is your absolute commitment to your nation I must truly respect. I've agonized about something for the past few weeks and have decided to share some information with you, Colonel. I already anticipate how you will react, and I hope you'll channel that energy into what we'll discuss shortly."

"What is it you wish to tell me, Director?" asked Sassani

"Israel has decided to attack and kill every man, woman, and child in Iran, Colonel." said Director Mizrahi.

"What!" Sassani shouted.

"Colonel, the information you've provided has made us realize we have no other options. First, we might convince the Americans to strike Iran with nuclear weapons before your submarines leave port, but the associated fallout would find its way into neighboring nations, including perhaps Pakistan and Israel. A nuclear attack on Iran is simply not a viable option, plus I seriously doubt we could ever convince the administration in Washington to launch a nuclear first strike. The American government most often moves tediously," said Director Mizrahi

He held up his left hand and raised two fingers.

"Two," he said, "conventional weapons are also not an option, since your nation's nuclear missiles are on transport trucks parked deep within the Alborz and Zagros mountain ranges."

The Director held up a third finger.

"Three, Israel's neutron weapons have been ruled out of consideration, because while many Iranians would die in such an attack, the neutron bomb will not destroy your transport trucks. Within a week, other VEVAK or Revolutionary Guard personnel would man those vehicles and launch against us."

The Director's hand shook a bit as he raised another finger.

And finally, four, we have decided to utilize our one remaining weapon against your nation. It is called 'Plague Ten,' Colonel, and when that lethal virus is released into Iran's population, every living soul in your nation will die. Israel will then remain secure, because there will be neither agents of your VEVAK nor Revolutionary Guard troops available to drive those trucks out of their impenetrable bunkers."

"In the name of Almighty Allah," said Sassani, "do you mean to tell me that I'm to be the cause of this madness? I faithfully provided you and the Americans detailed information, so that diplomacy and logic would prevail. I've revealed my nation's deepest military secrets to you, including our timetable to attack Israel and the United States. I trusted you, Mizrahi! And with my naïve assistance you've now decided the only course of action is to wipe my beloved nation off the face of the Earth. If I had a weapon in my hand right now, I'd kill both of you."

Yaakov bristled at that, his survival instincts awakened.

Director Mizrahi held up both hands, a peace sign.

"Colonel, please," he began, "there is much more that I need to share with you. The Americans have agreed to cooperate with Tel Aviv, and once the people of Iran are infected and begin to die, some will decide to flee your nation. That's when the American military is to step in. They have been enlisted to shoot any aircraft out of the sky that may attempt to leave Iran. The plan is to isolate the Islamic Republic of Iran and allow you all to expire, Arshad. This Plague Ten virus is unstoppable, and from a purely military point of view, the plan is feasible. I frankly have put my own stamp of approval on all this, because Israel has no other option. We cannot sit here and await the day Iran will launch nuclear weapons against us, Colonel, so the decision has been made to strike first."

"Why are you telling me this?" asked Sassani. "Perhaps you loathe the fact that I've betrayed my nation, and this is your way of whipping me?"

"No, not at all, Colonel Sassani." said Director Mizrahi. "I have the deepest respect for you. You have vision, sir, and you have been able to look beyond doctrine and blind loyalties. You realize that to institute a bloodbath is no way to move a nation forward, and in that respect, you are rare. I am also a man of vision, gentlemen. It is my honest opinion that Plague Ten will not be controllable, and that the plan to have this virus kill only those in Iran will go awry. If unchecked, we could unleash a virulent disease that will spread well beyond Iran's borders, and it may very well spread around the globe. Unwittingly, the State of Israel may be about to release the ultimate doomsday device."

Shlomo Mizrahi rubbed his eyes for a moment.

"I am in charge of planning all this, gentlemen. And the more I engage in details of this attack on Iran, the more I realize that, if a single element goes wrong, this virus will be transmitted to others outside your nation, Colonel. Israel's top research scientists assure us that this deadly virus will only live twenty-eight days, but what if it somehow mutates and continues to replicate and spread? What if a single aircraft gets through the American umbrella, or a truck carrying refugees is able to successfully cross a border. The list of 'what if's' has grown exponentially, and my conclusion, while I have admittedly endorsed this plan as my nation's one remaining option, is that we are on the brink of a monumental catastrophe."

"That's why the two of you have been summoned here today. There is another option, gentlemen, one that I much prefer. If we are able to mount a highly perilous operation to destroy Iran's nuclear weapons by penetrating those two bunkers in which they are located prior to the scheduled release of Plague Ten, there will be no need to release the virus. I've been in contact with Shannon Parks, Deputy Director of the

Central Intelligence Agency. She shares my concerns, as apparently does the Secretary of the United States Navy."

"Colonel Sassani, it is my opinion that we must structure and mount an operation that calls for simultaneous attacks on Iran's two nuclear weapons bunkers. Our commando force will consist of U.S. Navy SEALs, Mossad agents, and Israeli paratroopers, the very best people from both our nations. And we would like you to lead that mission, Colonel. You have intimate knowledge of these nuclear weapons sites, and your participation is vital. If your mission should fail, Plague Ten will be released by Israel on schedule, and all in the Islamic Republic of Iran will then die. But **if** you succeed, reason and order will possibly prevail, and millions of lives, lives you cherish, will not be sacrificed."

"Director Mizrahi," said Colonel Sassani, "you do realize you're asking me to assist in the destruction of the weapon we refer to as, 'Allah's Sword,' do you not? Without nuclear weapons, we fear we may be exposed to Israeli aggression or attack."

"Colonel," said Yaakov, "we all know Iran hasn't created those weapons as a deterrent, but rather as a first strike option. The proof is the schedule of attacks looming before us this July. So please, Arshad, let's not confuse mindless doctrine with hard reality. If we do nothing, Israel will attack Iran without mercy in April. If you agree to this mission, there is a chance those in your nation will live. Isn't even an unlikely chance worth the risk?"

"You're right, Yaakov, of course," said the Colonel. "I've been hit with a barrage of information, and I'm still in a state of shock." He hesitated for a moment before speaking again. "Yes, gentlemen, I shall return to Iran and help you destroy our nuclear weapons. But, of course, we have the technology to continue to produce them, and it's only a matter of time before we will prepare once again to strike at Israel."

"We'll let the IDF and the U.S. military deal with that probable contingency later, Colonel," commented the Director. "For now, let's concentrate on what Mossad will call, 'Operation Cobra,' a rapid strike to kill the victim before it can react. Colonel, I'll have someone pick you up at 6:00 AM, and training will begin tomorrow. We'll need as much information as you can provide about what to expect within those two mountains, and obviously, the more details the better. You'll command this operation and lead one group, and Yaakov will lead the other, since he is also fluent in Farsi."

Director Mizrahi stood and extended his hand.

"Arshad, I'm sorry to give you this horrific news, but your nation has initiated this chain of events. We and the United States refuse to sit and await nuclear war, and it will be up to you and the Special Forces personnel committed to this operation to prevent the Plague Ten option from being utilized. The fate of your nation truly does rest in your hands."

The extended hand was accepted, and as Colonel Sassani turned to leave, the Director said, "Yaakov, stay for a moment, please."

The two men were now alone.

"Yaakov, the plan to release Plague Ten is far more extensive than I've actually led the Colonel to believe. On Passover morning, our nation intends to attack fourteen Arab nations simultaneously and kill all who reside there. The State of Israel and the Americans are weary of Jihadist attacks and a conflict against an invisible enemy that hides amongst its women and children. So the concept that a war of that nature will finally be over, because all who might wage it are dead, is a logical, albeit rather hideous conclusion."

"Fourteen nations?" asked Yaakov.

"Yes, our concern is that once other Arab nations realize Israel has killed all who reside in Iran, they will attack us," said Director Mizrahi. "The Saudis, we are sure, possess nuclear weapons, and perhaps Egypt will also obtain those weapons from Russia. We cannot start a conflict that, in the end, may go badly for us. So the decision has been made to strike at all Arab nations simultaneously, in order to control the outcome."

"Containment of this virus will be impossible," said Yaakov.

"Yes, I agree. Too many airports and borders, too many roads and unguarded, isolated ways to travel from one of these nations to a non-Arab state. The goat herders' path you used to enter Turkey is but one of perhaps ten thousand ways for people and this virus to enter another country.

"I'm sure you feel as I do, that we also can't expect full cooperation from nations bordering Iran such as Turkmenistan or Azerbaijan, or nations in Africa such as Chad and Sudan that border Libya and Egypt. Those borders are highly porous, and people will flee into those nations unabatedly. And the pandemic will then begin."

"Shlomo, if you and I instantly realize that Plague Ten can't be contained, even though our most meticulous efforts, then to proceed with its release is madness. How can others within our government not understand this?"

"Gadi Eisenkot said something in our meeting early last month," said Mizrahi. "He said to do nothing is like mindlessly shuffling into cattle cars in the early 1940s, just to be taken to places like Dachau. He's right. We must do something prior to the scheduled Iranian strike date in July, and Plague Ten seems the only option available to us. Operation Cobra is the only way we can prevent the release of this virus."

"Why are you putting an Iranian in charge of this operation, and how are you so sure we can trust him?" asked Yaakov.

"He is an Iranian patriot, Yaakov, and I believe he will follow through with the plan to destroy those nuclear missiles in order to save his countrymen," said Mizrahi. "I've given him the title of 'Commander' to play upon his ego, but you, in reality, will be the one in charge of this operation. If the Colonel seems to have a change of heart about our killing Revolutionary Guard troops in the course of destroying missiles, at that time you may consider him expendable."

"But won't we be many miles apart," asked Yaakov, "while we're simultaneously attacking two different weapons installations?"

"Yes," said Mizrahi. "The U.S. Navy SEAL commander will be at Sassani's side at all times, and the two of you will coordinate."

"How do you propose we'll infiltrate into Iran?" asked Yaakov.

"The Americans have committed to furnishing their latest RAH-88 Comanche stealth helicopters, eight of them, and each will carry ten men," said Mizrahi. "One group will enter Iran by flying low over the Caspian Sea from a base in Azerbaijan. The other group will launch from an American aircraft carrier in the Persian Gulf. Exfiltration will be the same way you came in, and you should be on the ground for at most an hour. It can't be more. Revolutionary Guard reinforcements will be massive."

The Director stood and the two men shook hands warmly.

"Where are we to begin training, Zayde?" asked Yaakov.

"At Masada."

CHAPTER 4

February 3, 2028 … Masada, Israel, 0915 Hours

In the year 37 BC, Herod the Great built a fortress in Judea on a tall, impregnable plateau named Masada. Construction lasted for six years and included a high, thick wall that encompassed the entire plateau, storehouses, a system of large cisterns to collect rainwater, barracks, a palace, and an armory. Long after Herod's death and decades later, at the beginning of the Jewish revolt against the Romans in 66 AD, a group of Jewish extremists called the Sicarii overcame the Roman garrison at Masada and were later joined by others after the fall of Jerusalem in 70 AD.

In 73 AD, the Roman Governor Flavius Silva led the Tenth Roman Legion against the Jews at Masada, and the siege began. The fortress could not be taken, and in the spring of 74 AD, the Romans constructed a massive ramp of stones and earth against the western approach to the fortress. A battering ram was positioned to breach the wall the following morning.

The nine hundred and sixty Jewish Zealots that defended Masada made a decision that day, to die in freedom by their own hands rather than die tortured deaths at the hands of the Romans. First, all the men killed their wives and children. They then drew lots, and ten were chosen. Those ten killed all the other men, and another group of lots gave one of the remaining ten the task of killing the other nine. He then set fire to whatever he could and fell on his own sword.

When the Romans broke through the western wall of the fortress at Masada eagerly prepared to slaughter the Zealots, they realized they had been cheated of that opportunity.

Free people willfully had taken their own lives.

To Israelis, that lesson has great significance.

It was just after 9:15 AM.

As Yaakov and the Colonel slowly toured the Masada plateau and the Israeli pointed out remnants of what was once a palace, they observed a group of young men and women running toward them, in single file. They were dressed in tan and brown fatigue pants and white T-shirts. These were new recruits of the Israel Defense Force, and they were completing the run up the seven hundred stairs from the base of the mountain to the top of the plateau. The Colonel noticed with obvious disbelief that nearly half of them were young women. So different from his native Iran, he realized.

The recruits stopped and formed ranks. An older man, obviously an officer, slowly moved among them, staring into each set of eyes.

Now at the front of their formation, he turned and faced his young men and women.

His voice was filled with determination as he barked these words: "What do you pledge?"

In unison, they loudly replied,

"‏שנית מצדה לא תיפול שנית!‏" "

A few moments later, the recruits left the plateau and in single file again, they disappeared quickly from view as they descended the steps.

The Colonel was curious.

"What did they shout in response?"

"Their response in Hebrew was, 'Masada shall not fall again,' " Colonel. Try to understand the meaning of that phrase, sir. The survivors of the Holocaust helped create the State of Israel, and we Jews of this modern age justifiably feel surrounded and besieged — as were our ancestors here at Masada besieged by a Roman legion nearly two thousand years ago. We are completely encircled by hostile nations today, and unlike those who died in the Holocaust and went meekly to their deaths, Masada, just like Israel, represents Jews who will not go quietly to their demise ever again."

The colonel shook his head.

"And so you are prepared to practice genocide and kill all the inhabitants of Iran, in order to preserve your nation," he said.

"Never Again," replied Yaakov.

"I despise the path the State of Israel is taking," said Sassani, "but I do actually understand the logic your leaders employ, Yaakov. If I were given the same two options, your entire nation's demise or the deaths of all in my beloved Iran, I would not hesitate to make a similar choice."

"Good, then we agree the way to prevent the Plague Ten option is to prepare thoroughly here and to execute Operation Cobra with precision," said Yaakov. "Perhaps, if we succeed and our nations narrowly survive annihilation, sanity will prevail."

"Agreed, Yaakov. That is my prayer."

The thirty American Navy SEALS arrived around noon in a swirl of dust caused by the huge rotors of their two Chinook helicopters. Another Chinook arrived twenty minutes later with their base camp gear. Yaakov and Colonel Sassani watched them organize their camp, set up five large tents, string camouflage netting and settle in, all in under an hour.

"Impressive," said the Colonel.

"Yup," said Yaakov, "almost as efficient as are those fellows over there, from the 35th Israeli Paratroopers Brigade."

The subtle competitive humor was lost on the Iranian.

February 3, 2028 … Tehran, Iran, 1700 Hours

They finally located her.

"Arrest them all," he commanded.

"Yes, General," was the immediate reply.

Eight VEVAK agents left their headquarters and drove toward a middle-class neighborhood in northern Tehran near Tajrish Square. It was evening. The family and their guest were gathered at their table, about to enjoy a simple meal.

The door burst open. Agents scooped up the three children as their mother screamed.

"No, do not do this," she wailed. But it was to no avail as two other agents began to drag her husband toward the door. He struggled, and one of the agents reached toward the dinner table. He seized a ceramic water pitcher and smashed it down on his victim's head. The man collapsed, unconscious.

Samira cried out, and her tears began to flow. Blood flowed down her husband's cheek, and she stared wide-eyed at the trail of bright red as his captors dragged him out the front door.

Agents escorted the two women out of the dining room, their hands steel vices on delicate, graceful arms.

In moments, the cars left the peaceful residential district behind and accelerated toward their destination, Evin Prison.

Samira was thrown into a cell and the metal door was slammed shut. She heard the lock engage. She was naked, the ultimate insult to her faith. As she raised her shivering body off the floor and looked at the stark, darkened interior of the cell, her eyes locked on one of the two narrow beds.

It was occupied. A man shifted slowly and sat up. He was large and filthy, and he stared between her legs.

She stood and walked shakily to the other bed, her feeble attempt to cover herself with bare hands an incomplete effort. Samira sat down facing him, and waited for the moment he would force her to submit to his desire. She shivered uncontrollably.

The man slowly stood and walked toward her. He towered above her, and as her eyes moved up and met his, he slowly began to unbutton his shirt.

"Please," she begged.

He removed the shirt and handed it to her.

"You are cold. Put this on," he said. He turned and walked back to his bed.

She donned the shirt and hastily buttoned it. She rolled the sleeves up quite a bit to locate her hands, and the front of the shirt flowed nearly to her knees.

"Thank, you," she whispered.

"Allah be praised," she mumbled.

"What's your name?" he asked.

"Samira. And yours?" she asked.

"Parviz." said the large man. "Doesn't 'Samira' mean 'entertaining companion'?" he asked.

"Yes. And 'Parviz' means 'lucky,' " she added.

He laughed, and so did she. Relief flowed through her.

"Why are you here, little butterfly?" asked Parviz.

"I don't know. VEVAK came and took us away. They took my three children!" She started to cry.

"What did you do?" he asked.

"We did nothing," said Samira. "We were about to share a meal, and they burst in on us and threw us in cars. My husband was at work all day. He had just returned, and his cousin and I and the children were just sitting down at dinner when the agents broke down the door."

"What did your husband do?" asked Parviz.

"Nothing out of the ordinary." said Samira

"You mentioned your cousin. Who is he?" asked Parviz

"It's 'she,' " corrected Samira.

"What did she do?" asked her persistent cellmate.

"Nothing," said Samira. "She's been staying with us for a while now. She helps me with the children. They love her, and so do we. She left her home in Tabriz about a month ago. She is a photographer, mainly wildlife and sunsets. Nousha is a wonderful person, as her name suggests. She has been working on what she describes as a looking glass into the Iran that the West has never seen. She believes she can create something that will help others understand our heritage by having photographs of our people and our architecture published. Some of the photographs she has taken are quite beautiful."

"Has she ever taken photographs of any military installations or VEVAK personnel at work? That could be the cause of all this," said Parviz.

"I can't be sure, but I don't think so," said Samira.

"You mentioned her name is 'Nousha.' What's her surname?" asked Parviz.

"Sassani. Nousha Sassani," said Samira.

"Sassani, Sassani," Parviz pondered out loud. "Isn't there someone in our military establishment with that name?"

"Yes," was the immediate reply, "Arshad Sassani is a Colonel in the Intelligence Directorate, and when he hears his younger sister has been arrested and thrown into Evin Prison, heads will roll."

I think not, thought the VEVAK agent. He realized Samira would not reveal anything of value within the confines of normal conversation and that it was time to squeeze information from her. He glanced in the direction of the hidden camera above the cell door frame and briefly shook his head from side to side, an indication that nothing of substance had been revealed.

Moments later, the cell door was unlocked. Two guards held Samira firmly while a third slowly unbuttoned her shirt. He stared at her breasts for a moment before they dragged her out of the cell. The shirt was thrown in the lap of the VEVAK agent, and the huge man shrugged, as if to say, "Oh, well, I tried."

Samira was sobbing as she was forced to sit on a wooden chair. Her hands were tightly bound to the upper portion of the chair, and she appeared to be in a position of continual surrender. Her ankles were pinned firmly against the front legs of the chair with duct tape.

Samira's chest heaved and she was unable to fight off the panic and fear that grasped at her. An older man appeared and he slid a metal chair across the room so that he could sit directly in front of her. The sound of the chair sliding across the concrete floor sounded like worn fingernails scraping across a chalkboard.

He sat down, looked her over slowly, and spoke tenderly, as if they were having a casual chat in a coffee shop.

"You are quite beautiful, Samira," he said. "You need to tell us everything you know about Arshad Sassani. You see, he has vanished, and we of VEVAK know that people have conspired to kidnap him. Tell us everything you know, and you'll be back in your home in plenty of time to tell your children bedtime stories."

"I know nothing," said Samira. "This is the first I've heard of his leaving our beloved Iran. I don't think his sister knows anything, either. She would have been nervous and afraid, and in the weeks she's been with us, she's shown not a single sign of those traits. If you've checked about me, you'd know I have degrees in behavioral psychology, and I can assure you that Nousha knows nothing of her brother's plans or his business."

The man's eyes were locked on hers and, as he calmly issued his command, his eyes never wavered.

"Bring in the youngest child," he said.

Samira's eyes widened.

Less than a minute went by, and then the door to the room opened. A man in a drab business suit entered the room, holding a little girl, at most three years old. She was bucking, kicking and screaming, but the man's grip was firm.

"Mommy, Mommy," pleaded the child.

"Tell your daughter to sit in the chair against the wall," said the man who still stared into Samira's eyes. He smelled of garlic.

"Do as the man says, Jasmine," said her mother.

The child obeyed. Another minute went by as Samira returned the man's gaze. Calmly, quite gently, he issued an order.

"Shoot the child in the head," he said.

As the guard who stood near the child obeyed, her mother tugged and lurched against her restraints.

"Noooooo!" she screamed.

The gunshot resonated off the stone walls and was deafening, and the blood splatter formed an elliptical pattern on the wall directly behind the dead child.

"That was to improve your memory, Samira," said the man, so very gently. "You have two more children in the next room, and we have so very many bullets."

Samira was out of control and gasped for air. She prayed to God to allow her to die, right then and there, and to kill the man seated in front of her. But He did neither, and the questioning continued.

"Samira, let me ask you again. Who assisted Colonel Sassani in his exodus from our glorious Republic?"

Samira's mind flew at the speed of light.

"It was one of his most trusted assistants at Oghab 2, an officer," she said. "He helped Arshad get to the border in order to defect."

"Which border?" asked the man.

"I think our border with Iraq," replied Samira, "but I'm not sure about that."

"How did Colonel Sassani get close to our border with Iraq?" asked the man.

"I think the officer drove him there," said Samira.

"Who is that traitor, Samira, the officer who drove Arshad Sassani to within walking distance of our border with Iraq?" asked the man.

"I don't know his name," said Samira. "Please believe me; I'm telling you the truth, as God is my witness."

"Of course you are, and thank you," said the man.

The man gave her a warm, fatherly smile.

"Bring in the boy," he commanded.

"No, no, please, I beg of you, please, please don't do this!" Samira shouted.

The door opened, and a boy was ushered in. He was perhaps six years old and had a mane of dark hair and dark, flashing eyes. He was instructed to sit in the chair against the wall and he obeyed, his eyes were fixed on the body of his younger sister on the floor and the slowly expanding pool of blood surrounding her head. He looked up in horror and began to hyperventilate.

"His asthma," said his mother. "He needs his inhaler."

The tall man who stood next to the boy thought that was amusing, as did another man nearer to the door. They both chuckled.

"Shoot the boy!" was the command, and it was done.

Samira's eyes bulged and the veins in her neck stood out, as she struggled against her restraints. The man leaned forward and patted her on the shoulder, a completely empty assurance in the midst of madness.

"Samira," he said, "Colonel Sassani drove his own truck north from Tabriz. It broke down and was discovered abandoned along the side of the road. Someone was with him, and together they trekked through snow covered mountains toward our border with Turkey. We were in position to stop them, but American helicopters swooped in from a base in Turkey and while they were engaged in combat with our troops, Colonel Sassani and his companion escaped. So we know that at least the Americans were involved in this plot, and probably also the Jews. Tell me who was with Arshad when they managed to leave our Republic."

Samira's mouth was so dry that she could barely speak. Dried spittle was encrusted on her lips, and blood trickled down from her bound wrists. It slowly dripped onto the floor from her elbows.

"Nousha must know," she mumbled.

"Bring in the other woman and the third child," said the man, and the order was obeyed.

The man stood, and Nousha was bound to his chair as Samira was bound to hers. She was also naked. The eldest child, a ten-year old girl with flowing auburn hair and dimpled cheeks, was placed in the same chair that was used to execute her brother and sister. Her eyes were glued on their bodies, and there was so very much blood, she kept thinking.

The elderly man spoke as though he were a judge delivering a sentence to someone found guilty of heinous crimes.

"Nousha Sassani," he said, "your brother, a trusted member of our armed forces and a trusted officer of Oghab 2, has defected and is now in the hands of the Americans. We need to know who assisted him in that endeavor, and we need to know his plans."

Nousha looked in horror at the bodies of two children she loved as her own, but she nonetheless remained calm.

"Please tell them everything you know," begged Samira.

Nousha thought for a moment and decided there was no harm in sharing the little she knew.

"Yes, it is true," she said, "my brother has left Iran. He told me it would be a few months, but he'd somehow send for me. All we have on earth is each other since his wife passed away several years ago. He has no children, our parents are dead, and I am widowed. The CIA helped him escape, and Arshad promised we would be reunited and live out the rest of our lives in a place called Denver. I've not heard of this place, but Arshad says it is beautiful, with mountains and valleys just like here in Iran. He is tired of a life tied to the military and constantly being watched. He knows he would never be allowed to leave Oghab 2 without being followed every minute of every day, so he has decided the only possible way to live a life of peace and tranquility is to live that life in America.

"Whatever knowledge he possesses will remain within him, I can truly assure you. He is a patriot and has always been fiercely loyal to this nation. He plans to give the American military only things they already know in return for asylum."

"Why did your brother not seek asylum during any of those scheduled meetings we've had in Brussels or during his three separate trips to Washington?" asked the old man.

"He did mention that to me," said Nousha. Arshad decided to defect sometime after those trips to Washington, and there are none scheduled again in the foreseeable future. Sometimes, when you have enough of a situation, you wake up the next morning and make plans."

She looked over at the bodies of the children. "Why would you do this?" she demanded. "You are monsters!"

The old man's response was as cold as it was brutal.

"I don't think you would have been so candid with us, unless you saw bodies of some of those you love on the floor," he said.

The aging man with a voice as soft as gentle rain seemed satisfied.

"Take Ms. Sassani back to her cell and give her clothes," he suggested softly. "Then return."

When the two men returned, the older man quickly withdrew a pistol from a shoulder holster nestled in his left armpit. He whirled and shot the ten-year old young girl squarely between the eyes. Her body flew backward and struck the crimson wall, and then the limp form collapsed on top of her dead brother's body.

Samira gagged and vomited onto the floor to the right of her chair as the room grew silent.

The man in charge headed for the door. He turned.

"The two of you have an hour to enjoy all that lovely Samira has to offer. It's a shame to waste so beautiful a woman without giving her life some purpose and meaning. Then shoot her and leave her next to the children over there."

Two hours later, Samira's husband was led into the room. He fell to his knees as he viewed the bloody remains that were once a family. As he wept, one of the men slid a bucket of water and mop across the floor. Four packages were thrown at his feet.

Body bags.

"Put this trash in these bags, and then mop the floor and wall. We'll be back in thirty minutes, and for your sake the work had better be completed by then."

Gagging and sobbing, the anguished man complied.

When the two men returned, one said, "Good job. Your lovely wife would be proud of you."

He laughed as the other man withdrew his Glock.

The agent then shot Samira's husband three times in the chest.

The grouping was very tight.

CHAPTER 5

February 3, 2028 ... Masada, Israel, 1400 Hours

"Gentlemen, my name is Major Yaakov Rafaeli. I am also a senior agent with Mossad, and for convenience, you may call me Yaakov."

Yaakov looked at the men seated in neat rows in their makeshift mess hall ... a large sand-colored canopy on four poles. Every pair of eyes was focused on him at that moment, and they all realized that scuttlebutt and conjecture were about to become old news.

"Precisely five months from yesterday, on this coming Fourth of July, Iran intends to launch missiles with nuclear warheads at Washington, D.C. and New York City. These missiles will be brought to approximately one hundred miles off the East Coast of the United States by submarines of the Iranian Navy. Their plan is to launch precisely at noon on that day. Eleven days later, Iran will launch a massive nuclear attack against the State of Israel on our Sabbath, in an attempt to wipe this nation off the face of the Earth."

"Sir, a question, please," asked one of the SEALs. "Doesn't Iran realize that a nuclear attack will be met with a nuclear response? We have the capability to level Tehran and all their other cities."

"That is correct," came a voice from the rear row of chairs. The man stood and walked forward to join Yaakov at the front of the room.

"My name is Colonel Arshad Sassani, gentlemen, and I'm the one who shared my nation's plans with Tel Aviv. Until recently, I was also second in Command of 'Oghab 2,' Iran's counter-espionage agency. We are chartered to protect our nation's nuclear facilities from threats. I am, therefore, intimately familiar with the location of all my country's nuclear missiles and the fortifications surrounding those sites. To answer your question, young man, the madness in all of this is that those in Tehran are unconcerned about the obvious consequences of initiating nuclear war. They are Jihadists, and the greatest glory any of us may achieve is to die in the pursuit of Jihad.

"Sadly, my nation is ruled by extremists, and I cannot fathom the logic they employ. I have murmured the right phrases and endured their radical speeches for decades now, simply as a means to achieve personal survival, and it's worked well for me. I have averted my eyes to the insanity of a father strapping explosives to his precious child in the name of some vague principal, because he's been instructed it is the righteous thing to do. I have watched the foolish ways in which the United Nations has attempted to peek in upon our nuclear program. And now, with my country's successful development of nuclear weapons, my nation is about to use them in the fathomless name of ultimate glory. At the highest levels of Iran's government, we are a nation of madmen being led by fools. The only real glory in death, gentlemen, is to avoid being one of those who die in combat while you systematically take the lives of your enemies."

With that, several of the commandos in the huge tent nodded. This Iranian, they realized, was not of the mold they envisioned as the enemy.

"Gentlemen, I am a patriot, and in proclaiming myself one, my thrust and concentration must necessarily be to work toward saving millions of Iranian lives, rather than methodically work to have them consumed in a nuclear travesty. I have seen and lived in your part of the world, in London actually, while working on a Master's Degree many years ago. The Muslim conscience within me has often been repulsed by what many in my country term, 'Western Decadence.' On the other hand, we are a nation of extremists as well, although clearly in the extremely opposite direction. In my world, for example, we have accepted for centuries the quite cruel and barbaric practice of female circumcision. This practice is referred to as 'Khafd' and is performed supposedly to control a woman's sexual urges. But this is blatant and systematic mutilation of innocent girls, nothing more. At the one extreme, Europe has red light districts where pleasure is a form of worship, and in the Muslim world, we maim our women to assure they'll never have a moment's pleasure. Surely, logic dictates that the better, far healthier path is some middle road for us all. At least that's my observation."

"Forgive me, Mate," explained one of the SEALs in a tortured Cockney accent, "but what does cuttin' into a lady's genitals have to do with imminent nuclear war?"

Several of the men in the room laughed in agreement. It seemed to them the Colonel was a bit off the wall.

"I'm merely trying to help all of you gentlemen understand that the differences between Western culture and the mindset in Tehran are extraordinary. Your goal in this operation is first of all to succeed, but just as importantly, you'd each prefer to return to your families alive. The men with whom you will engage in combat don't care if they live or die, and many of them look forward to death with far more zeal than your strongest desire to survive. You are soon to face an enemy, and I have great difficulty referring to my own people as the enemy, but that they are nonetheless. Those in Tehran are the enemies of life. For we all know the immediate consequences to the citizens of Iran, should any of their nuclear weapons somehow succeed in reaching a designated target.

"There is no room, gentlemen, to achieve *near* perfection in this operation. You who are Israeli understand it is unacceptable for us to destroy all but one of the missiles that may then vaporize Tel Aviv. And those of you who are Americans will most assuredly find it unacceptable if that one warhead detonates over Washington."

"Thank you, Colonel," said Yaakov, who now began the business of mapping out the mission.

"We'll have two groups of forty men," he said. "One group will launch from the USS *Ronald Reagan* on station in the Persian Gulf and will be comprised of the thirty Navy SEALs and nine agents of Mossad. Colonel Sassani will lead that party. I'll be in command of the other group, and we'll have ten Mossad agents and the thirty Israeli paratroopers. All our Mossad agents are fluent in Farsi, by the way. The second group will start our mission from a base at Baku, in Azerbaijan, and our wing of four helicopters will fly south over the Caspian Sea and then inland. Our objectives, gentlemen, are two underground fortified bunkers in Iran. One is at the base of Mount Qash-Mastan in the Zagros Mountain Range near Yasuj. The other is located at Mount Damavand in the Middle Alborz Mountains near Kodir. You probably don't recognize any of those names, but to give you some perspective, Mount Damavand has an elevation of 18,400 feet, and Mount Qash-Mastan is a bit smaller, at 14,500 feet. Both of these locations have been chosen quite well by the Iranians, gentlemen. These mountains are perpetually encased in snow and ice, and the terrain greatly limits our abilities to conceal ourselves.

"At the entrances to each of these mountain strongholds there are massive blast doors, and there is only one road that approaches each of our targets. Within roughly five to ten miles of these locations, there are an estimated one thousand elite motorized Revolutionary Guard troops billeted and on call at all times. Inside each mountain is a winding road carved into solid rock that's nearly a mile long. There are two more sets of blast doors and finally, a parking area where trucks carrying Iran's nuclear missiles stand prepared, at a moment's notice, to be driven into the open if an order is given to launch. Colonel Sassani has assured Tel Aviv that Iran's additional nuclear weapons, those not already mounted on transport trucks, are also stored at these two locations."

"Gentlemen," added Colonel Sassani, "the plan is to have four U.S. stealth helicopters at each of these sites drop us onto a small ridge that flattens out slightly. On Qash-Matan, that site is nearly two thousand feet above and somewhat east of the entrance to the fortification. On Mount Damavand, it's a similar situation, but our drop point is to the west. Each drop-off point will be very narrow and snow encrusted, and the plan demands that we hit the ground undetected. We'll then have to rappel down silently and dispatch any troops at the entrances before they can sound an alarm. They'll have vehicles, and we'll simply mount them, drive down into the heart of the mountains and destroy Iran's nuclear weapons. We'll then drive the captured vehicles back toward the entrances and immediately rendezvous with the helicopters before any of the Revolutionary Guard detachments may arrive. The two groups, I might add, must initiate their attacks simultaneously, but we will be totally unable to assist one another in the event of a crisis. The two sites we're attacking are nearly a thousand kilometers apart, so each group will be completely on its own."

One of the men spoke up, a SEAL Master Chief.

"So at each location, it may be forty of us against however many are inside the mountain, plus a thousand Revolutionary Guard troops if we don't get out of Dodge in time, right?" he asked.

"Sounds like a fair fight to me, with the odds in our favor," joked one of the Israeli Paratroopers.

A few of his fellow paratroopers laughed, but most did not.

"Why are we here at Masada?" asked another.

"To practice rappelling," responded Yaakov.

"Those mountains in Iran are primarily limestone, and as you may already know, limestone is an organic sedimentary rock. It's extremely soft, and it crumbles quite easily. You've all rappelled, but swinging out and hitting a rock face hard with your boots as you descend will be unacceptable. The limestone will break apart upon impact, and falling rocks will make noise. The men at the bottom will cut us to ribbons if there's any hint of what's going on, so we're here to practice a new art form, gentlemen. Within a week or so, you all will be experts at rappelling gently and soundlessly on limestone. We'll also be doing this in Iran at 3:00 AM, so you'll be required to exercise your newly acquired art in complete darkness."

"After a week of training," said Colonel Sassani, "we'll practice rappelling off the plateau here at Masada while we are all blindfolded. Our trainers will be able to observe, in order to scrutinize your skills, and they'll then help you make adjustments. You must all realize that silence as we descend at both sites in Iran will be absolutely essential. If those at the entrance to either of those installations are alerted, we will be massacred."

One of the Israeli paratroopers spoke up.

"Why are we doing this?" he asked. "We've all been inoculated already, and in another few weeks our entire nation will be resistant to this virus. Why don't we simply release Plague Ten and have a picnic while all those who despise us die and disappear? This sounds like a suicide mission to me, by the way, with all due respect, sirs."

Veins bulged in Arshad Sassani's neck at the concept that killing everyone in Iran and several other nations was meaningless to this young man, but before he could respond, Yaakov interrupted.

"All of you, listen to me. Greater minds than ours have major reservations about the success of releasing and containing the Plague Ten virus, he said. "What if someone exposed manages to escape his dying nation, and he ends up in Europe, Asia, or North America? What if the virus mutates and is no longer harmless after twenty-eight days, as our scientists assure us will be the case. What if the virus also mutates into a new strain, one that is not resisted by the inoculations we've all had? Then all in Israel will also die.

"Plague Ten may very well kill all life on earth, and this mission is the only cork that will keep that deadly virus contained in a bottle in a laboratory. If we fail, it will be released, but if we succeed, the innocent in all these Arab nations will not die. Those of us who are Israeli well remember the attempted genocide of the 1940s at the hands of the Nazis, and we all should loathe committing the very act we despise.

"The plan we've laid out is certainly one filled with risk and may even be labeled under the heading, 'desperation,' but it is nevertheless the plan, and it is our duty to execute it to the best of our abilities."

"Hooyah," said one of the SEALs.

"Hooyah," repeated the other twenty-nine in unison.

"May I say something, sir?" asked one of the Mossad agents. He was very young, but his eyes revealed the fire within him.

"Yes, you may," said the Colonel.

The young agent named Ari removed a small card from his wallet.

"I keep this with me when I'm here in Israel," he said, "and when I'm on a mission, I keep it in my head. I'm a history buff, and this is a quote from the American Indian, Crazy Horse, just before the battle at the Little Big Horn. It's quite famous. He simply said, 'Today is a good day to die.'

"But it's the actual meaning of that quotation that inspires me, gentlemen. The Lakota Sioux went into battle that day with the U.S. 7th Cavalry, trusting in a power far greater than that possessed by all their warriors combined.

"They believed, they *knew*, that whatever the outcome, it would necessarily be good. Those of them who passed away that day did so in completeness, and those who survived knowingly did so at the discretion of their Creator.

"The world will remember for generations what we are about to do in those mountains in Iran, provided we succeed. If we fail, there might be no one left alive to criticize our efforts. I am honored to be a part of this group, and if it is God's will for me, that day in the mountains of Iran will be my own personal very good day to die."

"Thank you, young man," responded the Colonel.

Arshad's eyes were a bit misty.

Their specialized training began early the following morning.

February 6, 2028 ... Washington, D.C., 1330 Hours

"Mr. President, thank you for seeing me on short notice," said the Director of the CIA.

As they sat down on two muted yellow and white striped sofas in the Oval Office and faced one another, another man quickly joined them, the Chairman of the Joint Chiefs of Staff. As he sat down next to Director Brennan, General Dunford addressed the man seated on the opposite sofa.

"Good afternoon, Mr. President," he said

"Same to you, Joe. What's up, gentlemen?" said the President.

"Mr. President," began the Director, "Shlomo Mizrahi, the top man at Mossad, is in the process of mounting an operation to take out Iran's nuclear weapons well in advance of the date Israel has committed to release their Plague Ten virus. He's assembled a group consisting of thirty Israeli paratroopers, twenty agents of Mossad, and the part of that operation we're here to discuss is that we've already agreed to send thirty of our Navy SEALs to participate heavily in the operation. We've also agreed to commit eight of our latest stealth helicopters to the Mossad plan, sir, the new RAH-88 Comanche. Our commitment to participate in this operation, was orchestrated by Shannon Parks on our side. I've reprimanded her, Mr. President, for not going through the proper channels and clearing all this with me. I would have killed our participation, but the SEALs are already on the ground in Israel, training for the mission. When I discussed this matter with General Dunford, we agreed to bring this to your attention. So the question we have for you is twofold. Do we (A) pull out the Navy SEALs and wash our hands of this highly perilous and unsanctioned mission, or do we (B) choose to continue our participation?"

"Shannon agreed to participate in a clear act of war against Iran, without going through the proper protocols? What's her explanation?" the President asked.

"She believes that time is of the essence," said the General, "and that going through channels, including the likelihood of getting you and Congress to sign off on an act of war, would have taken far too long."

The President was silent for a moment and then looked at the two men seated before him.

"Gentlemen," he said, "I share Director Mizrahi's obvious concerns about his nation's plans to release this virus. He must have grave misgivings about releasing a deadly plague; otherwise he'd not be mounting what sounds like a quite desperate mission to me.

The President hesitated, then added with apparent anger, "And Shannon Parks had the audacity to agree to participate in this plan? Does she not realize that if any of these men, our men, are captured or killed, that part of the world will explode in our faces?"

"Ms. Parks remains firm in her evaluation of the situation and in making those decisions, Mr. President," added Director Brennan, "and she's offered her resignation for this completely uncharacteristic breach of protocol, sir."

"Don't accept it," decided the President. "I agree with her. Any operation, to ward off the Israeli's deployment of Plague Ten, however desperate, is worth the risk of failure. To get Congress involved would take weeks, if not months. I want you to give the Israelis all the assistance they may require, gentlemen, and put Shannon in charge of our side of this operation. This virus scares the hell out of me, and I'm clearly not alone in that analysis. I do have one stipulation, however. It occurs to me that part of this plan by the Israelis might include infiltration into Iran by our people, dressed in military uniforms. I ask that they not do that. I want our people to wear our uniforms, and I want a red, white, and blue patch on their shoulders that proudly displays our flag. And screw the notion of 'plausible deniability.' Let these bastards know who is there to kill them, gentlemen; let them know we're there to send them all straight to hell."

"And one more thing, gentlemen," he continued. If this mission is successful and we can avert Israel's release of Plague Ten, I want

Shannon Parks in this room, so I can personally present her with the Presidential Medal of Freedom. The lady has balls."

The President stood, handshakes were exchanged, and as the door to the Oval Office closed behind them, Director Brennan and General Dunford breathed a sigh of relief.

"You really knew nothing of Shannon's discussions with the Israelis?" asked the General.

"Of course I did, Joe," said Brennan. "She and I share the same concerns, and running this by the President initially might have been a disaster. This isn't the first time you or I have played our Commander in Chief like a fiddle, my friend."

General Dunford chuckled.

"You folks at Langley play the fiddle as an art form," he said.

"Our middle initial *does* stand for 'Intelligence,' Joe," said Brennan

"Give Shannon my regards, John," said the General

"I'll call her as soon as I get to my car," said Brennan. "She's a bit nervous about putting her ass on the line, so she'll be relieved that it went well."

February 6, 2028 ... Tehran, Iran, 1900 Hours

"Where is his sister now?" asked Minister Mahmoud Alavi.

"We've removed her from Evin Prison and she now resides in a walled safe house here in Tehran," replied General Firouzabadi. "She is the only bargaining chip we have, if we want to control Colonel Sassani now that he's defected to America. We guard her very closely."

"We originally thought he'd been kidnapped. Why would a man like Sassani choose to defect?" asked Alavi. As the head of Iran's Intelligence Directorate, his questions required immediate answers.

"His sister says he wanted to leave what he apparently terms a 'closed, extremist society.' He thought that, if we ever allowed him to retire from the military, he'd be watched every minute of every day. She claims he wants to live in an American state called 'Colorado.' In order to assure his silence, we need to have his sister contact him. I'm sure she knows how to do that. Once we locate him we'll send VEVAK agents to America to execute him."

"He has intimate knowledge of our plans in July," said Minister Alavi as he slowly shook his head in disbelief that so trusted a career military man would choose to defect. "What if he reveals all he knows, in return for asylum?"

"His sister claims Colonel Sassani will reveal only minimal plans and details, things the Americans essentially already know. He seems to think he can get away with that and still gain asylum, and his sister has assured us he remains patriotic to our Republic."

"He is a fool, General. The CIA will squeeze everything out of him, I promise you. And do not mention his former rank again in our glorious armed forces. Arshad Sassani is now an enemy of our nation. As we move forward, we must assume the Americans know every detail of our plans to help celebrate their date of independence and that the Jews also know the launch date against Tel Aviv."

General Hassan Firouzabadi was fuming. He and Arshad Sassani had been friends, he thought. And now the man was a traitor and had been entrusted with deadly secrets. How would the CIA and the American Pentagon react to the news of an imminent nuclear launch against their nation? And the Jews? No, not so much to be concerned about Israel, he decided. They have little capabilities, compared to the Americans.

"Minister Alavi, I have an idea," began the General.

CHAPTER 6

February 12, 2028 … The Pentagon, 0730 Hours

"Gentlemen, we have a problem."

All eyes at the conference table were glued on Shannon Parks. She stood, adjusted the jacket of her tailored business suit, and slowly looked around the room.

My God, she thought, *I'm the center of the universe now, and this room is filled with more brass than one might find in a souvenir shop in Jakarta.*

Her urge to flee and hide under a bed in her parents' home in Wichita was a brief, fleeting thought.

This, after all, wasn't Kansas anymore.

She raised a finger, a signal to an agent who was using a laptop, and an image appeared on a screen on the wall behind her.

"Sorry about the crisis alert calls at 0515 Hours, gentlemen, but this is, as you'll soon realize, a crisis," she said. "This high-resolution photograph was taken on four January of this year. It is of the Iranian naval base at Bandar Abbas where the Persian Gulf meets the Gulf of Oman at the Strait of Hormuz. Among other dormant vessels at anchor there are clearly shown three submarines of the Islamic Republic of Iran's Navy. Their navy operates a total of six of these ships and they were procured from Russia over a three-year time span, from October of 2021 through early December of 2024.

"Russia has also assisted Iran in upgrading and modernizing this fleet of diesel-electric submarines, and Iran's interest in these boats was highly opportune for the Russians. Diesel technology has given way to nuclear power in Russia's continuing race for equality with our navy and that of China, and just as the Russians were about to send these diesel boats to their scrapyard, Iran gave them the proverbial 'offer they couldn't refuse.' But Iran's contractual stipulation with Moscow contained some secret modernization provisions that have now been implemented, and the terms of that contract were satisfactorily completed by one January, 2027. We don't actually know precisely what improvements were negotiated and performed, other than the logical assessment that enhancements, which required two years to conclude, must have been substantial."

"Shannon, I hope you didn't bring us here at this hour to recite a history of the Iranian Navy." said the Secretary of Defense, in a decidedly edgy voice.

"No, Mr. Secretary," said Shannon, "please allow me to continue, sir." Shannon raised a finger to indicate she had much more pertinent information to share.

"As you gentlemen can see, the photographs we're showing you are essentially the same. They were all taken in January, on the eighth, the twelfth, the sixteenth, and the twentieth."

She signaled once again to her associate and spoke rapidly.

"There was more of the same, on the twenty-fourth and on the twenty-eighth of January, gentlemen, and again on one February and on five February. Then, from our satellite pass on nine February, you'll note a change. Hold on this photograph, please, Phillip. You'll notice that just three days ago, there unexpectedly appeared a fourth submarine in a slip at Bandar Abbas. We thought that alarming, so we tasked a satellite to take daily photographs of the naval base.

"Phillip, please. On ten February and again yesterday, there were no changes and you'll note that four of Iran's six submarines remained tucked quietly in their slips. There was no unusual activity to report on either the tenth of February or yesterday, but we were still puzzled by the inexplicable appearance of a fourth submarine at that naval base. You're here this morning, gentlemen, to see the results of this morning's satellite pass, when this and other images were recorded. Phillip, please display the last photograph."

"They're gone!" said General Dunford loudly.

"Yes, General," said Shannon Parks, "the four submarines of the Iranian Navy have set sail within the past twenty-four hours, since the last set of satellite images were taken yesterday morning. Our concern at Langley is that Tehran has thrown aside the Fourth of July timetable, because they assume Colonel Arshad Sassani has revealed Iran's plans to us. We don't know if they somehow managed to affix towed array canisters containing nuclear weapons to the four subs before those submarines set sail, but our best guess is that they did not. Our feeling is that those boats left Bandar Abbas in a hurry, and that they'll rendezvous somewhere with a transport carrying the towed array devices and their missiles."

"There's a lot of conjecture in all this, Ms. Parks," said the Secretary of Defense.

"Yes, Mr. Secretary that's correct. But the information we're able to provide you this morning is only a few hours old. We'll find those submarines, sir, and with a little more time, we'll understand their entire plan and revised timetable."

The Secretary of Defense was clearly displeased, and the drumming of his fingertips on the conference table was now incessant.

"Gentlemen," began the Secretary of the Navy, Ray Mabus, "based upon all intelligence reports I've read, we are talking about fairly sophisticated submarines, which are operated by a hostile nation. And which may very well be heading for the Eastern Seaboard of the United States. We've all read the reports furnished by this Iranian Colonel, and we must assume those four submarines now carry or will later be equipped with nuclear weapons targeted at this nation."

Secretary Mabus stood for emphasis.

"This will not happen on my watch, gentlemen, I assure you," he said.

Later, as they were concluding the meeting, Ray Mabus called Shannon Parks aside.

"Ms. Parks," he said, "I want your solemn commitment to share with me, personally, every piece of information, including seemingly inconsequential scuttlebutt, about these phantom Iranian submarines. No one knows our SOSUS detection system better than me, and this situation will potentially be many thousands of times more devastating than the attack on Pearl Harbor by Japan nearly ninety years ago, young lady.

"Do you read me, loud and clear, Shannon? I don't want some young Ivy League spook at Langley to decide what's important and what's not important to share with me, understand?"

"Yes, sir, we'll share *everything* with you, sir," said Shannon as she turned to leave.

"Fry goddamned Washington and New York City, will they? These fellows in Tehran are pickin' a fight with the wrong boy from Mississippi," said Mabus, with his teeth clenched.

She knew the man addressing her was so much more than his occasional sleepy drawl indicated. To the halls of power in Washington from rural Mississippi, she mused. With a Master's Degree from Johns Hopkins and a degree from Harvard Law wedged quite securely in between, Secretary Mabus was never one to be taken lightly.

February 12, 2028 … The Arabian Sea, 2100 Hours
Captain Ghorbani took a deep breath. The cold night air was a respite from what they had been breathing while submerged for the past seventeen hours.

His mind raced back to the meetings of the past three days, the hurried plans, and the rush to leave port undetected. He knew every inch of this "boat" and her long list of innovations, technology which should allow the submarine to move into hostile waters undetected. The Captain's confidence soared as he closed his eyes for a moment and proudly pictured the Persian name carefully painted on both sides of his submarine in delicate white strokes.

دست صالحان

Righteous Hand, an excellent name, he thought, symbolic of the mission before his crew. With God's assistance, he knew, they would deftly slip through the American Navy's SOSUS network and strike daggers into the heart of the infidel beast.

They were running due south on the surface now at flank speed and would do so until just before dawn.

The powerful diesel engines of the Islamic Republic of Iran's *Righteous Hand* were running perfectly, and he hoped the other three captains were having as much success as he was. Their instructions had been quite clear; there was to be no communication between the four submarines, and they were to run as though they were alone.

The Captain opened a sealed metal box affixed to the interior wall of the submarine's conning tower and depressed a yellow button. "Dive, dive!" he yelled into the microphone.

He quickly locked the box and slid gracefully down the ladder.

A sailor moved up the ladder and immediately secured the circular hatch that leads to the tower. He spun the wheel on the inside of the hatch and tightened it.

"Hatch secured, sir!" he yelled.

Captain Ghorbani watched and waited as those around him performed their well-rehearsed ballet.

"Forty-one seconds," he said, as he showed his stopwatch to the boat's Executive Officer.

"Our goal is to be under thirty seconds, is that clear?"

"Yes, Captain."

"Level off at thirty meters, run for sixty minutes, and then we'll surface and enjoy the canopy of clouds overhead. They are perfect camouflage for us tonight, Asad." His XO smiled confidently.

When the submarine surfaced, she was greeted with a roiling sea and rumbling, menacing storm clouds that carried torrential rains in the distance, but she steadfastly maintained her course.

February 13, 2028 … Langley, Virginia, 0610 Hours

"Shannon, here, you'll need this," were the words spoken by a soft, friendly voice.

She looked up sleepily and her arms remained folded beneath her chin on the desk.

"What time is it?" she asked.

"0600 Hours."

"Any news? I guess I crashed and burned around 2:00 AM, Paul," said Shannon. "Thanks for the coffee … how do I look?"

"Let me remain politically correct, Ms. Parks," said Paul. "You are, at the moment, not your normally immaculate self."

Two sips of coffee and it was time for the ladies' room.

On the way back to her office ten minutes later, she wagged a finger at Paul Vander Vere. As Shannon sat and placed her wire-rimmed spectacles on the bridge of her nose, Paul sat down in one of the two chairs at the front of her desk. He studied her while she logged in and wished she would pay more attention to him. In his eyes, Shannon Parks was magnificent in every conceivable way. At thirty-two, she maintained the body of a well-toned athlete, and she possessed the delicate facial features of a Bernini sculpture.

Paul studied her exquisite face as she puffed several times at a long strand of auburn hair that kept drifting annoyingly toward her right eye. He decided that a regal sculpture of her, similar to that of Ludovica Albertoni reclining gracefully within the Church of San Francesco a Ripa in Rome, might be used to improve the images that adorned the Fontani de Trevi.

The brief thought of a white marble replica of the alluring Ms. Shannon Parks, with water perpetually squirting from her nipples into the fountain's pool, made him smile.

Shannon seemed to read his mind and glanced at Paul. She often displayed a quiet brilliance, he was instantly reminded, and when those green eyes searched the face of a man, she seemed to have the ability to gaze into his soul. It was frustrating to work so closely with a woman he adored, to have her always seem to know what others around her were thinking, and yet not have a clue about what was going on in her head.

"Tell me something really good, Paul," she said, "like we know the location of those four submarines and their destination."

"Here's the math, Shannon," as he began to cite from memory.

She knew enough to begin scribbling as he spoke.

"The last diesel-electric submarine produced by the U.S. Navy was the USS *Blueback*," he said, "and that was in late January of 1960, nearly seventy years ago. If that ship were nuclear powered, we wouldn't be having this discussion, because nuclear powered vessels essentially have limitless range. But there's relevance to look at the Blueback's numbers, because they can give us some insight about the range of those diesel-powered Iranian submarines.

"The Russians produced a similar vessel to the Blueback, and that's what Iran has purchased. It's much more modern than the Blueback, as it was produced through 2016. It's called the Kilo-Class fourth-generation diesel-electric submarine. Kilo-Class boats are about two-hundred and thirty-five feet long, very similar to our diesel submarines like the Blueback, which was two hundred and nineteen feet long. Assuming a Kilo is not towing an array of missiles, which would drastically reduce its speed and range, we estimate it to have a range of within ten percent of the older Blueback's, which was nineteen thousand miles without refueling. If we give the slightly larger Kilo the benefit of a somewhat greater fuel capacity than the Blueback and we also assume the Iranian boats are traveling at full rather than at flank speed, we conclude that the range of the submarines that have sailed from Bandar Abbas is at most twenty-one thousand miles. Much less if they are, if fact, towing those arrays."

"Give me the bottom line, Paul," said Shannon.

"The bottom line is this," said Paul. "We believe those submarines must be heading due south from Bandar Abbas into the Arabian Sea. They sure as hell aren't going to perform a hard-right turn at the southernmost tip of Yemen, parade through the Suez Canal and then manipulate the Strait of Gibraltar. So that means they'll head south and then somewhat southwest into the Indian Ocean. They'll give Cape Town a wide berth and eventually sail northwest into the South Atlantic Ocean."

"Bottom line, please," said Shannon. "Not a geography lesson

"A vessel traveling from Bandar Abbas south," said Paul, "at the time it is positioned well south of Cape Town and has turned in a northerly direction, will have traveled roughly six thousand miles. It will then travel another six thousand five hundred miles in order to reach its refueling destination. That's the key to all this, Shannon … the absolute need to refuel, and the only logical place to do that is at the Russian Naval Base at Puerto Caballo, Venezuela. Those Iranian submarines, especially if they are towing containers loaded with missiles, cannot ignore the South American continent and continue into the North Atlantic. They don't have the range to get within striking distance of our Eastern Seaboard, launch missiles, and sail south again into the sunset.

That plan simply isn't feasible without their first refueling in Venezuela."

"Why are you so sure they're heading for Venezuela, Paul?" asked Shannon.

"Because," said Paul, "it's an additional nineteen hundred miles for those submarines to ignore and travel past the South American continent to get within their planned striking distance of Washington and New York. If they're actually towing those arrays, that means if they launch without having refueled, they will not have enough fuel to return to Bandar Abbas. Clearly, they cannot possibly intend, after launching nukes at us, to run out of fuel and become bobbing corks on the high seas. Not a chance that's their plan. Logic dictates they must necessarily refuel *before* continuing into the North Atlantic, and we also believe that will be the time and place when those submarines will be equipped with the containers containing missiles.

"The only place that's a friendly enough port in South America for all that to be accomplished is at the Russian naval base at Puerto Caballo. The Iranians will also have a sense of security when docking there. In order for us to attack those submarines at that point in time, we'd essentially be declaring war on Russia by attacking their naval base and killing Russians in the process. Their destination cannot be anywhere else than the base at Puerto Caballo."

"Okay," said Shannon, "how long before they arrive in Venezuela?"

"At full speed," said Paul, "a Kilo will travel at ten knots surfaced and twenty knots submerged. A good assumption is that each twenty-four-hour period will include roughly twelve hours of travel each way. They'll travel submerged during the day, of course, and on the surface at night. That means the Iranian submarines will travel at an average of fifteen knots, or roughly seventeen and a quarter miles per hour. To travel twelve thousand five hundred miles at that speed will take them about thirty days.

"Assuming maximum efficiency at their refueling destination of one day," said Paul, "and that they set sail immediately into the North Atlantic at an average reduced speed of twelve knots while towing those arrays, they will be in a position to launch those missiles against us in an additional six days. It is our best estimation, boss, that we only have between thirty-five and forty days before nuclear weapons are used against this nation."

Shannon's expression was grim.

"Then let's assume we have less than thirty," she said.

"There's one other important piece of this puzzle, Shannon," said Paul. "Under the current 'oil-for-goods' program that's been going on for the past thirteen years, there is a constant flow of ships in and out of Bandar Abbas. One ship, however, has attracted my attention. She arrived on five February, and it's typical for any cargo ship to be in that port for at least fifteen days. Apparently, Iran's stevedores don't work with much haste. Bandar Abbas is *not* New Jersey."

"What's special about that ship?" asked Shannon.

"She sailed on ten February, boss," said Paul, "and I can think of only one reason for her prioritized loading … she's carrying the arrays to be towed behind Iran's submarines and a complement of missiles and nuclear warheads.

"We're tracking that freighter now, and she's obviously heading for a passage through the Suez Canal. It's my opinion that this cargo ship will traverse the Mediterranean Sea and sail through the Strait of Gibraltar. If her intended course is the North Sea and a Russian port, that ship will then head north and become unimportant to us, but if I'm correct, she will head southwest toward Venezuela."

"How far away are we from that determination?" asked Shannon.

"Gibraltar is fifty-three hundred miles from Bandar Abbas," said Paul, "so that vessel will either turn north or southwest twenty-three days from the day she sailed, on the tenth of February. So we'll know if I'm correct about that vessel twenty days from today, on the fourth of March."

"We have to keep exploring all other possible scenarios, Paul," said Shannon. "You're seldom wrong when it comes to analysis, but we'll have nothing if that cargo ship heads into the North Sea toward a Russian Federation port in early March. I'm scheduled to meet with the President this afternoon and the Chairman of the Joint Chiefs. I'm expected to give those gentlemen facts and not anything laden with hypothesis or conjecture."

"Then you'd better tell the President and General Dunford one very specific fact," said Paul. "The name of that ship we're tracking is the '*Yuriy Arshenevshiy*.' She is painted bright red, so there's no way of mistaking her in a sea of other vessels. She sails under the flag of the Russian Federation. That ship contains those towed arrays and missiles armed with nuclear warheads, and she is headed for the Russian Naval base at Puerto Caballo, in Venezuela.

"On the fourth of March she will turn and head southwest, and the *Yuriy Arshenevshiy* will dock in Venezuela on the morning of the fifteenth of March. History tends to repeat herself, Shannon, and the date of that vessel's arrival in Puerto Caballo should be a warning to this nation."

With that, Paul turned and went back to his desk.

The Ides of March, thought Shannon.

An ominous chill swept over her.

CHAPTER 7

February 15, 2028 … Masada, Israel, 1400 Hours

"Gentlemen, well done," commented Major Edwin Powell.

Several days of grueling training were now behind them, but they'd already suffered a casualty. On day three of their exhausting six-descents-a-day schedule, one of the Mossad agents destined to be on Colonel Sassani's team broke an ankle and was relieved of his participation in the mission.

A quick call to Washington gave them their eightieth man once more. Ed Powell was assigned to fill the gap.

Edwin James Powell was fiercely proud of his heritage, and as the grandson of General Colin Powell, he had great shoes to fill. Initially, he was to be merely on loan to this desperate endeavor, and as the lead instructor for the past four years at the Special Forces Advanced Mountain Operations School (SFAMOS) located in Ft. Carson, Colorado, Major Powell was well-equipped to teach skilled combat troops the art of climbing and rappelling.

But the course in Colorado he normally taught at the Army Mountain Warfare School was designed to be six weeks, rather than the highly abbreviated practice at Masada, and that concerned him greatly. The great equalizer was that these men he was training on Masada were the very best to have ever graced his ropes.

That evening, in their mess tent, as Major Powell mulled over the fact that he was to be the only black man in a fighting force of eighty, he looked up at the SEAL seated across from him and flashed a broad grin.

"This dance we're about to attend is gonna be like an NBA All Star game," he said, "but in reverse, don't you think?"

"What do you mean, sir?" was the polite reply.

"I mean, sailor, that if this was an elite group of NBA greats, there'd most likely be seventy-nine who looked like me, and perhaps one of the light-skinned variety … just the opposite of the little team of all stars seated here this evening.

"We're all one color here, Major" said one of the Israeli paratroopers. He raised his cup in salute. "Gentlemen, in the ensuing days, I pray that I may do honor to my rank, my country, and that I make my grandfather proud."

"One color, one cause, one victory," said one of the SEALs.

This time, all the men raised their cups in salute.

I wish others in my nation could observe these men, thought Colonel Sassani as he also raised his cup.

It was 4:30 in the afternoon, and they were all gathered on the plateau near the eastern face of Masada. The drop off behind Major Powell was severe.

"Gentlemen," he began, "as you've been informed, we have two other expert climbers within our group. Colonel Arshad Sassani and Yaakov Rafaeli have been sport climbing and rappelling for several years, and they have excellent skills.

"We've practiced the art of the rappel, and you all are now quite adept at controlling the rate of your descent in a relatively short, two-hundred-foot practice route and gently pushing off a rock face on the way down. We're not going to ask any of you to descend blindfolded as our practice schedule becomes more intense, by the way."

The Major laughed.

"It was actually my idea to have Colonel Sassani mention that, to see if you all had the stomach to carry on here. We've already lost one member of our team to a broken ankle, and the risk of additional injuries is too great to do something stupid like asking you to fly at night."

Several of the men breathed a sigh of relief. Give them a target to acquire and they were all capable, but the fear of the unknown and operating without all their senses intact was really unnerving.

"Today, we will practice the actual descent plan," said Major Powell, "as mapped out by detailed satellite topography at both locations in Iran. What's involved is a series of two hundred- and fifty-foot pitches, eight in all. I've vetoed the idea of descending in four five hundred-foot pitches. Here's the logic of that decision. First, ropes of that required length are extremely cumbersome, and we're to commence our descents from a somewhat awkward and narrow plateau. Second, if our pitches are each five hundred feet, your metal rappel devices will become extremely hot from friction as your rappel rate escalates. The exterior fibers of our ropes will then begin to melt. That's an unacceptable hazard for those coming behind you, and I'd personally hate to be the last man down that rope in one of those longer pitches. So a series of eight pitches is what we've agreed upon, and it's essential, as you go from pitch to pitch, that you spray your rappel device with this substance, which will instantly cool it. It's water based, by the way."

He held up a small spray can.

"Unhook from a rope, spray your rappel device, and then hook onto the next rope. I'll be the first man down in Colonel Sassani's group, and Yaakov will be the first man down in his. Anchor placement will be essential, and all forty men in each group should complete the full descent within two hours' time. We're going to practice today in deep shade on the eastern face of Masada as evening approaches, and we'll do that for the next three days. Then we'll practice for another two evenings with full equipment, and your graduation ceremony will be to perform these eight pitches beginning at midnight the following night while carrying all your gear. Remember, silence is absolutely mandatory during your descent.

"There are two separate sets of ropes with eight separate pitch points set up behind me. Your groups will descend separately, and I'll provide the beer and peanuts for the group of you that gets to the bottom first … provided no one is injured or killed in your attempt."

Major Powell glanced at his watch.

"Silence and safety, gentlemen. Silence and safety. You may start … now."

February 16, 2028 … Tehran, Iran, 2350 Hours

She stared at her cell phone on the bedside table. They allowed her to keep it, and she didn't understand why they had been so generous and accommodating. Day after day it beckoned to her, like a perfect apple in the Garden of Eden. She longed to pick it up, hold and caress it, and dial her brother wherever he might be. She wanted desperately to hear Arshad's voice, to have him assure her that everything would be all right and they would be reunited soon. Perhaps, somehow he'd whisk her away and she'd open her eyes to see the majesty of Colorado.

But Nousha Sassani sensed the worst was about to occur. The images of Samira's precious children being shot dead, just to prod a confession or information from their mother, were to be etched into Nousha's mind and soul for ten thousand eternities.

She also knew, with absolute certainty, that both Samira and her husband were dead, and the lingering images of this pointless carnage made her race to the bathroom and vomit once again. This pattern of barely eating, drinking water minimally and vomiting often had been repeated for the past several days without pause, and she had quickly become a gaunt shadow of her former self. A doctor had been summoned the prior afternoon, and after he gave her a sedative, a nurse administered an IV containing sustaining fluids.

That was yesterday afternoon, and a somewhat stronger Nousha Sassani this evening failed to resist the urge to call her brother, just as those at VEVAK hoped she would.

Colonel Sassani stared at his cell phone and prayed that it might stop ringing, but he realized his sister would not have broken her promise to contact him unless things were going very poorly.

He accepted the call.

"Nousha, you cannot contact me. Surely, VEVAK is listening to us right now!"

"Arshad, please. They found me, and they threw us in cars and took us to a damp prison. I don't know how I wasn't raped by the man in my cell, but then they dragged me to an interrogation room. Arshad, they shot at least two of Samira's little children in the head in an effort to extract information from her, but she knew nothing and they kept shooting her children anyway!

"These men are really monsters, Arshad. They are monsters!"

"Where are you now, Nousha?"

"In a house somewhere in Tehran. It has a big wall all around it. There are five men living and sleeping in this house with me, but so far they have not treated me poorly or molested me. I think there are others outside in the courtyard, and they seem to come and go in shifts. The voices I hear outside change once in a while, but I don't know how many of them might be out there at any one time. Please come and get me out of here, Arshad. I'm terrified, and I can't get the images of those dead children out of my mind. There was so much blood everywhere, and I thought Samira's eyes were going to pop out of her head when they kept executing her children. She wailed and made inhuman sounds, Arshad. When will you come to get me, brother?"

"Soon, Nousha. Don't make any trouble and be patient, and never, please, never call this number again."

Colonel Sassani hung up, fearful that his location might have been pinpointed by Iranian Intelligence.

He was correct.

"He is in Israel, perhaps in a safe house somewhere less than two hundred kilometers south of Tel Aviv," said the VEVAK agent. He checked the monitor on his desk and depressed a few keys.

"Yes, that is correct, sir. I've confirmed the trace. Less than two hundred kilometers south of Tel Aviv."

"And his sister claimed he planned to defect to America and would give them nothing but meaningless information! Now, we learn he's been in the hands of Mossad for six weeks? Six weeks!" roared the senior VEVAK agent in charge of the monitoring station.

"We must notify General Firouzabadi of this development, immediately."

"Sir, it's nearly midnight."

"Then awaken the General, you imbecile!"

February 17, 2028 … Tehran, Iran, 1100 Hours

"He's been in Israel for the past six weeks?"

"Yes, Minister Alavi," replied the General nervously.

"So the Jews and the Americans most assuredly know all aspects of our July plans for them, don't you agree, General?"

He glanced at the head of the Iranian Intelligence Directorate warily, and hoped he would not be severely punished for this highly disturbing piece of information. The General spoke cautiously.

"I did have some faint hope," he said, "that Arshad Sassani might do as his sister suggested and only release trivial information, but now that we know he's been in Israel all this time, I fear he's revealed everything. I'm also glad you agreed with my plan that our submarines should leave our naval base at Bandar Abbas immediately and head toward Venezuela, Minister. When they are poised and armed and are within striking distance of the United States, I'm sure the Americans will hesitate to strike at us. That is the leverage we must always maintain, and it's something with which the Americans are very accustomed. Mutually Assured Destruction from the Cold War with the Soviet Union created a precarious but vital balance, and neither nation dared strike at the other. Washington must be made to realize that if they attack our beloved Republic, our submarines will immediately leave Puerto Caballo and head north toward their coastline."

"Do you think they will dare attack our submarines while they are in their berths at Puerto Caballo, General?" asked Alavi.

"No, I do not, Minister Alavi," said the General. "That naval base is officially a part of the Russian Federation. The entire area has been formally deeded to Moscow by Caracas, and to attack that installation is truly to attack Russian soil. If the Americans think they have a problem now, they will have a much larger issue if the Russian Federation has been attacked and their personnel have been killed by the U.S. military. This would be Pearl Harbor all over again, Minister, but this time, it's the Americans who would initiate the attack. In reality, it doesn't matter that Tel Aviv and Washington may know the exact date of our proposed launch against Israel. The Americans must stand down, for fear their actions against us will precipitate our submarines leaving port and destroying New York and Washington. They will feel powerless and will do nothing as we annihilate the Jews. But I don't think we should wait until July to release the Sword of Allah, Minister. Their Passover is in early April, and I propose their Angel of Death visit all who reside in Israel on that date, or perhaps even beforehand."

"I agree, General Firouzabadi," said Alavi, "but we must first await the arrival of our submarines in Venezuela. Equipping them with the towed arrays, which contain our nuclear weapons, is now of the utmost urgency. Then, I agree, there is no real need to await July. Arm our submarines quickly, General, and we'll send warnings to the American President that if they intervene, we will decimate their cities. When the Americans quake with fear at the might of our great Republic, Allah's sword of vengeance can be swung to kill all in Israel whenever we choose."

The General settled into the rear seat of his staff car after being dismissed by the second most powerful man in the Islamic Republic of Iran. Thankful he hadn't ended up in Evin Prison, he allowed himself to luxuriate in his 915 RC Peugeot V12 limousine.

"Take the long route, Aziz," he told his driver, "I think I'll have lunch at that café I love in the mountains today, and afterward you can take me home."

"Yes, General Firouzabadi, of course, sir," said the driver.

Urging Minister Alavi to allow four of their submarines to sail for Venezuela had been a brilliant strategic maneuver. Success was not yet certain, but if achieved it would probably save the General's life, and he knew it.

And it felt so very good to be alive on this crisp, clear day.

February 23, 2028 … Masada, Israel, 1000 Hours

Shlomo Mizrahi listened to the report from the makeshift tent garrison on the plateau at Masada. He hung up the phone and sat for a few moments in silence. His next action, he knew, would put men in great danger, and that probably, some were about to die. Throughout his career, at a time such as this, he had hesitated, prayed for the safety of those he commanded, and then proceeded.

He dialed a number.

"Mr. Prime Minister, we are ready. Operation Cobra can now be initiated, whenever you and Gadi ask us to proceed," he said.

"Thank you, Zayde," said the Prime Minister.

"And Joshua," said Mizrahi, "they all realize there are so many things that can go wrong, but to a man they are prepared to die, if necessary, in order to succeed. They understand the fate of this nation is in their most capable hands."

"I also pray we can avoid the release of Plague Ten," said the Prime Minister. "Even though we're clearly being backed into a corner and have no other choice, it is reprehensible to me to become the author of a chapter of history that will be labeled, 'Genocide.' "

February 23, 2028 ... Washington, D.C., 0915 Hours

Director Brennan spoke first.

"Mr. President, the SEAL and Israeli strike team has concluded their training on the cliffs at Masada, sir. Director Mizrahi has been keeping us in the loop, and Ms. Parks has been communicating on a daily basis with Major Edwin Powell of our Army Mountain Warfare School. He concurs that they're as ready as is possible."

"I certainly won't second guess the head of Mossad and Colin Powell's grandson, John" said the President. "Now the issue is really a matter of timing, and when we decide to send these people into harm's way, isn't it?"

"That's correct, Mr. President. Even though this is an Israeli operation, Tel Aviv would like you to personally give it a green light since we have Navy SEALs and our aircraft involved."

"There's one other piece of information that we need to share with you today," said the Secretary of the Navy. The President gave him an icy stare.

"More good news, I trust, Ray," he said.

"Afraid not, sir." said Brennan. "Shannon, please proceed with this segment of the briefing for the President."

"Of course, sir," said Shannon. "Mr. President, as you're aware, a large Russian freighter abruptly sailed from the port of Bandar Abbas in Iran on ten February, after only being in port for five days. The name of that vessel, as we've mentioned in a prior briefing, is the *Yuriy Arshenevshiy*, and we're tracking her. She's been plodding on at a modest pace of ten knots, and she's currently poised to exit the Suez Canal and enter the Mediterranean Sea early tomorrow morning."

As she was talking, Shannon opened her dual-screened laptop, placed it on the coffee table in front of her, and turned one of the screens to face the President. She used a light pen to illustrate the route she then began to describe.

"Five days ago, Mr. President," she said, "a task force comprised of four surface warships of the VMF Rossii, the Russian Federation's Navy, set sail together from their Black Sea Fleet's naval base at Sevastopol. They've traversed the Black Sea at a steady twenty-five knots and sailed through the Bosporus Strait into the Sea of Marmara. The warships have entered the Aegean Sea, navigated the string of islands off the coast of Greece and then sailed past the eastern tip of Crete. These four warships are now at anchor, Mr. President, at the city of Suez, in Egypt."

"So you've concluded they are to be some sort of escort for the freighter that left Bandar Abbas on the tenth of this month?" asked the President.

"Mr. President," answered Ray Mabus, "as your Secretary of the Navy, let me please add to this discussion. It's not just the fact that there are four warships awaiting the *Yuriy Arshenevshiy*, sir. It's the actual *type* of vessels they are that really concerns me the most. Two are sophisticated guided missile destroyers, the *Bespokonyy* and the *Nastoychivyy*, and the other two Russian Black Sea Fleet ships are the *Admiral Chabanenko* and the *Admiral Kharlamov*. Those are modern, deadly antisubmarine warfare ships, and they are not lightweights, sir. The *Chabanenko* and the *Kharlamov* are not ASW destroyers; actually, each is larger than a Russian Kresta-II class cruiser. Moscow's clear intent here, Mr. President, is to make sure that freighter sails successfully into Puerto Caballo unscathed."

General Dunford of the Joint Chiefs cleared his throat.

"Mr. President," he said, "Secretary Mabus and I have spent several hours kicking all this around. We believe the CIA's opinion about that freighter's destination is correct. I agree we'll know for sure on the fourth of March, since that's the projected date at which time the vessel will either turn north toward the North Sea or head toward South America, but that fact is clearly less up in the air now. Those warships are not at the mouth of the Suez Canal for R and R, nor are they there to escort that bright red freighter into the North Sea. They are there to make sure one of our submarines does not sink that freighter, before it reaches its destination in Venezuela."

"General Dunford and I absolutely concur, Mr. President," said Secretary Mabus, "that the Russian mentality in this is most revealing. They believe we could easily sink that freighter, which is correct, and then we'd deny that we've done so. They're absolutely convinced that will be our plan, as evidenced by the highly capable flotilla of warships that they've assigned to prevent us from doing so. Sir, General Dunford and I have come to the conclusion that the Russians fear the *Yuriy Arshenevshiy* might be sunk by an unseen and supposedly unidentifiable submarine for one additional reason: This scenario precisely emulates their plan to attack the continental United States. Those Iranian submarines will dock at Puerto Caballo. They will be outfitted with the towed arrays when that freighter arrives — and those submarines will then proceed to launch a nuclear attack on this nation. Iran and Russia will vehemently deny any complicity in the attack, since immediately afterward, those unidentified submarines will slide gracefully into the depths and then return within a few days to Puerto Caballo. Both those nations will claim the submarines' absence from port was merely a 'training exercise' and some other nation must have attacked us. In a Court of Law, Mr. President, our contention that those two nations are to blame for that heinous attack would be like attempting to obtain a murder conviction without finding the murder weapon or the murderer. And what will be our response, if all this plays out? Do we destroy that naval base in retaliation, perhaps nuke Moscow and Tehran and initiate World War III? We are about to be viciously attacked, and the Russians are cooperating greatly with those maniacs in Tehran because they believe that, in the end, we will do absolutely nothing in response."

"They think we are spineless?" asked the President.

"Indecisiveness will be interpreted that way in Moscow," said Shannon Parks.

The young lady does have balls, thought the President.

"What are our options?" he asked.

General Dunford immediately responded.

"Mr. President, we've prepared a list of options, sir. One ... we sink that freighter and, if necessary, take on those Russian warships in order to execute that mission. Two ... we allow the freighter to reach the port in Venezuela, and when the submarines have arrived, we attack those vessels in their berths at the Russian naval base. Three ... we allow the submarines to be armed with those towed arrays and missiles, and sink them once they sail clear of the Russian base at Puerto Caballo. This scenario, sir, is the one in which we would not directly confront and sink a freighter flying the flag of the Russian Federation. Perhaps we would, however, also destroy a few of that nation's warships. This approach to our dilemma would also avoid causing numerous Russian casualties in an attack on their naval base. It is, however, clearly the alternative which carries the greatest risk to our nation, Mr. President, because we'd deliberately allow those four Iranian submarines to be armed with nuclear missiles. If just one of those boats should get through, her missiles might be successfully launched, with a catastrophic result."

"But in your option three, General Dunford," said the President, "is it correct that if we allow those subs to be armed and wait until they sail, we would not directly confront armed forces of the Russian Federation? We'd be sinking Iranian submarines in International Waters, and there'd be no possible Russian casualties, right?"

"That's correct, Mr. President," added Secretary Mabus.

"Ray, if we elect to wait until those submarines are armed and highly dangerous," said the President, "are you sure we can track and destroy those four Iranian subs, without equivocation?"

"No, Mr. President," said Mabus, "regrettably, I am not. As you recall, part of the deal Iran made with Russia when they purchased those six boats was that sophisticated technology was to be added to each of these submarines. Further, those modifications took approximately two years to complete. That's a great deal of time, and we have little intel on the technology that's been installed in those boats."

"That's true, Mr. President," added Director Brennan.

"John," said the President, "you mean to tell me that our fabled CIA has no resources to provide information on a naval project inside Russia that took *two years* to complete, for Christ's sake? Not a single piece of intel?"

"That's correct, sir," said Brennan. "Similarly, we don't know how good the latest Russian technology might be onboard those ASW warships that would go up against our nuclear submarines if we elect to engage that Russian freighter. Unfortunately, we're talking about decades of growth in sophistication. I'm afraid the proverbial proof of the pudding would be the mission to sink that damned freighter, during which time we would or would not successfully avoid the perils presented by her protective umbrella of warships.

Director Brennan raised his hands, a sign of frustration. "It's a similar situation in successfully detecting and destroying those Iranian diesel-electric submarines, sir," he said. "That's when whatever technology that's been installed on those boats will be activated, and at that moment, it'll be our advanced electronics versus whatever Moscow has perfected over a long period of time. Everyone in this room truly believes our armed forces are the best and most advanced in the world, but we've never gone toe to toe against the Russian Navy yet."

"I see," said the President. "I would much prefer not to sink Russian ships, including that freighter and possibly some or all of the warships accompanying her. And I'd also clearly prefer not to institute an attack on a Russian naval base. Those actions would absolutely be denounced as an act of war and would bring us to the brink of a larger conflict, perhaps nuclear, with a major adversary, the Russian Federation. The fact that Vladimir Putin is aging poorly and has been unpredictable of late is an additional complication. If we sink his ships or attack one of his naval bases, the old bastard is just crazy enough to launch his missiles at us. And four subs heading our way with eight nuclear missiles will look like a Sunday walk in the park, compared to what Russia can send our way."

"May I interject something, sir?" asked Shannon.

"Yes, Ms. Parks."

"Mr. President, it's my opinion that we should not consider sinking that freighter and quite possibly, in the process, engaging the Russian warships accompanying her. It's our conclusion at Langley that if we did that, since Iran has as many as forty or more additional nuclear weapons in her arsenal, it would very likely send several by air to Puerto Caballo and not skip a beat in arming their submarines. So all we'd accomplish by sinking the *Yuriy Arshenevshiy* is to let the Russians know we're aware of their plans and create a state of war between our two nations, while not at all diminishing the threat to our Eastern Seaboard. I'm sure that Tehran fears Colonel Sassani has revealed a great deal to us, but if we leave that freighter alone and allow their submarines to dock at Puerto Caballo unchallenged, we believe Tehran will be lulled into a false sense of security, sir. It's also unrealistic for us to attack a Russian naval base and then control the situation. Your evaluation of Vladimir Putin's mental health lately mirrors our concerns at Langley, Mr. President, and the course of action we suggest is option three, as described by General Dunford. We at the CIA acknowledge that if we agree upon option three, there is great risk to our cities and if we make the wrong call here, several million Americans will perish, but we cannot risk a confrontation with the Russian Federation."

"I'd like there to be unanimous agreement on this," demanded the President. "We're deciding here and now that it's not worth the risk to kill naval personnel of the Russian Federation while that freighter is at sea. We're furthermore dismissing the idea of attacking those Iranian submarines while they are highly visible and vulnerable in their comfortable berths at the Russian naval base at Puerto Caballo, for fear of an unpredictable and potentially massive responsible by those in Moscow. Correct?"

All heads nodded in solemn agreement.

"Then my final comment on this matter is that we'd damned well have better technology than the Russians, folks," said the President. "If any of those four submarines slides through our defenses and launches, we are signing death sentences for those who reside in this Capitol and in New York City. We are faced with untenable choices and unpredictable outcomes today, and I do not want to go down in history as the American President who knowingly allowed nuclear detonations on our soil, due to a trembling fear of the Kremlin. I feel quite despicable at this moment, and I personally loathe the role of a coward."

The President turned his attention to the Secretary of the Navy.

"Ray, anything it takes," he said. "When those four Iranian submarines set sail from Venezuela armed with their nuclear weapons and are in international waters, you sink those sons-of-bitches. And if Moscow decides to send a hundred goddamned warships in an attempt to provide cover for those subs, you have my permission to engage those ships as well. That must necessarily be the tipping point, the moment in time when diplomacy and our purportedly greater concerns about Russia shall be thrown to the winds, gentlemen."

"Understood, loud and clear, sir," assured Ray Mabus. "We will engage them at the appropriate time, Mr. President, and we won't disappoint you."

"Tell that to the residents of New York City and Washington, Ray, if you fail. And one other thing," said the President as he turned his gaze to Shannon. "Ms. Parks, I want you to inform the Israelis to commence their Operation Cobra. Let's at least eliminate Iran's other goddamned nuclear weapons, ASAP."

"Yes, Mr. President," she replied.

"One other thing, Shannon," said the President. "What's the estimated date of arrival for the Iranian submarines and that Russian freighter in Venezuela?"

"The submarines on the twelfth of March, Mr. President, and the *Yuriy Arshenevshiy* on the fifteenth." said Shannon.

The President looked slowly from face to face, breathed a sigh of resignation and stared down at his folded hands.

"It just has to be on the Ides of March," he said. "Perfect, just perfect."

At her desk at Langley barely an hour later, Shannon dialed a number in Tel Aviv. It was picked up on the second ring.

"Director Mizrahi," she said, "this is Shannon Parks. I've just returned from a meeting at the White House. The President of the United States agrees that your Operation Cobra has a green light."

"Thank you, Shannon," said Mizrahi, "I'll call the team at Masada."

After she wished him well, the old man sat in silence, and reflected about the unlikely mission before them and the fine men he was about to put on icy mountains. He dialed Yaakov Rafaeli's cellphone and as it rang, he recalled Shannon Parks' last comment before their connection ended.

"The fate of our two nations is in your capable hands, and also the lives of all those in fourteen Arab nations, if Plague Ten must necessarily be released," she said.

"From your mouth to God's ears," he mumbled, a moment before Yaakov answered the call.

CHAPTER 8

"… and let slip the dogs of war, that this foul deed shall smell above the earth with carrion men, groaning for burial."

Act III, Scene I
The Tragedy of Julius Caesar
William Shakespeare

February 25, 2028 … Masada, Israel, 1630 Hours

The two groups of men exchanged handshakes. Many were certain that once their missions began, they'd never see one another again.

Yaakov motioned to Major Edwin Powell to join him outside the mess tent. On his way outside, Yaakov tapped one of the SEALs on the shoulder.

"Come, walk with us, Captain Donoghue," he ordered.

The SEAL Team Leader obeyed.

"So formal … this must be serious," he grinned.

"Sorry, Peter,' said Yaakov. "Tough to be on a first-name-basis in the field with anyone other than an Israeli."

"So what's up?" asked Major Powell. He set down two perfectly coiled climbing ropes and gave the Israeli his full attention.

"Gentlemen," said Yaakov, "the two of you are in Colonel Sassani's group and, as you already know, I'll be commanding the all-Israeli force. The Colonel's involvement is pivotal, but when we're faced with the task of taking out VEVAK and Revolutionary Guard personnel, Tel Aviv is concerned the Colonel may soften or hesitate. For all we know, you'll turn a corner in the middle of a mountain and he'll come face-to-face with someone who's his cousin."

Yaakov glanced at Captain Donoghue.

"I don't have to explain to a SEAL," he said, "that a moment's hesitation by any of us may cause an alarm to sound, and that may spell the end of the mission. It's been explained that Colonel Sassani is in charge of this entire operation, but that's not quite the case. That actual responsibility is mine, not his, and I thought you'd both feel relieved that your group will not be in the hands of a man who's been your mortal enemy for most of his life."

The other two men nodded. That aspect of the mission had been bothering them greatly.

"But even though I'm the one Tel Aviv is relying upon," said Yaakov, "that's a minor detail in the scheme of things. Captain Donoghue … sorry, Pete … my group is going to be engaging the enemy a thousand kilometers away from the task before your group. If you feel that the Colonel is making poor choices, you are to relieve him of his duties. If you feel he is softening or putting your men in harm's way, you are to view him as no longer necessary to the mission. And if you feel he is vacillating in his loyalties once again, you are to consider the man expendable. Are we absolutely clear on this?"

"Aye, aye," responded the SEAL.

"I'll watch your back, Captain," commented Major Powell.

"Thank you, sir," said Donoghue."

"And I'll keep the Iranian in my sights, as well," added Powell.

"We leave Masada at 0700 Hours," said Yaakov as they turned and headed back into the mess tent.

It had been light for over an hour as the eighty men filed into two huge Israeli Sikorsky CH-53E Super Stallion helicopters. Their destination was Hatzerim Airbase in the Negev desert, where two U.S. Air Force C-130J Super Hercules transport planes sat on the tarmac, awaited their arrival.

"Don't worry about checking gear yet, gentlemen," said Yaakov as he instructed his group to board one of the planes. "Some of it is already on board, and the remainder awaits us at the U.S. Air Force base in Baku, in Azerbaijan."

At that same moment, Pete Donoghue gave similar instructions to his group of Navy SEALs and the Mossad agents on board the other transport plane. Colonel Sassani gave the Captain an odd look when the SEAL commander stood and issued orders. Sassani thought it highly inappropriate and rude that the man failed to ask for permission to speak.

When the SEAL sat down as the plane began to taxi forward, Colonel Sassani rose and addressed the men under his command.

"Gentlemen, we are flying to a U.S. base in Kuwait City now," he said, "and from there two American CH-47D Chinook helicopters will take us to the USS *Ronald Reagan* aircraft carrier in the Persian Gulf. The stealth helicopters that will bring us into Iran are already on board the Reagan, and that leg of our journey, I'm told, will be roughly two hours. Our flight this morning will be approximately four hours and thirty minutes, since this aircraft is a turboprop rather than a 757 equipped with jet engines. We'll travel at roughly four hundred miles per hour, the cruising speed of a Hercules, so relax, sit back, and enjoy yourselves. The stewardess will be around shortly after takeoff to obtain your drink orders."

Several of the men laughed, and as the Colonel sat down, he was immensely proud of his attempt at humor. He felt much closer to these men he led and decided they were bonding quite well.

Both flights were routine and uneventful.

The C-130J Hercules was the transport workhorse of the U.S. Air Force, and there were many flights each week from Israel to points throughout the Middle East. Ever since the Gulf War of 1991, Kuwait naturally remained a staunch ally of the United States. An aircraft flying into the American base there was not at all unusual, and neither was crossing into Saudi air space en route to Kuwait City.

The flight plan of the other Hercules was more complicated, however. It dared not fly over Syria, so it flew due north over Cyprus and entered Turkish air space. As the plane neared the city of Konya, it banked sharply to the east and headed for the newly constructed American Air Force base at Baku, in Azerbaijan. It crossed over the friendly skies of Armenia in the process.

That particular U.S. Air Force base at Baku had become a highly annoying thorn in Vladimir Putin's side, as it was created in clear desperation by Azerbaijan after the Russian Federation annexed neighboring Georgia in the late spring of 2025.

There was little doubt about Moscow's intentions concerning Armenia and Azerbaijan, and the huge garrison of troops and equipment at an ever-expanding base in Grozny was a clear omen of what was about to occur. Because they anticipated a Russian invasion in the summer of 2026, the Azerbaijanis turned to the United States, and construction of an American base began in their capitol city of Baku. Presumably, that caused President Putin to hesitate. The other reason Moscow balked at swallowing Azerbaijan had to do with geography and the foreboding Caucasus Mountain Range that separates Russia from neighboring Azerbaijan. But it was mainly the presence of the American military in Baku that caused Moscow to delay their planned invasion, rather than the presence of an ominous mountain range. Their forces at Grozny were billeted and awaited orders.

Due to the indirect route necessarily taken to Baku, the C-130J carrying the Navy SEALS and the agents of Mossad landed safely after a long flight, seven hours from the time of their departure from Israel. Yaakov's men were tired and hungry when they landed.

To these men, the barracks provided for their use seemed like a Ritz Carlton, especially after they'd lived in tents for many days and endured a most uncomfortable ride in a transport plane.

They ate and slept.

That evening commenced a cyclical "new moon" which resulted in a complete absence of moonlight. Mossad decided their mission would begin the following night, with just a fine sliver of moonlight to help guide them on their ropes. The men also needed a day to check their gear and prepare for the mission.

For some of them, it was to be their last day alive.

February 26, 2028 … Baku, Azerbaijan, 2300 Hours

The four RAH-88 Comanche helicopters took off as one from Baku and headed south toward the open sea. At a cruising speed of a hundred and sixty miles per hour, their flight time was to be nearly two and a half hours.

The helos skimmed the motionless waters of the Caspian Sea, and at a hundred and fifty miles off the coast of Iran, they activated their stealth mode technology.

At that same moment, four other Comanches left the deck of the USS *Ronald Reagan* and instantly reverted to stealth mode, since their landing point was only an hour away from the aircraft carrier's current position.

Colonel Sassani's group disembarked from their helicopters on the flattened ridge at Mount Qash-Mastan in the Zagros Mountains without incident. Yaakov's group was less fortunate. Their designated landing point on Mount Damavand was smaller and much more treacherous than the site on Qash-Mastan, and one of the Mossad agents suddenly slipped and disappeared into the abyss below. The man elected to fall silently and stifled a scream of absolute terror when he realized he was about to die.

"Silence is mandatory," his brain demanded as he plummeted so quietly to his death.

Yaakov and the others stood in silence on the icy mountain for a moment, in tribute to their friend who had just died.

"His name was Ari Rosenthal," said one of the men softly.

Ari was the young man who carried the quotation from Crazy Horse with him at all times, and that night became his own personal very good day to die.

Yaakov hoped that Ari's death would be their only casualty.

They quickly organized their gear and began to rappel, with a bare hint of moonlight to help guide their path downward.

On Qash-Mastan, Major Powell was the first to rappel, and Colonel Sassani's group began their descent.

Each of the Navy SEALs, by presidential edict, wore American uniforms, and the Mossad agents wore uniforms of the elite Saiqa Special Forces Division of the Iranian Revolutionary Guard. Each of the Mossad agents' belts was equipped with a device that would identify them as a "friendly" when in the laser sights of the American SEALs or their other Israeli comrades in arms. Yaakov's group of Mossad agents was equipped in the same manner, but the Israeli Paratroopers proudly wore the desert sand uniforms of the 202nd "Viper" battalion underneath their snow-white climbing jackets. Prime Minister Joshua Ben-Gurion, as did the President of the United States, wanted the Iranians to know who was there to send them to hell.

The four pitches went flawlessly, although twice during the descent on Qash-Mastan, a booted foot struck the wall hard enough to chip away limestone. To the SEALs, the falling debris sounded like thunderclaps, but no one seemed to be alerted on the ground.

The men at both locations eagerly relieved themselves of the rappel harnesses that kept digging into their legs during the descent and then removed their heavy white jackets.

The commandos assumed their designated attack positions and waited for the order to move onto the road below.

Colonel Sassani spoke quietly into the microphone attached to his headset.

"Yaakov, this is very strange. There are no guards at the entrance to the facility here on Mount Qash-Mastan, and the blast doors are sealed shut. We're positioned to attack, but we must wait for some activity below our position. Those blast doors cannot be breached with the explosives we carry."

"It's the same here on Damavand, Arshad," said Yaakov. "Absolute silence and the place is sealed shut. We'll just have to wait until the regular guards come outside, I guess. You told us there's a continuous twenty-four-hour security perimeter here. Perhaps Tehran feels these facilities are so secure that they've decided there isn't a need to post guards outside during the night."

"Not true, my friend. I designed the security protocol for both of these locations, Yaakov," said Arshad. "There should be guards with vehicles at hand to streak into the mountain and warn others to close the two huge sets of blast doors, but there is no one out here."

"Arshad, I see lights in the distance coming up the road from the direction of the Revolutionary Guard base," said Yaakov.

Colonel Sassani adjusted the focus on his binoculars.

"Same here, Yaakov," he said, "I can see at least a dozen or more distinct sets of headlights coming up the road."

"What the hell is going on, Arshad?" asked Yaakov.

Colonel Sassani looked at his watch.

"I think I know," he said. "Just a few more minutes for me to be sure, Yaakov."

It was exactly 0500 Hours.

The silence was broken by a highly-muted claxon.

It emanated from within the Damavand fortification. At that same moment, the contingent of Revolutionary Guards arrived and began to disembark from their vehicles. There were at least a hundred of them, all armed with AK-47 automatic weapons, and their heavily armored vehicles each had Dushka 12.7mm machine guns manned and ready.

A red light began to swirl and flash above the blast doors.

"Arshad, the blast doors are beginning to open," said Yaakov.

"It's the same here, Yaakov," said Arshad "There are heavily armed troops here now, and a bright red light is flashing above the blast doors as they're opening. The alarm from within the bowels of Qash-Mastan grows louder and louder as the doors are opening."

"What's going on, Arshad?" asked Yaakov.

"It must be a launch drill, Yaakov," said Arshad. "It's a standard practice for the Intelligence Directorate in Tehran to issue orders to perform these drills without prior notice, just as a submarine captain will perform an emergency dive drill to keep his crew alert. A launch drill must take less than thirty minutes to accomplish."

"Does that mean the trucks carting your missiles will come out of their caves, Arshad?" asked Yaakov.

"Yes, that's correct," said Arshad. "All ten at each location should come out and then line up in a firing position. They will then tilt their missiles toward the sky. When the hydraulic systems on the transport trucks are fully engaged and the nuclear missiles are in a vertical position, the timing of the drill will end."

"Pete, come in," said Yaakov.

"Yes, sir," said Captain Donoghue.

"Pete," said Yaakov, "we're in position at a time when the enemy is about to perform a missile launch drill. That means at any moment the trucks carrying Iran's missiles will roll out into the open and will be exposed. There should be ten trucks at each site, and once they're out in the open, we'll commence our attacks."

"Aye, aye, sir," said the captain.

"There are at least a hundred Revolutionary Guard troops at each location to guard those trucks, Captain,," said Yaakov, "plus however many more Iranians who may come out of these mountains during the drill."

"Got it, sir," said Donoghue.

"Now I'll also inform Sassani that's the plan. Watch him, Peter," said Yaakov.

"Will do," said Donoghue.

Yaakov rekeyed his mic.

"Sassani here," said the Colonel.

"Colonel, we're going to wait until all ten trucks are in their launch positions, and then we'll commence our attack here" said Yaakov. "I suggest you do the same and that we time our attacks to coincide with one another. Are your men in position, Arshad?"

"Yes, I agree, and we are ready," said Donoghue.

The SEALs hidden in the rocks on the elevated side of the road waited, as did the Israelis at both locations. Each of them carried multiple weapons, including 9mm MP8SD submachine guns with stainless steel sound suppressors and FN Scar assault rifles equipped with FN60 high-explosive grenade launchers mounted on the lower rail of the rifles. Each man also carried the most powerful weapon ever placed in the hands of a combatant, a battery-operated laser rifle. It had a range of two hundred-plus yards and could cut a good-sized tree in half when swung to and fro. Six SEALs also carried MK14 Mod 0 Sniper Weapon Systems, as did six of the Israeli Paratroopers in Yaakov's combat group.

The trucks began to rumble from their sanctuary deep within each mountain. They slowly pivoted, backed up, and parked next to one another, facing north.

"Arshad, there are only nine trucks here at Damavand, not ten," whispered Yaakov into his microphone.

"The tenth must have some mechanical issue. It is definitely there, with a missile mounted on it," said the Colonel.

"We'll have to get in there and take it out, along with the other nuclear weapons, then," said Yaakov. "But first things first."

"Agreed," said the Colonel.

"Your call, Colonel, just give the command," said Yaakov.

"Open fire," said Colonel Sassani.

The first wave of their assault was deadly and took less than fifteen seconds. Eight of the Israelis in Yaakov's group and the same number of SEALs on Qash-Mastan had been positioned to address the Revolutionary Guard troops. They stood in unison at both locations and methodically raked their laser weapons back and forth, an action similar to watering a lawn with a garden hose.

The sound of the activated laser rifles wasn't particularly loud, but these weren't conventional battlefield weapons. Deployed by the United States, primarily to Special Forces personnel in early 2026, these weapons didn't need a skilled marksman to operate. Just swing and kill, swing and kill. Wave after wave of instantaneous death was raked through the ranks of the Revolutionary Guard troops.

Most of the laser weapons were leveled at waist height, and many of the Revolutionary Guard troops were cut in two. Their screams were the only sounds on the otherwise lifeless mountains.

One of the SEALs noticed a lone Iranian soldier standing there smoking a cigarette, for the moment oblivious to the carnage around him. The SEAL adjusted his aim slightly upward and deftly beheaded the man from more than a hundred yards away.

"That's for more than twenty years of Jihadist bullshit, asshole," mumbled the SEAL as he turned to acquire another target.

Some of the Iranian troops, when the carnage around them began, sought shelter behind their transport vehicles, an assortment of Russian armored personnel carriers and UAZ-469 Jeep-like small trucks. With a sheer cliff behind them and nowhere else to possibly seek shelter, they began firing wildly toward the rock face where the Americans and the Israelis were well concealed.

The SEALs unleashed a barrage of self-propelled rockets, from devices similar in concept to the World War II bazooka, but more compact and many times deadlier. The Israelis on Mount Damavand had identical equipment, and Revolutionary Guard vehicles exploded all around the soldiers who attempted to hide behind them. Those who somehow survived the explosions were immediately cut down by laser weapons. A few dazed stragglers at each location were taken out by sharpshooters using their Mod 0 sniper weapons.

The entire battles at both locations took less than three minutes, and the Revolutionary Guard contingents suffered more than three hundred casualties. There were no wounded on the battlefield that needed assistance. Laser weapons leave only slices of lifeless corpses behind, and the victims have no chance of survival.

In war, dominant technology will prevail.

The two attack groups stormed from their positions onto the road surface. On Mount Damavand, Yaakov's group discovered that one of the missile transport drivers was still alive. The trembling man's fate was decided, after some debate.

"Let me kill him, Yaakov," demanded one of the paratroopers. "He was driving a truck armed with a missile that can kill all those in Tel Aviv, and he deserves to die."

"No," said Yaakov. "Handcuff him and we'll leave him inside the mouth of the cavern. Our Prime Minister wants Tehran to know the State of Israel did this. Tell him to remember our unit number ... the 202nd Viper Battalion, and that we were flown here on the wings of eagles."

A Mossad agent stepped forward and relayed the message in Farsi to the wild-eyed Iranian soldier. The man kept shaking his head, an assurance the message would be delivered intact.

Several Israelis walked methodically around the corpses and viewed chunks of men who had previously been whole. When they came upon the corpse of a soldier killed by a conventional weapon, two taps to the man's head from a silenced MP8SD assured their victim was dead. The entire road surface was bright red.

Other Israelis were already through the blast doors, inside the mouth of the cavernous facility. There were two UAZ-469 Russian Jeeps parked immediately inside, and Yaakov and some of his men quickly mounted them. They gunned the engines and headed down the winding roadway, deeper and deeper into the cavern.

"Hurry, before they close the other blast doors," urged Yaakov.

Other paratroopers raced behind the two vehicles on foot.

Surprisingly, there was no resistance, no pockets of armed troops to dispatch along the way, and the two additional sets of blast doors described by Colonel Sassani were wide open and unmanned.

The two speeding vehicles turned a corner and a huge room came into view. It was the obvious nest for the Iranian missile trucks, and Yaakov realized Arshad was correct. Off to one side was one more truck, with its hood open. Two men worked hurriedly inside the vehicle's engine compartment, and they didn't even look up when the two Jeeps roared into the room. Paratroopers dismounted and immediately gunned down the two defenseless technicians.

Yaakov led the search for additional nuclear weapons, and his men immediately found a broad hallway, just beyond where the lone truck was parked. As four paratroopers walked toward the large sealed door at the end of a dimly illuminated hall carved out of bare rock, machine gun fire from the walls abruptly cut them down.

The Israelis realized there were guns mounted on the walls of the hallway, undoubtedly computer-controlled by men within the room beyond. Their rate of fire was extraordinary, and the four motionless paratroopers were testimony to their accuracy.

Other Israelis arrived, the ones on foot.

"Yaakov, we have to first take out those machine guns."

The paratrooper peered carefully around the corner of the hallway and easily identified the locations of the four guns in the walls beyond. They were red hot from their brief use moments earlier, and the Israeli's infrared scope pinpointed them in the walls.

"I need a trooper on the right side of the entrance, and I'll take the other side," said Yaakov.

The two men carefully took up their positions, with the other Israelis off to either side and out of sight of the machine guns.

"Now," said Yaakov. Both men aimed carefully and FN60 high-explosive grenades hit the two front machine gun emplacements and eliminated the threat.

"Again," he ordered, and the two rear guns were also destroyed. Four paratroopers immediately raced to aid their fallen comrades, and it was quickly verified the men were dead. They were carried out and placed gently on one of the Jeeps.

High explosives were attached to the door down the hall by two paratroopers, and with a nod from Yaakov, the steel door's hinges were blown from their mounts. The entire hallway was filled with smoke and rock dust, but that didn't deter the Israelis.

Eight FN60 grenades were aimed into whatever space or room was beyond the door, and the violent explosions were deafening.

A dozen paratroopers charged down the hall.

From the mouth of the hallway, Yaakov and the others heard short bursts of gunfire from the room beyond.

"Clear," came the single word in Hebrew.

When Yaakov and the others arrived, they surveyed the room.

There were twenty-three Iranian soldiers on the floor, and three of the paratroopers systematically administered two taps to each already motionless head. In a neat row off to one side there were twelve identical large aluminum cases on pallets and two heavy-duty fork lifts. Yaakov opened one of the cases and verified that it contained a warhead for a missile. He was sure it was a nuclear weapon, per the information provided by Colonel Sassani.

They set to the task of attaching explosives to the warheads. Disarming warheads was far too lengthy a process, and if left intact, Iranian scientists would quickly rebuild them. So brute force was the Israeli method of choice, and if there was a bit of fallout along with massive explosions, at least the fallout would be within Iran. Tel Aviv simply didn't give a damn.

Ten minutes later, the Israelis and their Russian Jeeps were poised at the mouth of the huge garage designed to house the missile transport trucks. One of the paratroopers pressed a button and several enormous explosions erupted from the weapons storage room. As they turned to head back through the sets of blast doors, Yaakov pressed a button and the disabled truck armed with a nuclear missile ignited in an inferno. A split second later, the truck's fuel tank also exploded and another, more violent explosion occurred. But by then, the Israelis were nearly a hundred yards away, heading for open air. Their two UAZ Jeeps burst into the faint glow of morning light, and several minutes later, the Israelis who were on foot also arrived.

The nine neatly parked transport trucks were in flames, their missiles mangled and warheads now useless. One explosion after another occurred as missile fuel and truck diesel fuel ignited.

The lone Iranian survivor of the raid was strapped to a rail within the mouth of the cavern as the Comanche helicopters were called in. Headlights in the distance, many sets of headlights, danced in their race up the mountain road.

The Comanches left their perch immediately. Six minutes later they landed gracefully, two at a time, and retrieved the commandos.

Sixteen minutes later, the Revolutionary Guard reinforcements arrived. There were bodies everywhere and their missile trucks burned out of control. The lead UAZ raced at high speed into the unguarded mouth of the complex and screeched to a halt when the Iranians spotted a man, hands zip tied behind him and tied securely to a rail on a wall.

A Revolutionary Guard Major jumped down and two others helped untie the man.

"What happened here?" demanded the Major.

"It was the Israelis, sir," replied the terrified transport driver.

"The Israelis?" asked the Major.

"Yes, sir," said the driver. "It was their 202nd Viper Battalion, Major. They specifically wanted you to know that's who they are."

"How did they get here?" asked the Major. "Did you see them arrive?"

"They told me to also tell you they came here on the wings of eagles, "They want to let Tehran know that's how they arrived."

"On eagles?" said the Major, "You are a fool!"

"No, sir. They arrived on the wings of eagles," claimed the driver with conviction.

The Major removed his revolver from its holster and shot the startled man squarely between the eyes.

On Qash-Mastan, the execution of the plan was a mirror image of the engagement by the Israelis on Mount Damavand, except for their casualties. Peter Donoghue suffered a shoulder wound when the Revolutionary Guard troops were shooting wildly in the direction of their assailants. It was a clean through-and-through. As Captain Donoghue clutched at his injured shoulder, Major Powell immediately stood and killed the three Revolutionary Guard soldiers who were firing in their direction.

That instinctive move cost Major Edwin Powell his life. A long burst from an Iranian AK-47 as the soldier died caught the Major squarely in the neck and chest. He died instantly.

Five SEALs were also gunned down in the hallway to the nuclear weapons storage room at Qash-Mastan. The installation of those machine guns in the walls, Sassani explained later, must have been sometime after he had been extricated from Iran. An urgent message from Yaakov, in an attempt to warn the other group of several well-concealed machine guns in the hallway, was not received. The transmission from deep within a mountain failed to get through, and five SEALs suffered the tragic consequences.

While the group on Qash-Mastan awaited the arrival of their Comanches, Captain Donoghue watched Colonel Sassani, as he walked slowly through the sea of Revolutionary Guard corpses strewn around their vehicles. In the bright light of burning missile transport trucks and the crimson blood that bathed everything in sight, it was quite apparent that Arshad was crying.

Donoghue understood. He had six comrades to mourn.

Arshad Sassani had nearly a hundred and fifty.

The Comanche helos swooped in and soon withdrew once the Commandos and their dead were aboard.

Silence prevailed.

CHAPTER 9

February 27, 2028 … Washington, D.C., 0900 Hours

Shannon Parks declined a cup of coffee. She'd already had more than enough at Langley.

"Mr. President," she began, "our Navy SEALs and the Israelis in the strike force have executed Operation Cobra flawlessly, sir. Iran's nuclear missiles mounted on transport trucks and their additional stored warheads have all been destroyed."

"Did we incur casualties, Shannon?" asked the President.

"Yes, Mr. President, we did," replied the Secretary of the Navy.

"How many, Ray?" asked the President.

"Five of our SEALs on Qash-Mastan, plus one agent of Mossad and four Israeli Paratroopers on Mount Damavand, sir. Captain Peter James Donoghue, the SEAL Team Leader, was wounded, but he should make a full recovery," was the solemn reply. Director Mabus hesitated. "There was one additional casualty on Mount Qast-Mastan, sir. Major Edwin Powell was also killed, I'm afraid."

"Eleven good men," mused the President. He shook his head. "How many of these bastards did our forces kill?"

"Roughly three hundred and fifty," said Shannon.

"And you're sure we destroyed all their nuclear warheads?" asked the President.

"Absolutely, Mr. President," responded the Director of the CIA.

"Well done, gentlemen," said the President. "And thank you, Shannon, for the work you did to coordinate our side of the operation."

"Thank you, Mr. President. Just doing my job, sir," said Shannon.

"Now we have to concentrate on those damned submarines and await their arrival in Venezuela. We're not out of the woods by any means yet, sir," said Ray Mabus. "The Navy's part of this operation is about to commence."

"Thank you for this briefing," added the President. "Now if you'll excuse me, I have to place a call to my friend Colin Powell and tell him his grandson is dead. I loathe hearing his reaction to this news."

"He died while saving Major Donoghue's life," added Shannon.

The President nodded as they left the Oval Office. He took a deep breath and reached for the telephone.

It was just after 11:30 AM that same morning, and Shannon was at her desk, trying to unwind. Paul Vander Vere knocked twice on the door frame of the open door. He didn't await permission to enter her sanctuary.

"Shannon, why don't you go home and get some sleep?" asked Paul. "You've been here for the last three days and nights, and the mission is over. Our SEALs are back on the Reagan, and the Israelis are safely at our base at Baku."

"What I need now is a good stiff drink" said Shannon. "Care to join me?"

"It's not quite noon," said Paul. "A bit early for us to hit the sauce, boss."

Shannon's eyes locked with his.

"Not for me right now, Paul," she said. "My internal clock says my most recent day has just been nearly seventy-two hours long, and for me, it's officially 'Miller Time.' You've been here by my side through this entire mission, my young genius. So you've earned the afternoon off, too. If you'd prefer, I'll check with your boss to make sure it's all right for you to leave early today."

Shannon picked up the phone receiver on her desk. She pretended to dial a phone number and had a brief, mock conversation with someone on the other end of the line.

Shannon smiled.

"Yup, she says it's okay with her," she said. "We'll take my car."

They now descended to the parking level and, a few minutes later, her BMW 555i was speeding east on Route 66. They exited at Lee Highway and Shannon turned right onto George Washington Memorial Parkway.

"Where are we going?" asked Paul.

"We'll be there in a few minutes," she said..

She turned onto Memorial Avenue and slowed as they drove through the huge wrought iron gates. He looked at her and saw tears welling up. One descended down her cheek and lingered on her chin.

Shannon turned left onto Eisenhower Drive, left onto Bradley Drive, and right again onto Roosevelt Drive. The car slowed, and she parked along the curb. To Paul's left, in the distance, was the Tomb of the Unknown Soldier.

They sat in silence for a while surrounded by manicured lawns, and Shannon focused on her folded hands. He felt her pain.

"Shannon," he said very softly, "there must be sacrifice in order to preserve this nation. We'll always have dialogue, but that's how old men indulge one another, and they term it progress. I understand why we're here at Arlington today. You want to pay tribute to our real heroes, Major Powell and the five Navy SEALs who just died in Iran. I come here often, just like you do, and I always feel better when I leave. The knowledge that this nation has been preserved, gives life and meaning to the brave men and women beneath this ocean of white headstones, and I'm constantly reassured they have not died in vain."

"Eleven fine men just died because of my directives, Paul," said Shannon. "Their mothers mourn, perhaps as many wives are now without husbands. Some guy tried to hit on me in the grocery store the other day. When he asked me what I do for a living, I wanted to say, 'I send men to their deaths, pal.' And that was before eleven more names were added to my personal list of casualties."

"Men in combat will die, Shannon," said Paul. "That's the way it is."

"I know that," said Shannon. "Now we have to prevent Iranian submarines from nuking New York and Washington. When we accomplish that, the next time I come here, perhaps I'll feel that none of the thousands of people buried here will have died pointless deaths."

"We live in a free society, Ms. Shannon Elizabeth Parks, " said Paul, "often as a result of your brilliance."

"Thank you, but look at all these headstones, Paul," said Shannon. "This is what I do for a living. I send people to their deaths, so that more and more headstones can be placed here. Sometimes I wonder if I'm the actual monster in all this madness."

"Shannon, I think it's time for us to have that drink," said Paul. "You're certainly not the villain in all this. You are quite the hero."

She turned, reached out, and touched his hand gently.

"On second thought, Paul," she said, "I'd honestly rather take you home and have you make love to me. You're the smartest man I've ever met, and the term, 'tall, dark, and handsome' describes you perfectly."

She started the car and headed for the gates. It was a short drive to her townhouse in Tyson's Corner.

She poured them two no-nonsense Johnny Walker Blacks on the rocks, and they sat for a while on one of the two matching creamy loveseats in Shannon's family room. They somewhat awkwardly held hands while they talked about the mission in Iran and the sacrifices made by the Navy SEALs, Major Powell, and the Israelis.

When she finished her drink, Shannon said, "Let me show you what's upstairs."

Later, she commented, "Why are your hands so clammy? Do I make you nervous, Paul?"

"Yes," he replied as he kissed her tenderly. "I've never made love to a goddess before."

With that, she straddled him.

Just past 9:00 PM, Shannon fell asleep in his arms, and her horrific nightmares began anew. She pictured herself at the center of Arlington National Cemetery, with white headstones in one long, endless line. The headstones were pulsating as though alive, awaiting her to scrawl a name in red ink on each of them. In her dream, she realized it wasn't ink that she was using. It was blood.

February 27, 2028 ... Tel Aviv, 1800 Hours

"Prime Minister Ben-Gurion will give the eulogy tomorrow at the funeral for our people, Yaakov," said Director Shlomo Mizrahi.

"Ari Rosenthal and our others who died in Iran believed any day they fought and died for their country was a very good day to die," said Yaakov. "I pray all those men did not die in vain."

"Our nation still exists, and that's the only measure that's at all meaningful," responded the Director of Mossad. "Iran's deadliest weapons were about to be used against us, and you and your men valiantly eliminated that threat. Our Operation Cobra was a complete success, and Iran is no longer a nuclear power. Well done, son, well done."

"My concern now is that they have the ability to produce more missiles and nuclear warheads," said Yaakov, "and they have two more submarines that can be equipped with nuclear weapons.

"This is by no means over, Shlomo. I fear that now that we've attacked them, their commitment to destroy us will be amplified."

"I agree, and I've already been discussing next steps with the Americans. But first, they need to locate and destroy the submarines that are about to threaten their cities."

March 2, 2028 ... Tehran, Iran, 2150 Hours

Four days had passed since the devastating raids destroyed the stored nuclear weapons at Mount Damavand and at Qash-Mastan. The

VEVAK guards in the house and the rear courtyard arrived every day and departed punctually, according to the schedule they dutifully followed.

But their usual small talk had given way to more focused discussion over the past several days, and their topic of conversation remained unchanged. The agents also felt there was no particular need to keep their voices down as they discussed the attack on their nuclear weapons storage facilities.

Nousha quietly eavesdropped each day and evening, and then she made a courageous decision. That evening, she bathed and waited.

At 11:00 that night, one of the VEVAK agents was alone in the courtyard. He sat on a bench smoking a cigarette. Nousha opened the door from her bedroom and went outside. She sat down next to the startled young man. She smelled of lavender. She placed her left hand gently on his leg and slowly began to caress his inner thigh. His eyes opened wide.

"What are you doing?" he demanded.

"You are so very young and handsome, and I haven't been with a man for two years, since my husband died," she responded sadly.

He looked up at the canopy of stars overhead and prayed for guidance. He wondered what to do. He had never been with a woman before, and he was not one to violate Sharia Law.

Her hand moved higher and his body immediately responded.

"Stop this, please," he begged.

"No, I will not," she whispered. "I want you to come to my bedroom tomorrow night and service me, and I'll teach you how to please a woman. When you marry, your future wife will appreciate the lessons I'll provide you."

He closed his eyes and moaned softly.

"I've watched the schedule, and I know you're the only guard here in the rear courtyard from ten to midnight," she said. "You'll be back at your post with a smile on your face, Rahim."

"How do you know my name?" asked Rahim.

"I listen very well," said Nousha, "and I simply had to know the name of the most handsome man of my dreams."

Nousha gave him one final squeeze. She stood up and went inside.

March 3, 2028 … Tehran, Iran, 2230 Hours

It was nearly 10:20 PM, and just as she was about to give up, Nousha's bedroom door to the courtyard was opened delicately. She walked over to Rahim and kissed him passionately. Nousha reached up to the straps on her nightgown. They were simple ties and when she untied them, the soft cotton material slid down her body and nestled around her ankles. She moved her hands to Rahim's belt and coaxed him toward her bed.

At 11:45 PM, he was back at his post. He promised he'd return each night for additional lessons. The other VEVAK agent arrived at precisely midnight, as always.

March 4, 2028 … Tarifa, Spain, 1040 Hours

After they negotiated the Strait of Gibraltar at a predesignated point well to the south of Tarifa, the *Yuriy Arshenevshiy* and her four escort vessels prepared to change course.

The *Admiral Kharlamov* bravely led the way.

The five vessels turned and headed southwest.

SSN 780 and SSN 781 awaited them.

The USS *Missouri* and the USS *California*, both nuclear powered Virginia Class fast attack submarines, had been ordered to leave their base in Groton, Connecticut six days prior to March fourth. Their orders were to shadow the Russian warships and the freighter and await further orders.

The Russians knew the Americans were there, and instructions from Moscow were issued to sink the American submarines if they turned and assumed an attack position. The four warships and the *Yuriy Arshenevshiy* maintained their course, and the U.S. Navy nuclear submarines remained beneath the waves at an ever-menacing distance of two thousand yards.

March 4, 2028 … Tehran, Iran, 2205 Hours

Nousha was in bed, awaiting him.

He undressed hurriedly, and in a moment he was beside her.

At 11:05 PM, she breathed a sigh of satisfaction and suddenly became irritated with herself. She was actually enjoying this virile young man, and, of course, he was completely satisfied with her. He had just achieved a second orgasm, and Nousha curled up against him. She draped a leg over his torso.

"Rahim, what's going to happen to us?" she asked.

"What do you mean?" asked Rahim, "I will never tell anyone about our times together, and I trust you won't either. There are severe penalties for this, but I find you irresistible. I cannot get enough of you."

"No, Rahim, I didn't mean just the two of us," said Nousha. "I meant to our beloved Republic."

"I don't understand your question," said Rahim.

"Of course you do," said Nousha. "I couldn't help overhearing the daily, lengthy conversations in the courtyard lately. I know now that Israel has attacked us, Rahim, probably with assistance from the Americans. You all speak too loudly, so don't deny any of this. I also know that our arsenal of nuclear weapons has been destroyed during their attack on us. What is distressing is that you've all mentioned that our nation has two more nuclear warheads nearing completion, and we intend to immediately launch them at Tel Aviv in retaliation."

"You've heard too much, Nousha," said Rahim. "If you mention any of this to anyone, VEVAK will severely punish all those with loose tongues."

"I promise not to get you in trouble, my love," said Nousha.

"You love me?" asked Rahim.

"Of course," said Nousha. "When I'm in your arms, I feel quite complete, Rahim, and I think about you every minute of every day."

Rahim hesitated for a moment.

"I feel the same way about you, Nousha," he said.

"Rahim, you do realize that if we launch two nuclear missiles against Tel Aviv, the response will be massive, don't you?" Nousha asked.

"We are taught that to die for a just cause is glorious," said Rahim.

"Tehran will be vaporized in a nuclear inferno, Rahim," said Nousha. "How can that be at all glorious? And then you and I will also die. I want to spend the rest of my life in your arms. I want us to grow old together and not perish in a few days or weeks."

"I want that, too," said Rahim.

"How long do we have, Rahim?" asked Nousha. When will our beloved Republic destroy the Israelis?"

"Soon after our submarines are armed with nuclear weapons on the fifteenth or sixteenth of March," said Rahim. "Our government needs to first perfect a nuclear threat poised to strike at the Americans, so that they will not become involved in the conflict when we destroy Tel Aviv in a firestorm."

"Rahim, please listen carefully." She leaned over and kissed him tenderly, then more passionately. "I must ask you to tell me where those nuclear warheads are being perfected."

Rahim looked at her coldly.

"I cannot betray my country, you slut," he said. "I have betrayed my faith and allowed you to seduce me, and I cannot stand the sight of you. You've used me, Nousha."

He stood, and the rage within him was clearly evident.

"Rahim, the feelings I have for you are real," she begged. "I swear that, my precious Rahim. We will all die by nightfall on the day after our Republic launches missiles at Israel. And it will be at the hands of the Americans that we will die in a retaliatory nuclear inferno. They have an agreement to defend Israel, and surely Tehran and perhaps many more cities in our nation will be destroyed if we allow missiles to be dispatched at Tel Aviv. Think, Rahim, please!"

He sat down as anger gave way to logic. He looked at her cell phone on the bedside table.

"If I give you this information, you'll call your brother and they'll come back and destroy the other missiles, won't they?" he asked.

"Yes," said Nousha.

"You know, I was the one who discovered your brother's truck on that road north of Tabriz, Nousha," said Rahim. "We sent eight helicopters to set up a barrier at our border with Turkey in front of Colonel Sassani, and a contingent of Revolutionary Guard troops closed in on him from behind. The man leading him out of this country was either an Israeli agent or someone from the American CIA.

"We had them trapped and our troops were about to flush them out and force them to flee into the waiting arms of nearly a hundred of our VEVAK agents. We had eight helicopters and all those agents ready to capture them.

"But then, the Americans came. They swooped in from a base somewhere in Turkey, and our people were massacred. You cannot imagine what I saw, and I don't know how I also wasn't killed. But I somehow survived. The American military strength is unbelievable, and I agree they'll retaliate immediately after we destroy Tel Aviv. I also don't really believe that four Iranian submarines armed with nuclear missiles sitting like ducks at a base in Venezuela will deter the Americans, Nousha. They will attack our Republic, as you've clearly explained, and then their navy will deal with our submarines. Our Generals should study the history of conflict more thoroughly. There is a substantial difference between being concerned about four small submarines and being afraid about nuclear retaliation by the former Soviet Union. Tehran clearly has overinflated the importance of our tiny navy, and I agree with you. Once we launch those two new warheads toward Tel Aviv, we are doomed."

"So don't you want to live, Rahim?" asked Nousha. "Do you think it's right that my future with you will be only ten days or perhaps ten weeks? Can you not imagine me in your arms in a month or a year from now? It is wrong that you and I and many millions more are about to die. There will be no glory in any of that, I assure you. If we allow our nation to launch nuclear missiles at Tel Aviv, we are signing our own death sentences."

Rahim leaned back and rested his head on a pillow. As Nousha lovingly kissed his cheek, she reached down and touched him gently. He closed his eyes. He was in love with this beautiful and passionate woman, and he desperately wanted much more than a scant few days or weeks with her in his arms.

"Can you get an encoded message to Colonel Sassani, without VEVAK figuring out what you've told him?" he asked.

"Yes, we developed a secret code when we were children," said Nousha. "It's in Avestan, an ancient Persian language. If I send Arshad a coded text in Avestan, VEVAK should not be able to decipher the message."

"All right, then," said Rahim, "the two nuclear warheads are in the final phase of development. The missiles are ready, and when we merge the warheads with our missiles, two transport trucks will arrive. Once the missiles are placed on the transports, we will launch immediately."

"Where is all this construction being done, Rahim?" asked Nousha.

Rahim stood and began to dress. It was 11:45 PM, and he needed to be at his post when the next guard to be on duty arrived. Rahim walked toward the door to the courtyard. He turned.

"At our nuclear plant in the city of Bushehr," he said.

The door closed softly behind him.

Nousha decided to send a coded text in Avestan to her brother at noon the next day, when many guards were present within the compound. Her heart demanded that she protect Rahim, and she wanted VEVAK to have as many suspected traitors as possible.

CHAPTER 10

March 5, 2028 … Tehran, Iran, 1200 Hours

Nousha Sassani sent a seemingly innocent text to Arshad.

It mentioned their two first cousins on their mother's side by first name and said they've decided to relocate to a place much closer to the sea.

The VEVAK agents who were tasked with monitoring her cell phone were unable to interpret the meaning of Nousha's message.

A language expert was called in from the University of Tehran that afternoon, and although he was quite knowledgeable and adept in Avestan as well as several other languages, he failed to comprehend the subtleties or meaning of the message.

The discussion about her text to the traitor and what to do next went on well into the evening hours. A decision was made.

It was 1600 Hours.

Arshad's urgent request for an immediate meeting at Mossad's headquarters was granted.

"Thank you for seeing me so quickly, Director," he said.

"What is so urgent, Colonel?" asked Director Mizrahi.

"I instructed my sister never to contact me again on her cell phone," said Arshad. "It's far too dangerous. She understands that VEVAK must be monitoring her phone, and they're using her as a pawn to get to me. But something is happening in Tehran, gentlemen."

"She contacted you?" asked Yaakov.

"Yes, my friend," said Arshad. "She sent me a coded text in an ancient Persian language that can only have meaning to me. She referenced my two cousins on my mother's side. They are twins, they are obnoxious, and Nousha knows I detest them. She also said they've decided to move much closer to the sea."

"What does she mean by all this, Arshad?" asked Yaakov.

"If she understands that VEVAK is monitoring her phone," said Mizrahi, "then whatever she's trying to tell you is of great importance, Arshad."

"That's correct," said the Colonel. "It took me a while, but I know what she's trying to tell me. She knows I could not possibly care that two cousins I loathe are changing their place of residence. And then the word, 'twins' lingered in my mind. When I asked myself the simple question, *Who are the twins I loathe most?* I came up with the answer. My sister has placed herself in great danger, in order to tell me that the Islamic Republic of Iran has two more identical nuclear warheads. They are now being developed or they have been completed, gentlemen, and their location is the nuclear weapons plant at Bushehr. That plant is near the shore of the Persian Gulf. It was originally built with the assistance of Germany and later, Russia. There are only two Iranian power plants secretly working on nuclear warheads. The other one is well inland, in the city of Natanz, so my sister is trying to tell me the warheads are at Bushehr.

"And because Nousha understands that VEVAK will see her text to me, she's also trying to tell us that an attack against Israel is imminent."

"My God," said Director Mizrahi. "When will this end?"

"When Iran has no more nuclear capabilities, Zayde," answered Yaakov calmly. "I think you need to call Langley."

March 5, 2028 … Langley, Virginia, 1100 Hours

"I believe we can effectively attack the Iranian nuclear plant at Bushehr by using carrier-based aircraft, since it's so close to the sea," concluded the Secretary of the Navy during his briefing about the discovery of two additional nuclear warheads.

"They'll never know that we've flown in from the Persian Gulf. By the time the sounds of our stealth aircraft engines arrive, they'll all be dead," he assured the others at the conference table.

"Mr. Secretary," said the Director of the CIA, "with all due respect, sir, I understand you're itching for a fight with these people, but the truth of the matter is that only nuclear carrier-based weapons have the required detonative power to crush the thousands of tons of reinforced concrete that comprise a nuclear power plant. Ray, we have a proposed plan of attack, and it does include a combination of weapons delivered by aircraft from the USS *Ronald Reagan,* as well as much heavier, conventional weapons applied to the target from a wing of our B-21 stealth bombers."

"Then why use our carrier-based aircraft at all?" asked Secretary Mabus. He sounded more than a bit miffed at being told his fleet of warships and the Reagan's capabilities were inadequate to perform the mission as postulated.

Mr. Secretary," added Shannon Parks, "it is the Agency's opinion that we simply cannot allow Israel to immediately release Plague Ten, because that's the path they're leaning toward, now that they realize Iran has two additional nuclear weapons. They have no ability to attack and destroy underground nuclear plants, and if there is to be an imminent launch in as little as ten days against Tel Aviv, their one remaining weapon is the Plague Ten virus. In order to protect Israel and avoid their immediate release of an unpredictable, deadly virus, we must attack and destroy not only Iran's facility at Bushehr where their two newest warheads are in the final stages of development, but we must also attack their other nuclear plant, at Natanz, in Isfahan Province."

"That's correct, Ray," added Director Brennan.

Secretary Mabus sat back and frowned.

"Explain and justify your plan, please," he said.

"It's our contention that we must structure and execute one massive strike," continued Shannon. "We can't allow our SEALs to go in time after time and assume any degree of continued success. Those two nuclear weapons facilities can only be destroyed from the air, Mr. Secretary. This is our logic, sir. Iran is rather like an island, surrounded by a little water, but bordered by several of our allies and other nations, including Pakistan, that we do not wish to suffer the consequences of our actions against Iran. We dare not use nuclear weapons against Iran and have fallout drift and kill tens of thousands of innocents in Pakistan. That nation is a nuclear power, and they may construe radioactive fallout as a deliberate act of war against them, especially since we've not been on the friendliest terms with those in Islamabad for more than two decades. So the bottom line is this: We cannot consider using nuclear weapons of the Hiroshima and Nagasaki variety as an option against Iran. We will kill all those who work at both facilities without residual fallout drifting into other areas of Iran or into other nations. That's our proposed intervention by aircraft from the Reagan, but just at the target at Bushehr. The target at Natanz is beyond the range of our carrier-based aircraft."

"And that's, of course, why your plan calls for our B-21s", said Ray Mabus. He nodded at the logic.

"There's more, Ray," said Secretary Brennan. "A key aspect of this mission is, in fact, our stealth bombers. We suggest that, at the designated time, four B-21s from our 131st Bomber Wing will leave our Air Force Base in *Missouri*. Their flight path would carry them over our base at RAF Lakenheath in England, where they'd refuel in flight. They'd then turn southeast and maintain their course at extremely high altitude. Two B-21s will carry neutron weapons to be used against the nuclear facility at Natanz, in an attack similar to the one you'll launch from the Reagan against Bushehr, but the bulk of the four B-21s armaments will be a massive payload of conventional high explosives."

"I've studied the data about those two Iranian nuclear facilities," said Secretary Mabus. "As I recall, each of those facilities is deep underground, and the surface of the plant at Natanz is sixty feet of reinforced concrete, covered with about thirty feet of earth."

"Neutron bombs used there and at Bushehr will neutralize every living thing within a two-mile radius, sir," said Shannon.

"And the fact that the key structures at both nuclear plants are underground, Shannon?" asked Mabus.

"We've taken the liberty to discuss this concept with General Mark Welsh and two of his senior people earlier this morning," said Shannon "They flew in from the U.S. Air Force base at Colorado Springs yesterday.

"The plan is to have you and General Welsh meet with the President in the morning if we can all agree this plan is plausible. The Air Force does maintain their weaponry can penetrate reinforced concrete facilities and destroy them, Mr. Secretary, and the neutron weapons we'll employ cannot be parried by concrete, regardless of how dense it is."

"What would be their flight plan, Shannon?" asked Mabus

"As I mentioned, our B-21s would leave *Missouri* and be refueled over England," said Shannon. "They'd head for Natanz, and the first two bombers would deliver neutron weapons. At that same moment, in an effort to coordinate our attacks, F-35C Lightning IIs from the Reagan will perform a neutron weapons strike against Iran's facility at Bushehr. After our B21s unleash roughly half their conventional payload at Natanz, they'll redirect to Bushehr and exhaust their munitions at that second nuclear weapons site."

"Refueling, Shannon?" asked Mabus.

"After the mission has been executed," said Shannon, "they'll refuel within Turkish air space, overfly Greece, Spain, and Portugal at high altitude, and head back to *Missouri*. The total flying time will be in excess of forty-eight hours, and they'll travel more than sixteen thousand miles in the process, sir."

"And General Welsh is confident this is all doable?" asked Mabus. "And why didn't we simply all meet together, by the way?"

"Ray," responded Director Brennan, "the fellow here at Langley who concocted this plan is Paul Vander Vere. He's only twenty-eight, but his résumé includes a PhD in Astrophysics from M.I.T. Shannon and I put great credence into whatever Paul designs.

"We met with the top people in our Air Force to verify Paul's conclusions, and General Welsh's aides sat with laptops for nearly two hours before they agreed everything Vander Vere calculated is correct. Honestly, we didn't want you to sit tediously through all that legwork, especially if any doubts were expressed. You are the man in all this who has the President's ear, my friend, primarily because it will be your job to take out those four submarines before they make New York City and Washington radioactive wastelands.

"We'd like you to discuss this plan with the President tomorrow morning and convince him to give us the green light to proceed. There is no question that Israel will release Plague Ten a month before they originally planned to do so, especially since Iran has a new launch date of fifteen March, or shortly thereafter, according to the message by Colonel Sassani's sister, Nousha. Director Mizrahi has asked for our immediate assistance, since the State of Israel does not have the long-range capabilities we possess. And we at Langley agree that we must expand our involvement, and quickly. Sending B-21s into Iranian air space and bombing the hell out of their two key nuclear plants won't be construed as an act of war, Ray. We've already established that's our *de facto* relationship with Tehran when we agreed to participate in Operation Cobra. Perhaps Tehran will decide to turn their submarines around when they witness further unstoppable attacks on their nation's war machine. Who knows unless we proceed, Mr. Secretary? But if the President vetoes this, Israel will summarily wipe out all life in Iran and thirteen other Arab nations, and the only Iranian nationals left alive on the planet will determinedly sail those submarines toward our shores."

"I understand, John," said Mabus. "But before I sit with the President in the Oval Office and attempt to convince him to utilize B-21s and neutron weapons, I want to meet with General Welsh and his staff. I also want this Vander Vere genius of yours to be present at our meeting. Let's break for a brief lunch and get together this afternoon. I want to be damned sure of what I'm getting this nation into, before I convince the President of the United States to escalate this conflict. You all do realize, I truly pray, that these missions will kill Russians in addition to Iranian scientists at these two facilities. Vladimir Putin has become an unpredictable madman lately, and our President is very adept at studying the ramifications of our proposed actions."

"Lunch is already set up in the adjoining kitchen area, sir, and General Welsh, his staff, and Paul Vander Vere are scheduled to be here at 2:00 PM, Mr. Secretary," said Shannon Parks.

Mabus gave her a smile of satisfaction at her planning skills.

"What's for lunch, Shannon," asked the Secretary of the Navy.

"Mississippi-style barbeque, sir," she replied.

His smile broadened.

March 5, 2028 ... Tehran, Iran, 2210 Hours

The door from the courtyard to her bedroom opened softly, and Nousha was already in bed, anticipating his arrival. But Rahim did not begin to undress, and his eyes indicated there was something very wrong.

"Get dressed, Nousha. You have two minutes to pack, and take only things you can carry on your back."

"What do you mean? What's going on?"

"VEVAK has intercepted your coded message to your brother," said Rahim. "They even brought in a language expert from the university, but he couldn't help them, so they've decided to come here in the morning and bring you to Evin Prison for interrogation. They demand to know the meaning of your message, Nousha, and if they can't figure it out by spying, they will use direct means to ascertain its meaning."

"I've already witnessed firsthand their 'direct means,' Rahim," said Nousha. "The hideous images of those precious children with bullet holes in their foreheads will haunt me forever. What should I do?"

"I've decided to get you out of here," said Rahim. "I love you and cannot fathom you being tortured and killed. You'd never come out of Evin Prison alive, and I know you realize that."

"Yes, I do," she said softly.

He handed her a small backpack.

"Pack quickly," he urged.

He fidgeted while she took what seemed an eternity to pack.

It was 2225 Hours.

They escaped unseen and were on the road.

"I suggested to the guard who normally relieves me at midnight that I'll cover a portion of his shift, so he's not due in the courtyard until 4:00 AM," said Rahim. "But it's foolish to assume we'll be undiscovered until then. They'll realize I've helped you escape, and a massive manhunt will begin. The car we're driving is the Mercedes sedan owned by one of my neighbors. He works for the Ministry of the Interior, and the license plates will cause this vehicle to remain unchallenged, at least until he reports it's missing. But that shouldn't be until around 8:00 AM or a bit later."

"You seem to plan well," said Nousha. "But how can we escape and get out of the country?"

"We're temporarily driving south now on Route 7," said Rahim. "In ten minutes, you must send another text to your brother. We'll never make it to the shores of the Persian Gulf, where the American fleet sits off our coast. That's at least fourteen hours from here, and we don't have that much time. But I want VEVAK to believe that's where we're heading.

"They will track your cell phone, and they'll even be able to verify that you're in a vehicle speeding southward on this highway," said Rahim. "But when you then turn your phone off, we'll immediately turn and head north and drive toward our shoreline along the Caspian Sea.

"Your coded message to your brother must include that we're heading toward Ramsar, in Mazandaran Province. It's a small, sleepy little city, and it's only a six-hour drive to Ramsar from the point at which we'll turn around. Tell Colonel Sassani that we intend to steal a small boat once we arrive at the harbor there, and we'll head due north into the Caspian Sea. It'll be up to the Americans to find us. They have an air base at Baku, in Azerbaijan. Nousha, when my neighbor awakens and realizes his car is missing, I estimate that within an hour it'll be spotted near the docks at Ramsar. VEVAK will quickly realize we've commandeered a boat and we've headed out to sea. It'll be up to the Americans to find us before an Iranian Navy vessel tracks us down."

It was 2245 Hours.

Arshad Sassani heard his cell phone vibrate. He was awake and unable to sleep, because a flood of unending visions haunted him. The shock of witnessing the carnage all around him after the brief battle with those massacred Revolutionary Guard troops remained.

At night, with his tearful eyes closed tightly, the bloody body parts of men he might have once commanded came alive in his mind, dancing and waving to him.

Colonel Sassani stared at the text message and pieced its meaning together. He tried to think logically. He then dialed a number.

The cell phone rang just once. "Donoghue here," said the Captain.

"Peter, this is Arshad Sassani. How is your shoulder?" said the Colonel.

"Good, thank you, Colonel," said Donoghue. "I'm at the Landstuhl Medical Center in Germany now. I've had surgery and they tell me it went well. I have pain pills and two absolutely spectacular nurses, so things are pretty good over here. Arshad, I was briefed that we've discovered there are two more nukes to deal with, thanks to your sister. Very brave lady, to contact you when she knew VEVAK would be listening."

"That's why I'm calling you, Captain," said Arshad. "We desperately need the assistance of your people in Baku."

Pete Donoghue listened as Arshad told his story.

"I'll get back to you, Colonel … soon," he said. "I know exactly who to call. By the way, say hello to our new friends in Tel Aviv for me."

"We don't have much time, Peter," said Arshad.

"I understand," said Donoghue. They hung up, and Captain Donoghue dialed a very private cell phone number in Virginia.

Shannon Parks answered on the first ring.

CHAPTER 11

March 6, 2028 ... Ramsar, Iran, 0440 Hours

Nousha got back in the car and closed the door.

"I don't normally urinate in the bushes, Rahim," she said.

"Then just praise Allah that's all you needed to do, my love," said Rahim.

They both laughed for a moment as he drove for another twenty minutes into the city. Rahim decided to park the Mercedes behind what appeared to be an abandoned building. It was run down and there were crude boards over the windows with gaping spaces between.

Rahim retrieved their backpacks, and he also removed a large duffel bag from the trunk.

"What's in there?" she asked.

"Automatic weapons, ammunition, flares, spotlights, water, and some food. Also, two heavy parkas, and sorry, our entire food supply is just a loaf of bread, my dear. It's going to be very cold out on the water, so we'll need the parkas soon. The next step is to find my neighbor's boat, the one we'll steal, and head out to sea. It's always well prepared for his arrival, so I'm counting on the fuel tank being full. The rest will depend on your brother and on the Americans. Once we're out to sea, it will be time to pray. Let's head to the marina now. I'd like to cast off before anyone sees us board his boat."

"At least the water is cold," she said as her shivering hands tried to grip the plastic bottle. The next time you plan to escape a country, please try to remember to bring gloves."

Rahim looked at her and began to form an apology.

She suddenly turned and kissed him. "You are my hero, Rahim."

"Only if the Americans are out there somewhere," he mumbled.

It was 0750 Hours.

They'd been heading due north for nearly three hours. The mist of a reluctant dawn eventually had given way to a cloudless, brightening sky, and their small boat plodded forward at a steady twelve knots in order to conserve fuel.

It was 0940 Hours.

Rahim noted nearly half of their fuel had already been expended. Nousha noticed the look of despair on his face.

"My brother will not let us down. Have faith, Rahim," she said.

The sea was an endless palette of shimmering jewels as sunlight reflected off the water to their right. Its beauty lulled them into an unwarranted sense of peace and tranquility. Nousha turned her head and looked lazily to the southwest.

Her body instantly tensed, a primal instinct.

Two vessels bore down on them, still miles away but very clearly outlined in the distance. Smoke poured from their stacks.

"They are Iranian naval vessels from our base at Bandar Anzali," said Rahim. "I knew it would be a matter of just a few hours, once dawn arrived, for them to track our path and realize we've put to sea in Hassam's small fishing boat. From the size of those profiles bearing down on us and the amount of smoke they're generating, I'd say both ships are Bayondar Class Frigates, moving at flank speed."

"How long before they overtake us?" asked Nousha.

"Fortunately," said Rahim they move quite slowly, with a top speed of about twenty-five knots. We can increase our speed to perhaps fifteen or twenty knots to increase their closing time, but when all our fuel has been expended they'll close rapidly and we'll be captured. I'm afraid the end is near, my sweet Nousha."

"At twenty knots in this boat, how long before we're taken?" asked Nousha.

"My guess is those ships are at least ten kilometers away, perhaps somewhat less," said Rahim. We don't have any device on board to accurately measure the distance. To answer your question, at a difference of five knots, they'll be upon us in sixty to ninety minutes, assuming our current distance from those frigates is ten kilometers."

"Do we have enough fuel on board to maintain twenty knots for that amount of time, Rahim?" asked Nousha.

"Yes, I think so," said Rahim.

"Good," said Nousha. "I'm turning on my phone, and I'm going to call my brother."

"Don't," said Rahim.

"Why not?" asked Nousha. "I'm confident he can help us."

"I agree, but use my phone," said Rahim. "Yours can't possibly hold a signal this far out to sea. Mine has vastly better technology, compliments of VEVAK. Call him, and say hello for me."

She dialed a number using Rahim's cell phone.

Arshad listened and simply said, "Keep this phone on."

He handed his cell phone to one of the Mossad agents sitting at a terminal. Within seconds the GPS coordinates of the fishing boat were identified, and the information was transmitted to Shannon Parks at Langley. She passed the data to Air Force personnel at Baku, and a few minutes later, two stealth F-35 Lightning IIs streaked into the morning sky.

Nousha and Rahim maintained their heading and speed, and they watched helplessly as the silhouettes of the two frigates loomed larger and larger. Twenty minutes became thirty, and then forty. Their boat was within target practice range of the frigates, but Rahim knew that VEVAK wanted to take them alive. Torture would lead to invaluable information, and their lives would then be forfeit.

"Hawk Leader to Lightning Control, we have targets acquired. Do we have permission to engage, Control?"

"Affirmative, Hawk Leader. Engage both targets. ETA for the two RAH Comanche helos at your coordinates is twelve minutes. Do you copy, Hawk Leader?"

"Roger. Engaging. I'll take the one on the right, Matt."

"Roger, Hawk Leader. The one on the left is all mine."

"Fox Two," said the first pilot.

"Fox Two," repeated Hawk Leader to indicate he'd also just released one of his AIM-10X Block IV passive infrared missiles. A recent development by Raytheon, these latest air-to-surface missiles were designed to zero in on the heat generated by a warship's power plant, penetrate thick armor, and explode in the vessel's engine room. The weapon was designed to not merely cripple a warship with a single blow; it was designed to create a massive explosion that would take her to the bottom immediately, with all hands typically lost.

The nearly simultaneous repetition of "Fox Two" from both cockpits meant their second missiles were also running straight and true.

Rahim and Nousha instinctively shielded their eyes as each warship became an inferno. From more than two miles away, they could feel the heat generated as both frigates erupted. The center of each warship raised upward out of the water in protest as engines and diesel fuel exploded. The fatal wound became a subdued dance of death as each severed frigate settled back onto the ocean surface and then continued to submerge. Incredibly, in less than four minutes all signs of the two Iranian frigates were gone, the sea was once again dead calm, and

Nousha and Rahim sat in silence, stunned by what they had just witnessed.

The two Lightning IIs had been circling until all sign of the frigates were gone. The threat clearly eliminated, the aircraft streaked overhead and headed north toward Baku. Hawk Leader waggled his Lightning's wings for a few seconds, a farewell to the two they had been assigned to protect.

Eight minutes later, two spots in the distant sky loomed larger.

They were Comanche stealth helicopters from Baku. As one maintained a protective position, the other hovered carefully over the fishing boat. A bucket was lowered, and Nousha climbed in.

Rahim secured his larger duffel, and quickly tossed all his weapons and ammunition overboard. He kept two notebooks containing a scribbled wealth of useful information for the Americans, and with that he intended to bargain for asylum.

"We'd better hurry, miss," said the Airman who operated the hoist and bucket as he helped her into a seat.

"There are four Iranian warplanes headed this way, and there's no way we can outrun them," he added. "Our stealth technology won't help us if they have a visual, so we've called in for support."

It took three additional minutes to retrieve Rahim. The moment he was safely on board, the Comanches headed north northwest, barely twenty-five feet above the glimmering Caspian Sea. Nousha continued to stare out the open doorway of the helicopter in an attempt to see Iranian aircraft approaching from the south.

Hawk Leader responded immediately to the urgent distress call from the lead RAH-88 helicopter, and the two F-35 Lightning IIs abruptly reversed their course. At a distance of ninety miles from the four Iranian fighters, each pilot spoke briefly.

"Fox Three," was declared four times as each American aircraft released two AIM-120 AMRAAM air-to-air missiles.

Moments later, Nousha thought she noticed four faint wisps of smoke in the sky. The contrails seemed to indicate they were heading in a southerly direction at great speed.

Well within their accuracy limitations and traveling at Mach 4, the AMRAAM missiles all found their marks. The Iranian MiG-29 pilots failed to react in time. Less than two seconds of flashing red warning lights were given by their unsophisticated onboard defensive systems.

The two F-35s and the Comanche helos arrived safely at Baku.

An Air Force Major approached Nousha and Rahim just as the two of them exited the helicopter. The turning blades of the RAH-88 were eerily quiet as they slowly wound down. It occurred to her that a machine as large as this should make much more noise.

"How does it feel, Ms. Sassani?" asked the Major

Nousha looked at him quizzically.

"You're on American soil now, miss," said the Major.

March 6, 2028 ... NNW of Mauritania, 2030 Hours

The discussion continued on, not quite heatedly ... that would have been against protocol and impolite. The two officers were seated in the Captain's quarters of the nuclear submarine USS *California*.

"We are wasting time discussing these orders, Mason," said the Captain. "As you are well aware, they are never suggestions. They are commands."

"I understand that Captain," said Mason. "but it's insane to allow a Russian freighter carrying nuclear weapons to rendezvous with a squadron of Iranian submarines at a naval base in Venezuela, sir. We have the capability to sink that freighter and her escorts and end all this drama. I can't believe that Washington is convinced it's better to attempt to sink those submarines *after* they sail from Puerto Caballo, rather than prevent their connection to nuclear weapons here and now."

"You may be correct," said the Captain, "and I frankly concur with your assessment of the situation, *Lieutenant Commander*. Carter. We could take on those four Russian warships and sink them, and also send the *Yuriy Arshenevshiy* to the bottom. But this is not and cannot be a matter of debate, XO. As Executive Officer and Captain of this boat, we have to maintain the posture that our orders are logical and must be flawlessly carried out. Obviously, Washington feels that if we engage and sink Russian warships, the escalation will be unacceptable."

"I understand, Skipper, but the risk we're taking by allowing those Iranian boats to be armed is unimaginable," said Mason.

"We'll have our chance at them, XO" said the Captain. "That's for sure. I have some paperwork to do now. Dismissed."

The XO of the USS *California* saluted and left his Captain's stateroom a bit disturbed. There was an uncharacteristic edge to his Skipper's voice. What's more, addressing Mason Carter by his full rank in the discussion about orders was a clear reminder about who commanded this deadly Virginia Class nuclear submarine.

The XO headed for the Control Room.

Alone in his quarters, Captain Stanley Drummond couldn't contain himself.

"What the hell are you people thinking, anyway?" he said to the silent walls. "If we sink those ships we're tailing, there's no damned way the Russians will escalate this into a nuclear confrontation. Are we really this timid? We're to sit outside Puerto Caballo for just how many days and weeks, like jackals studying their prey, until those Iranian boats leave port, I suspect. That is *ridiculous*. C'mon, people, it's an unacceptable risk to assume we'll easily sink all four of those submarines, before one sneaks though our SOSUS network and its nukes are launched at Washington and New York."

"Absolutely unacceptable," he said once again for emphasis.

But orders are orders, he knew very well. Even stupid ones.

As he headed for the Control Room, all Captain Drummond wanted was to get a few Russian warships and the *Yuriy Arshenevshiy* in the USS *California*'s cross-hairs. His protective instincts called for him to eliminate the threat to the East Coast, especially since his wife and children were in Maryland, at their home in Bethesda.

Barb and the kids are just nine miles from ground zero if they hit Washington, he thought.

"My God," he muttered.

There was a similar opinion and equally deep unrest brewing onboard the USS *Missouri*, submerged more than two miles north of and on a parallel course with the *California*.

Her Captain prayed for better orders, but no new transmissions were received.

It was 2350 Hours.

The *Missouri* changed course slightly, accelerated for precisely thirty seconds, and she then crossed briefly within the minimum two-thousand-yard perimeter buffer required by Naval Submarine Base Command, New London. Her Captain realized he might very well lose his command for the decision to provoke the Russians, but he didn't give a damn. Todd Alexander was not one to ever back down from a fight, and his accomplishments were already legendary at Annapolis. As a Midshipman at the Naval Academy, he had been the primary ball carrier in the route of the Cadets of Army in the annual Army-Navy game twenty years earlier, and his nickname at Annapolis forevermore became, "Alexander the Great." His abilities on the gridiron were very well matched by his tactical skills as a nuclear submarine commander, and his crew respected and trusted him.

The thrust by the American submarine caused the anticipated result, and the Russians immediately parried.

On the bridge of the newly recommissioned Black Sea Fleet *Admiral Kharlamov*, the Officer on Watch processed the alarming news that one of the nuclear attack submarines was rapidly changing position. In his opinion, an attack was imminent.

"Battle Stations," he commanded.

Claxons and sirens roared as Russian naval personnel took up their positions on all four warships.

The USS *Missouri* surged forward immediately once again, intent on daring the Russian warships to engage her.

The Captain of the *Kharlamov* raced to the bridge to take command of his ship as the Officer on Watch made the decision.

"Fire One and Two," he ordered.

Two RPK-7 Vyuga Starfish II torpedoes were immediately spun into the water. Their motors activated and sophisticated homing devices immediately began to track and lock onto the *Missouri*.

"NO!" shouted the Captain of the *Kharlamov* as he realized he was too late to rescind the order to engage the American submarine.

Unstoppable at that point and without destruct mechanisms, the latest version of Russian Starfish torpedoes streaked toward the *Missouri* at nearly twice the speed U.S. Naval Intelligence thought possible.

"Dive!" commanded Captain Alexander.

"Come to course one-six-zero," he added.

"Release countermeasures," a few moments later.

Once they avoided the torpedoes, the *Missouri* would assume an attack position and blow those five ships to hell, he decided.

"Five hundred yards and closing, sir!"

"They shot first," would be his defense at the inevitable hearing at New London. Todd Alexander thought it a good plan.

But his stubbornness was to be his demise.

"Three hundred yards, sir!"

"How the hell are those torpedoes closing on us so quickly?" A fleeting thought, too late.

The first Starfish streaked by harmlessly at more than ninety miles an hour, its course parallel to the *Missouri*.

The second torpedo struck the rear of the submarine's conning tower, and six hundred pounds of high explosives ignited on impact.

In a flash, the USS *Missouri* was gone.

Captain Kushchenko on the *Kharlamov* sensed the entire world around him was a dream, an evil and disastrous nightmare moving in slow motion. His ship's sonar operator clearly indicated that the American submarine had been hit and destroyed, and the Captain realized what would happen next.

"Contact Fleet Command Sevastopol immediately," he ordered.

"Sir," a sailor said urgently, barely two minutes later.

Two Mark 50 Mod 8 CBASS torpedoes closed on the warship at sixty-five miles an hour and blew two massive holes in the port side of the Admiral *Kharlamov*, while the helpless sailors on her bridge watched their attempts to avoid the inevitable become futile. The entire warship exploded in one massive firestorm, and Captain Yuri Kushchenko's dying thought was that he should not have put so young an officer on the bridge that night.

Three minutes later, two more CBASS torpedoes ran straight and true. They impacted the Admiral Chabanenko with the same devastating result, and the warship erupted and sank within minutes.

Onboard the USS *California*, there was absolute silence in her Control Room. Sinking the *Chabanenko* and the *Kharlamov* was inadequate revenge for the loss of the *Missouri*.

"Send this to New London," ordered Captain Drummond as he quickly handed the boat's Communications Officer a handwritten text.

"I hope to God we haven't just started World War III," he added in a barely audible comment to his XO as he struggled to process the realization that the *Missouri* and her crew were suddenly gone.

The bigger question looming for the *California* and the U.S. Navy was whether or not to target and destroy the three remaining Russian Federation ships.

The submarine stalked the warships and freighter from two thousand yards, a fanged predator awaiting further orders.

The Russian ships quickly increased to flank speed.

CHAPTER 12

March 7, 2028 … Moscow, Russia, 1050 Hours

Vladimir Putin paced back and forth in absolute fury.

"Nearly a thousand lost," declared the President of the Russian Federation. He shook his head.

"Plus the Americans lost an entire crew, as well, Mr. President … those on their nuclear submarine *Missouri*," added a subdued voice at the conference table.

President Putin whirled on the man.

"Do you think I care how many American naval personnel died in this brief conflict?" he said.

He looked at the other faces.

"Do *any* of you think I care how many of them died in combat against Mother Russia?" he asked.

"Shall we instruct our remaining surface ships to engage the other American nuclear submarine, Mr. President?" asked another of Putin's operatives.

"*Nyet*," responded Mr. Putin after a thoughtful moment.

"Let them play cat and mouse all the way to the safe harbor in Venezuela, he said. "I doubt they will institute another attack, but if they do sink our remaining warships and the *Yuriy Arshenevshiy*, we will have to support Iran in other ways.

"The Americans have committed acts of war against our nation and our ally, the Islamic Republic of Iran, gentlemen.

"And those two coordinated missions to destroy Iran's nuclear missiles were truly a work of art, in my opinion. If we're to start a conflict with the United States, it cannot be on a direct basis. That concept will spiral out of control, and one of our nations may very well authorize the use of nuclear weapons as things escalate."

He reached over a man's shoulder and retrieved a grape from a large silver basket. It was one of several on the long, deeply polished conference table, which overflowed with fruit.

He popped it into his mouth, and as he chewed, President Putin looked at their faces.

"And, of course, the first to authorize nuclear war against anyone will be me," he said and laughed heartily.

Not one of the other fifteen men at the table said a word, nor did any of them smile. They were all terrified.

"At all costs, we will assist Iran in this plot to launch submarine-based nuclear warheads at the continental United States," said Putin. "That's how we will have our revenge for losing two of our warships and all hands yesterday, gentlemen. The Cold War of many decades ago is about to become quite hot.

"And just to make sure there is no tribunal later to implicate our involvement, it is your task to make certain those Iranian submarines never return to our base at Puerto Caballo in Venezuela. Once they launch their missiles at the American cities they've targeted, you are to sink those submarines, immediately.

"If our friends in Tehran run out of nuclear weapons at the hands of the American military, provide them whatever they need to launch their primitive attack on the United States. I will seriously consider any and all items on Tehran's proposed shopping list, including additional warheads and even missiles, should they request them. Their plan to launch against the continental United States must move forward, unimpeded.

"I want those in Washington to burn in hell. These Americans are not men of deep commitment, nor are they warriors.

"Their cities will burn, their Central Intelligence Agency will have reams of satellite photos showing our base in Venezuela assisted in arming the Iranian submarines with nuclear weapons, and yet they will do nothing to us in response.

"The fact will remain that the Republic of Iran has attacked the United States, rather than the Russian Federation. There will be no Iranian survivors of the attack to interrogate and link us to their plot, and the United States will quickly become a formerly ferocious beast, preoccupied with licking her wounds while we expand our might and influence worldwide."

As he reached for another grape, President Putin gave the group a most disarming smile and said two words quite graciously.

"Any questions?" he asked.

As the Politburo members and senior military planners of the Russian Federation filed out, President Putin added one final comment and again laughed loudly, quite amused with himself.

"I've never really cared for New York City," he said.

"It's far too crowded," he added, as his laughter echoed off the walls.

March 7, 2028 … Langley, Virginia, 1040 Hours

"It's much too quiet, Shannon," said Paul Vander Vere. "With all the bluster that flows from Moscow when someone there has a hangnail, there should be a shit storm of outrage about losing two of their warships."

"What do you think is going on, Paul?" asked Shannon Parks.

"I don't know," said Paul, "but whatever it is, I don't like it."

"A hundred and thirty-four men went down with the *Missouri* just after midnight last night, Paul," said Shannon. I have to meet later this morning with a justifiably furious President in the Oval Office, and you need to figure out why Putin is remaining silent about this. They lost nearly a thousand seamen in this mess, and they've not said a word."

"A wounded bear scares the crap out of me, Shannon." said Paul.

"Especially when that bear is rabid and has nuclear weapons," said Shannon.

The Secretary of the Navy walked in and sat down in the other chair in front of Shannon Parks' desk.

"I don't feel much like saying, 'Good morning,' right now, if you don't mind." Ray Mabus was clearly exhausted.

"Mr. Secretary," asked Paul Vander Vere, "Shannon and I have studied the report you provided from Captain Drummond of the USS *California*, sir. He clearly states that Captain Todd Alexander on the *Missouri* deliberately baited the Russians into attacking his submarine by two rapid advances in the direction of their warships. The Russian Federation has not yet made a statement on this matter, but when they do, it will be thunderous. If I may speak candidly, sir, why the hell did the Captain of the *Missouri* dare the Russian vessels to attack our submarine?"

"You know, and surely God knows, the Navy has processes upon processes, and frankly, sometimes orders don't always seem to make much sense," said Secretary Mabus.

"This opinion is based purely on conjecture, Paul. I've been trying to put myself in the shoes of a captain of a powerful nuclear attack submarine for the past several hours. These directives from New London, to do nothing and allow a Russian freighter carrying nuclear weapons to unload in Venezuela, would be reprehensible to me, as they were to Captain Drummond on the *California*.

"Presumably, Captain Alexander also felt the same way, and that particular captain has always been somewhat of a maverick. He's been tolerated and respected by Naval Fleet Command because Todd Alexander has been a legend at Annapolis for two decades, but we should have seen this coming. There was much too much of, 'give me the ball and I'll score a touchdown for you,' in him, however, and we never should have put a man who believed himself invincible in a position to potentially broadside Russian warships.

"At New London, their conclusion is the same as yours. The preliminary evidence does show the *Missouri* baited the Russians into firing first, so that she might then justifiably turn and take matters into her own hands. Sinking those four Russian warships and the freighter is child's play. Captain Alexander clearly needed an excuse to hone in on them, and his boat went down in the process."

"One conclusion from all this is clear. We don't have absolute intel about Russian technology and their latest weaponry. The captain of the *California* reported tracking the torpedoes that sank the *Missouri*, and his report is that those weapons were moving at more than ninety miles per hour, Mr. Secretary," said Shannon. "And errors in judgment, lack of knowledge of enemy capabilities, all may have started the wheels of World War III turning," she added.

"I pray that's not where we're headed," said Secretary Mabus. "Three naval vessels, a five-minute encounter, and 'poof,' it's the end of the world."

"World War I was started with a much smaller encounter, as you may recall," said Paul. "One bullet, actually, with the assassination of Franz Ferdinand, the Archduke of Austria-Hungary. Things in that era quickly went completely out of control, and we may be on that same disastrous path today."

Shannon scowled. She didn't think it at all appropriate for her subordinate to give the Secretary of the Navy a history lesson. She was also quite sure Ray Mabus had taken a few history classes at Harvard.

"Let's get down to business, please," said the Secretary of the Navy. "We've just lost a three-billion-dollar nuclear submarine, a hundred and thirty-four outstanding seamen, and in retribution the USS *California* immediately sent two Russian warships to the bottom. Their loss of life has been estimated to be nearly a thousand, and all our best analysts seem to feel that Vladimir Putin is unpredictable and perhaps insane. I know that's your assessment here at Langley, as well. Is there anything else the two of you would like to add to this gigantic pot of shit before we discuss these matters in the Oval Office later this morning?"

March 7, 2028 ... Washington, D.C., 1300 Hours
"Gentlemen, a Russian warship came to battle stations in the North Atlantic earlier this morning and attacked and destroyed our

nuclear submarine the USS *Missouri*. She was lost, I'm afraid, with all hands," said the President.

The members of his Cabinet sat in silence.

"Immediately, and as a counterstrike," said the President, "the attack submarine USS *California* launched four CBASS torpedoes at the *Admiral Chabanenko* and at the *Admiral Kharlamov* and sunk both of those warships. Langley has advised me earlier this morning that both crews manning those Russian Federation vessels went down with their ships. Let us have a moment of silence for the crew of the *Missouri*."

After an appropriate interval, the Chairman of the Joint Chiefs of Staff began to speak.

"Mr. President," he said.

"Yes, General." said the President.

"Sir, what has Moscow said about all this so far?" asked the Chairman.

The Director of the CIA answered.

"General, an absolute silence emanates from Moscow about this matter," said Brennan. "That is, as you all know, extremely uncharacteristic for the regime of Vladimir Putin. Perhaps it's too soon … it's only been a few hours since the incident occurred."

"Mr. President," said the Secretary of the Navy, "sir, while we await a statement from Moscow, let me please point out something. We, in fact, caused this incident. The captain of the USS *Missouri* used his boat in a manner to actively bait the Russians into thinking he was about to attack their warships."

"What the hell did he do?" asked the Secretary of State.

"He directed the *Missouri* to accelerate rapidly and begin to turn into an attack position. He performed that maneuver twice, and upon the second such movement, the *Admiral Kharlamov* launched torpedoes at the *Missouri*. The Russian Federation will clearly claim we caused this incident, and I'm afraid that analysis is correct."

"Who the hell was the captain of the *Missouri*, Ray, a competent naval commander or goddamned John Wayne?" asked the Secretary of Defense. His held his head in his hands as he realized a nuclear response by Russia might be imminent.

"No, Mr. Secretary, it was Captain Todd Alexander, a respected and tenured naval officer," said Secretary Mabus.

"I've always been led to believe that naval officers," said the Secretary of State, "and all other military personnel, for that matter, are taught to follow specific orders according to a very strict code of conduct. Is that not the case, Ray?

"And in this very conference room recently, a strategic plan was mapped out and agreed upon that called for two of our nuclear attack submarines to simply shadow the Russian convoy and allow that freighter to dock at the Russian base in Venezuela. We adopted that plan, in spite of its obviously inherent dangers, because we thought it an unacceptable risk to sink Russian naval vessels and be then forced to deal with the consequences. Now, you're telling us that one of your 'tenured' nuclear submarine commanders decided, solely on his own, to alter the rules of engagement this administration has outlined, what … perhaps because he didn't like them? What the hell kind of branch of service do you run, anyway? Do you have meetings and vote about whether or not to carry out orders? Can the swabbies and pilots on the John F. Kennedy or the Reagan sit and cast ballots about the need to launch their aircraft?"

"Mr. Secretary," assured Ray Mabus weakly, "this transgression was the act of one man, and it's unfair to condemn an entire branch of this nation's military establishment because of one man's actions."

"The hell I can't, Raymond," said the Secretary. "We're obviously not talking about some nineteen-year-old inductee who got drunk and missed the sailing of his ship, now are we? We're talking about a Virginia Class nuclear attack submarine commander, who the United States Navy selected to captain that boat, a commander who felt it in his purview to disobey orders from New London and his Commander-in-Chief."

"Gentlemen, gentlemen, please," interrupted the President, "this is a situational meeting this morning, not a witch hunt. For those of you who do not know the young lady seated at the far end of this conference table, I'd like to introduce you to Ms. Shannon Parks, Deputy Director of the CIA. Shannon, please let's get to the topics which are the bases of this meeting."

"Thank you, Mr. President," said Shannon, "Gentlemen, as we've discussed this morning, it is abundantly clear the USS *Missouri* took hostile action toward Russian warships in the North Atlantic. This turned into a tragedy, without question, for both our nation and the Russian Federation.

"Having said that, gentlemen, we have options to discuss while we mourn our dead. First, now that blood has been spilt, do we authorize the USS *California* to sink the remaining two Russian Navy warships and the *Yuriy Arshenevshiy*? The fact does remain that we are certain she contains a cargo of nuclear weapons, and four Iranian submarines are *en route* to Puerto Caballo to be armed with those weapons. So the first question is, are we to alter our plans and sink these remaining ships, thereby eliminating the threat to our Eastern Seaboard? Or do we continue to maintain the position that sinking additional Russian Federation warships may very well trigger an uncontrollable response by Moscow? Their current silence on the loss of two of their warships is, to say the least, alarming.

"The second question has similar concerns. As you are all aware, it has been discovered that the Iran has two additional nuclear warheads in the final stages of development at their nuclear plant in the city of Bushehr near the Persian Gulf. Our intel absolutely indicates that Iran intends to immediately launch those missiles at Tel Aviv, and the indicated date of that attack will be on fifteen March, just eight days from today, at the earliest.

"There has been a plan developed to eliminate that threat. It involves carrier-based aircraft from the USS *Ronald Reagan* and four B-21 long range stealth bombers from their base in *Missouri*. The plan is to destroy Iran's remaining nuclear weapons from the air, and to furthermore destroy the actual plants producing weapons of this type, the first at Bushehr and the other at a nuclear facility in the city of Natanz."

"However," interrupted General Dunford, "while one aspect of this plan is to have conventional high explosives from our B-21s rain down on both those facilities, the other aspect is to utilize neutron weapons to kill as many of their personnel and scientists as possible.

"From a military point of view, after we agreed to participate in the coordinated attacks to destroy weapons at their two primary nuclear weapons launch facilities, there exists a de facto state of war between our two nations, although not yet formally declared. And I for one would hate to wait for that formal declaration until after New York City or our Capitol has been vaporized.

"We can utilize the weapons in our arsenal freely, in my opinion, against a nation in the process of mounting an attack of this nature against us, and neutron weapons are in our arsenal. It is an irrefutable fact that Iran is at war with us, gentlemen, and we must treat them as a formidable adversary."

"There is one flaw in the plan to use air power to destroy those two nuclear plants in Iran," said the Secretary of the Navy.

"We will kill lots of Russians in the process," said Shannon.

"They have research teams, engineers, and lots of personnel at both those nuclear facilities," said the Director of the CIA.

After some rather heated debate, the President made a decision.

"Gentlemen, I do not intend to go down in history as the man who, through specious actions, baited the Russian Federation into military action against the United States of America.

"In our discussion this morning, one of you, I think it was you, Theo, asked if John Wayne captained the USS *Missouri*."

The Secretary of Defense, Theodore Worthington, nodded.

"Sarcasm aside," continued the President, "I prefer not to be the brunt of that or a similar joke. This day, we have taken Russian Federation lives, nearly a thousand. It is my belief that if we continue to peck at that nation, by taking more lives — should we elect to sink additional warships and that freighter — we will bait Moscow into the same manner of action that proved so disastrous for the USS *Missouri* and her crew.

"In a similar fashion, while we might adopt the position that in a B-21 attack on Iranian nuclear plants there will be 'collateral damage.' Some of those inevitably killed will be Russian Federation personnel. I cannot and will not condone a mission to use air power to destroy those two Iranian nuclear plants and kill Russians in the process, just as I will not authorize the USS *California* to sink more warships, and in so doing, take additional lives. I must now put myself in the shoes of Vladimir Putin, and continuing attacks against my nation would absolutely be met with significant and perhaps overwhelming force.

"We will hold firm to the original plan, gentlemen.

"We will allow that freighter to sail safely into the Russian naval base at Puerto Caballo. I hereby authorize our navy to seek out those four Iranian submarines on their way to Venezuela and sink the sons of bitches, if possible, before they reach their destination. I have no problem with that, at all. But in the event they are successful and reach Puerto Caballo unscathed and are then subsequently armed with nuclear weapons, we will seek them out and destroy them before they can launch missiles at our cities. As to the other matter, inform Tel Aviv we cannot authorize a B-21 strike against Iran at this time. They are on their own, I'm afraid."

Ray Mabus spoke up urgently.

"Mr. President," he said, "in as soon as eight days, Iran plans to launch their two remaining nuclear missiles at Tel Aviv. While Israel has a missile defense system, it remains true that if one Iranian missile detonates, Tel Aviv and all its inhabitants will be vaporized. Are we prepared to knowingly sacrifice all those in Tel Aviv, Mr. President? They are our ally, sir."

"Ray, I do understand it's impudent to answer a question with a question," said the Secretary of State, "but would this administration rather initiate an action that precipitates a nuclear response against this nation by the formidable Russian Federation?"

"The clear answer, Mr. Secretary, is 'no.' "

"My oath is to 'serve and protect' this nation, gentlemen," said the President, "and if I must be forced by circumstance to choose between Tel Aviv and an American city, I will not veer from the course given me by virtue of my holding the office of the Presidency.

"Tell the Israelis the plan to use our B-21s against Iran has been officially scrapped, and that decision is final."

March 7, 2028 … South Atlantic Ocean, 2300 Hours

On the bridge of submarine *Righteous Hand*.

He had been taught never to be prideful, to practice humility, and to serve Allah and his precious Republic without pause.

The *Righteous Hand* slid gracefully through the foaming seas, on schedule with her date with destiny, and Captain Ghorbani smiled and allowed himself a brief moment of satisfaction.

"With this new technology, Asad, we will easily slip through the American defenses and wound them deeply," he said to his Executive Officer.

There was a magnificent canopy of stars above, and the cool breeze delighted their senses.

"Five more days to Puerto Caballo, my Captain," reported the XO confidently, "and presumably the *Yuriy Arshenevshiy* will also arrive on schedule, three days afterward. One day or two at the most to affix our towed array system and load the missiles, and we'll be on the move again. Revenge will be sweet, sir."

"Yes, Asad, revenge will be extremely sweet," said the captain. "I'm going below to my cabin for a few hours now. Maintain a vigorous watch, Asad, and take her below at precisely 0430 Hours if I'm not back on the bridge by then."

"Yes, sir, and sleep well," said his XO. "We are in my most capable hands."

Asad grinned broadly at the trust displayed in him.

The *Righteous Hand* continued to plow relentlessly forward.

Her XO gripped the curved metal wall of the bridge tightly and leaned into the wind, as though the boat belonged solely to him.

His heartbeat accelerated.

CHAPTER 13

March 9, 2028 ... Andrews Air Force Base, 0800 Hours

The interrogation of Rahim Husayn Tabataba'i began in earnest. He had been locked in a holding cell since his transfer from Baku.

"Why are you seeking asylum, sir?" asked the aging CIA interrogator.

"As I've explained," said Rahim, "I am deeply in love with Nousha Sassani. When I learned VEVAK was about to relocate her to Evin Prison, I realized she would never be permitted to leave there alive. I helped her escape from the safe house where she was being guarded in Tehran ... and I saved her life. It was a plan of desperation, there's no question about that, but Colonel Sassani did convince you to come to our aid, just before those two Iranian frigates were about to capture us. The firepower your aircraft displayed is incredible."

"That's very noble of you to decide to save the damsel in distress, Rahim. Do you also own a white horse?" asked the interrogator.

Rahim didn't understand the reference.

The CIA interrogator had been doing this for nearly thirty years, and he didn't like the smell of this particular situation at all.

They were seated facing one another in what might have been a Hollywood set. The small windowless room had three barren cinder block walls and a fourth wall with an inset mirror that consisted of one-way glass. Completing the image was a plain rectangular metal table and two grey metal chairs.

Above the labyrinth of hallways and small rooms deep within the basement of the facility, business at the immaculate General Jacob E. Smart Conference Center at Andrews Air Force Base continued on, as usual.

Crisp uniforms were the traditional order of the day on the upper floors, but behind closed doors in the dreary rooms below, the only protocol was the relentless pursuit of truth. This restricted area was solely the domain of CIA operatives.

"What's wrong with Evin Prison, Rahim?" asked the interrogator. "I've heard it's a rather nice place to visit. They have tours, if I'm not mistaken, don't they?"

Rahim was confused. Perhaps his command of English was failing him, he thought, but before he could reply, his interrogator repeated the statement and questions in Farsi.

"Tours?" responded Rahim. "You must be mad."

"Tell me about Evin Prison, Rahim," asked the CIA operative.

"What do you want to know?" asked Rahim.

"I understand Nousha Sassani spent some time there." said the operative. "Did she like it? Did she purchase anything in the gift shop?"

This American is insane, thought Rahim.

"Nousha was brought there with a family she loved," he said. "Their three children were shot in the head by VEVAK agents while their mother sat horrified, strapped to a chair. Then the mother and her husband were also executed. Nousha was witness to much of this, and hideous nightmares return to her each night. And no, I'm sure she didn't visit the gift shop upon her release," he added

"What do you think of the VEVAK agents who performed those executions, Rahim?" asked his interrogator. "And please don't tell me they're really nice guys with sweet wives and cute little future VEVAK agent kids, and they were just 'doing their jobs.' That card was already played eighty-five years ago at Nuremburg, and it didn't work out too well for the fucking Nazis we subsequently hung for war crimes."

"The actions of any VEVAK agents cannot be considered as war crimes," said Rahim, "since we are not formally in a state of war with your nation or any other."

"So you condone shooting innocent children in the head?" asked the CIA agent.

"No, I didn't mean to imply that, sir." said Rahim. "I was just pointing out those actions cannot be considered war crimes."

"Do you prefer the term, 'crimes against humanity,' Rahim?" asked his interrogator.

"There are only crimes against my beloved country," said Rahim.

The elderly agent sat on the edge of the table and leaned forward, his face just a few inches from Rahim's. "As Nousha Sassani has tearfully described," he said, "three children were executed in an unsuccessful attempt to elicit information from their mother, and your concern is fucking semantics, is that correct, asshole?"

Rahim had no reply.

"How many children have you personally executed within the walls of Evin Prison, Rahim, in your role as a VEVAK agent?" asked the interrogator.

"None."

"Adults?"

"None."

"In the field?"

"None."

"So you're the merit badge award winner at VEVAK, do I have that right, Mr. Tabataba'i?" asked the CIA agent. "In all your years at VEVAK, you've been promoted time and time again, and yet there is absolutely no blood on your lily-white hands. Whenever there was an operation requiring your colleagues to perform 'crimes against humanity,' your story is that you always called in sick. Is that correct?"

Silence continued from the occupant of the other chair.

"Whose handwriting is this in these notebooks you've offered us in return for political asylum?" asked the interrogator

"Mine," said Rahim.

"Is it not logical to assume that if you were keeping a detailed record of situations and events, those entries would have been made over a protracted period of time?" asked the agent.

"Yes," said Rahim.

"Rahim, our analysts have studied these logs and determined their entries were all made utilizing the same pen," said the interrogator. "The entries were also made in apparent haste over a short period of time, perhaps as little as in just one day."

"That is correct," said Rahim. "Your analyst is very good."

"Thanks," said the agent. "I'll make sure someone gives him a big red cherry on his cupcake after lunch. Now explain."

"When I found out Nousha was to be taken from the safe house and I decided to help her," said Rahim, "I sat and wrote down everything I knew and had seen, in the hope the information would inspire you to grant me political asylum, sir. It took me several hours."

"I am totally uninspired, my friend," said the interrogator.

"What will you do with me?" asked Rahim.

The interrogator scowled.

"That's well above my pay grade, pal," he said.

Rahim was escorted to a cell, reminiscent of the Spartan and foreboding facilities at Tehran's Evin Prison.

Except this time, he wasn't the jailer.

March 9, 2028 ... Tel Aviv, Israel, 1630 Hours

"Good evening, Mr. Prime Minister.," said Shlomo Mizrahi. "I'd like to ask you to bear with us while we map out the situation before us and then we'll expand to the logic of our solution. I'd also like to introduce you to Ms. Shannon Parks. Shannon is the Deputy Director of the Central Intelligence Agency, Joshua. The gentleman seated next to her is Paul Vander Vere, one of Ms. Parks' associates at the CIA."

"Thank you for coming here so quickly," commented Prime Minister Ben-Gurion.

"Go ahead, Shannon," indicated Director Mizrahi.

"Mr. Prime Minister," she began.

Mizrahi interrupted her.

"Please call me 'Joshua,' Shannon. Things aren't quite so formal here in Israel."

"That's a bit uncomfortable for me, but all right, sir," said Shannon. "They'd have my head if I tried to be on a first name basis with the man in the Oval Office, I assure you. Joshua, we at Langley are not at all satisfied with the President's decision to allow Iran to complete and launch their two remaining nuclear weapons at Tel Aviv."

"So far, we are in complete agreement, Shannon," said Mizrahi.

"Per the President's directive, the United States military cannot act against the two Iranian nuclear weapons plants at Bushehr and Natanz. Washington will not dare kill additional Russian personnel and force Moscow to retaliate. That decision seems set in stone. However, there are many of us who find it reprehensible to sit idly by and allow Iran to annihilate the residents of Tel Aviv, and by 'us' I mean the CIA, the Secretary of the Navy, Mr. Raymond Mabus, and the Chairman of the Joint Chiefs of Staff, General Joseph Dunford, as well as our Secretary of Defense and the Secretary of State."

"On March 11, 1941," said Paul Vander Vere, "President Franklin Delano Roosevelt signed into law the 'Lend-Lease Act,' which allowed the United States to transfer arms or any other defense materials, and I'll quote, to the 'government of any country whose defense the President deems vital to the defense of the United States.' This Act allowed us to 'lend' Great Britain and other nations warships and warplanes, Joshua, essentially free of charge. The Lend-Lease Act kept the United States in a position of purported neutrality as World War II initially unfolded, by permitting us to supply other nations the weaponry they needed to fight the Axis powers. The obvious purpose of the Lend-Lease Act was to keep the United States at arm's length from the actual conflict, even though our interests were to engage a clearly perceived enemy.

"Ironically, the Lend-Lease Act did not have a termination date, although for all practical purposes its need came to an end as World War II reached its conclusion. Mr. Prime Minister, this legislation, although not acted upon for many decades, remains alive and well. It has, in fact, never been repealed.

"The United States Secretary of State, Theodore Worthington, has been in lengthy conferences with the President of Azerbaijan, Ilham Heydar Oghlu Aliyev. It took some arm twisting, but we've reached an agreement."

"Go on," said the Prime Minister.

"The nation of Azerbaijan is vitally aware," continued Shannon, "that the Russian Federation is preparing an offensive to engulf that nation and neighboring Armenia. That offensive may be conducted in less than three months, according to our analysts. Our Air Force base at Baku can be closed at the whim of the Joint Chiefs, and closing that base will be a clear invitation to Russia to march into Azerbaijan unopposed. For us to consider maintaining a presence at Baku, we urged President Aliyev to agree to our plan."

"In other words, you've decided to blackmail Aliyev to comply with whatever plan you've concocted. Well done, Shannon," added Director Mizrahi. "So what has Azerbaijan agreed to do?"

"We're lending them some equipment," replied Paul.

"And they, in turn, have agreed to immediately lend it to Israel," added Shannon.

"What equipment?" asked the Prime Minister.

"Two of the new Northrup Grumman F-35 Joint Strike Fighters are at the top of the list," said Shannon. "They are already at our Air Force base at Baku, and this is where it gets a bit complicated. Their mission is to fly into Iran and do as much damage as possible to the nuclear plant at Natanz. That's a distance of just over three thousand kilometers each way, and the newest version of the F-35 Lightning II is the only fighter in our inventory that has that kind of range. The strike will not be as devastating as one that could be unleashed from our B-21s, but some damage is better than no damage, as we see it.

"However, these two aircraft represent our nation's very latest technology, in many areas. We cannot agree to turn these planes over to another nation, even a staunch ally. Control of the generation six F-35s must be in our hands, at all times, and that's a non-negotiable condition, gentlemen.

"Israel is going to attack Iran, however, not the United States. That's where 'plausible deniability' comes into play. We have asked two of our finest pilots to resign from service, effective immediately, in order to conduct this mission and maintain U.S. control of the aircraft. The associated documents in their files will show their resignations have been accepted with regrets, and they are scheduled to arrive in Tel Aviv in the morning. You will make them citizens of Israel and immediately induct them into the Israeli Air Force.

"When these two pilots settle into the cockpits of their F-35s at Baku, it will truly be Israel that is about to mount the attack on Iran. And, of course, the aircraft will proudly display the Star of David on their wings."

"Plausible deniability, gentlemen, that's what it's all about," added Paul. "We're about to play the same game the Russians intend to play, by arming those Iranian submarines in Venezuela."

"I have a question, Shannon," said the Prime Minister. "In the Islamic Republic of Iran the state religion is Shi'ism, and that's also true in the nation of Azerbaijan. They are Shiites, and in a world where Sunni Muslims represent nearly ninety percent of those of that faith, it strikes me as doubtful that one nation of Shiites would assist in damaging another nation of that same faith."

"You're right, Joshua," added Paul. "Shiites would normally stick together, and past relations between Iran and Azerbaijan clearly support that thesis.

"But we're literally discussing Azerbaijan's existence as a nation here, and we've given their president no choice. Theo Worthington reported that, when he suggested we'd close our base at Baku without full cooperation, President Aliyev immediately asked for documents to review. And he signed them within an hour."

"There's a quote, supposedly attributable to President Lyndon Johnson, Mr. Prime Minister," said Shannon. "When you have them by the balls, their hearts and minds will follow," and that's how Secretary Worthington chose to deal with the Azerbaijanis, sir."

"May I also ask a question?" asked Director Mizrahi.

Shannon flashed a disarming smile.

"Of course, Zayde," she said.

Cute, very cute, he thought. *But the mind behind that perfect face is as sharp as they come. One didn't become the Deputy Director of the CIA at age thirty-two by merely looking good in tight jeans.*

"Shannon, I understand the complexity of your plan to eliminate," said Mizrahi, "at least for the immediate future, the manufacturing capability of the nuclear plant at Natanz. All the paperwork and details aside, your pilots and your latest aircraft will render that facility temporarily inoperable by doing superficial damage. But the much larger threat to Israel is from the nuclear weapons facility at Bushehr and those two warheads in the final stages of production. Does the remainder of your plan address that issue, as well?"

"Yes, Shlomo, it does," responded Paul calmly, "and it's much less complicated from a logistical point of view, by the way."

"I'm all ears, young man," said Mizrahi.

"As an additional aspect of our agreement with the government of Azerbaijan, they are receiving ten of our latest RAH-88 Comanche stealth helicopters, the same aircraft we employed in the first mission to take out Iran's nuclear missiles and their transport vehicles. We have all the necessary transfer documents here for Mr. Ben-Gurion to execute between your nation and the Azerbaijanis. Azerbaijan, in turn, will immediately 'lend' the Comanches to the State of Israel, gentlemen.

"The Star of David and other insignia of your IDF's 'Desert Birds Squadron' will be placed on those Comanches as early as tomorrow, and they're already on board the USS *Ronald Reagan* awaiting orders.

"We suggest that you select a force of perhaps sixty men. They'll launch their mission to destroy those remaining warheads at Bushehr from the Reagan, and exfiltrate the same way, by helo. Thirty minutes on the ground at most should be their estimated timetable, and your IDF commandos should be able to destroy those warheads and do significant damage to the Bushehr nuclear plant in that amount of time."

"And when the Russian Federation asks why you allowed the Israeli paratroopers and ten helicopters to mount an attack from the USS *Ronald Reagan*?" asked Prime Minister Ben-Gurion.

Shannon's expression was of absolute sincerity.

"We thought it was merely going to be a training mission by the IDF, Mr. Putin," she said.

"And when your two most advanced stealth fighter aircraft left an American Air Force base in Baku and bombed the hell out of an Iranian nuclear plant at Natanz, young lady?" asked Ben-Gurion.

"I'm afraid we have no knowledge whatsoever of that action, Mr. Putin," said Shannon. "Those two formerly American fighter aircraft are currently the property of the government of Azerbaijan, and what they do or where they go are issues completely out of our control."

The Prime Minister spoke next, challengingly.

"It has been reported," he said. Prime Minister, "that the F-35 fighters that launched the attack on Natanz from the American air base at Baku had Israel's Star of David displayed on their wings. Similarly, the helicopters that descended on the Iranian nuclear plant at Bushehr were also clearly labeled with Stars of David. How do you maintain that the

United States had no prior knowledge that your formidable weapons were about to be used against Iranian facilities and that the subsequent loss of Russian Federation 'advisors' would likely occur?"

Shannon took the bait and responded as if she were actually under cross-examination at The Hague.

"Again, sir," she said, "under the stipulations of the well-established Lend-Lease program, the United States has provided military equipment to our allies since the early spring of the year 1941. When we lent the government of Azerbaijan certain military aircraft recently, we were also made aware that they, in turn, lent some of those aircraft to the State of Israel. We did not participate in any negotiations between those two nations, nor were we aware of any covert missions mounted by either of those two governments. One proviso of the Lend-Lease program is that those using equipment lent them by the United States must clearly mark their own nation's insignias on that hardware, and by your own admission, all the aircraft you've so meticulously described bore Stars of David. What those aircraft may or may not have done in terms of engagements or missions is a matter between Baku, Tel Aviv, and Moscow, Mr. Putin. And Mr. President, let me remind you at this time that any action mounted by the Russian Federation against the sovereign State of Israel will be considered by Washington as an act of war against the United States of America."

Prime Minister Ben-Gurion sat back in his chair for a moment and scratched the back of his neck.

"Would you and Paul like jobs here in Tel Aviv, Shannon?" asked Director Mizrahi. A look of admiration was on his face.

"And you and these other Cabinet members have put all these chess pieces in place, without the knowledge of your President?" asked Mizrahi.

"Of course not, Shlomo," replied Shannon. "This entire concept of utilizing the Lend-Lease Act was the President's idea. Washington just needs a way to parry future questions at all levels and then deny involvement, if either of these two missions turns to shit."

"Cover thy ass," commented Paul. "It's sounds biblical."

"Old Testament, by the way," replied Director Mizrahi.

He gave them a grandfather's satisfied smile.

CHAPTER 14

March 11, 2028 … Andrews Air Force Base, 0930 Hours

"Good morning, Rahim. I trust you're enjoying the comforts of your cold, damp cell," said the interrogator.

"It's freezing in there," said Rahim. "Can't I please at least have a blanket?"

"We're saving up for one, pal," said the interrogator. "Walmart is having a big sale next week. Perhaps I can find something within our budget at that time."

"You are an asshole," spat Rahim.

"Perhaps you'd rather I shoot you in the head," said the interrogator. "Then you won't be cold tonight. But if you choose that option, you'll need to first provide me your mother's home address in Isfahan so we can send her a bill for the bullet."

"How do you know I'm from Isfahan?" asked Rahim.

The elderly man opened a manila folder.

"We know lots about you, Rahim," he said. "Soccer star, member of Iran's Olympic shooting team in 2016 at Rio, plus a Master's Degree in Economics from the famous University of Tehran. And now, you utilize those incredible skills to shoot little girls in the head."

"I do not shoot children in the head," said Rahim.

"Perhaps just in their shoulders, then," said the interrogator. "Why the fuck did you join VEVAK, Rahim? Didn't you learn anything about decency at that shit university in Tehran?"

"The University of Tehran is a fine institution, you CIA pig."

"Yeah, three-hundredth-and-fifth best in the world, you moron," said the agent, "just one peg above the University of Southeastern Cameroon."

"So where did you go to school, old man?"

"An obscure, mediocre university named Stanford, pal," said the agent. "And to think I left sunny *California* decades ago to end up in a barren room with a piece of shit like you is mind boggling. Confess that you're an Iranian spy, Rahim, and maybe you'll see sunlight again."

"He's telling the truth, Marcus," reported the agents behind the one-way glass in the adjacent room later that morning. "All our instruments show he's being completely honest, and the only stress he's exhibited is when you walk into that room. He's clearly terrified of you."

The agents all chuckled.

"As are we all," said one agent.

"This is bullshit," said their superior.

March 11, 2028 … The Persian Gulf, 2010 Hours

Yaakov Rafaeli was once again in command.

And once again, the attacks were to be simultaneous.

One hundred Israeli Paratroopers were chosen for the mission to attack the facility at Bushehr. In a group of nearly six hundred, when the mission parameters were explained to them and a request for volunteers was made, all had stepped forward.

The Chinook helicopters departed from the flight deck of the USS *Ronald Reagan* and headed back toward their base in Kuwait City, the sound of their rotors diminishing rapidly as they disappeared into the thick darkness. The Israelis set about the business of checking their gear.

Several men approached Rafaeli.

"Major Rafaeli, welcome to the Reagan, sir," began the XO.

"Thank you, sir" replied Yaakov. The words were an incomplete thought, for he had no idea who was greeting him.

"Sorry, Major. I'm Captain Brett Crozier, the Executive Officer of this carrier," said the officer who had just greeted him. "Do you and your men need anything?"

"No, Captain, we have everything under control right now," said Yaakov.

"Your pilots, I'm sure you're aware, arrived this morning and have been getting used to the RAH-88 Comanche," said Crozier. "It's very similar to the Blackhawk from an operational point of view. This is being logged as a training mission, Major Rafaeli, nothing more. If you and your men have munitions to load onto the Comanches, you'll have to do that yourselves. We're playing this one strictly by the book."

"We understand, Captain, and thank you," said Yaakov. "Our nation thanks you, as well, sir."

"What time are those F-35s taking off from Baku, Major?" asked Crozier.

"At 0300 Hours, Captain," said Yaakov. "That should put them over Natanz at about 0430 Hours, assuming they travel at Mach 2. They'll execute and turn back toward Baku in at most five minutes, and we hope the damage they'll cause will be significant. The attack will be conducted deliberately early, long before the plant can operate at peak capacity ... Tel Aviv doesn't particularly want to terminate a lot of Russian Federation engineers and scientists any more than your nation does."

"Understood, Major," said Crozier. "When will your group leave our flight deck and start your part of the mission?"

"At 0330, Captain. That should have us at Bushehr at the same time the aircraft release their payloads at Natanz."

"Godspeed, Major Rafaeli," said Crozier.

Curt salutes followed.

It was 0330 Hours.

Ten Israeli pilots lifted their Comanches with Stars of David on their sides simultaneously from the flight deck of the USS *Ronald Reagan* and proceeded to activate their stealth technology systems.

"Forty-five minutes on the ground, tops," dictated Yaakov in a brief transmission to the other nine helicopters.

The plan called for three of the helicopters to hover briefly above the main building at Bushehr, the research and development facility. They arrived undetected.

Thirty IDF paratroopers slid silently down their ropes and took up defensive positions atop the berm of earth that constituted the roof of the subterranean structure. The berm represented the only high ground in the area, and these paratroopers were tasked with providing cover fire, if necessary, for the other seventy men. They quickly set up heavy machine guns and dug in to the huge earthen mound that was at best twelve feet above the ground. It was easily the size of two football fields.

It wasn't much cover, they realized, but it would have to do. The thirty Israelis waited for the inevitable Iranian reinforcements to arrive and for their part of the mission to begin.

One of the other helicopters dropped to within thirty feet of the entrance to the nuclear plant at one side of the berm, and as its ten paratroopers slid down their ropes, they arced their laser weapons to and fro, and cut down the Revolutionary Guard sentries who guarded the gaping entry to the facility.

The Iranian soldiers died instantly and silently. None had the opportunity to return fire.

The other six helos touched down briefly, and men poured out.

Arshad Sassani had given Mossad a verbal roadmap and rough drawings of what to expect inside the Bushehr facility. The detailed information was so precise that Yaakov felt as though he'd been there before. The Israelis split into four groups, as planned.

As they descended into the heart of the complex, an alarm sounded from somewhere.

It was an ear-piercing, *WHUUP ... WHUUP ... WHUUP.*

Two of the Israeli groups were caught by surprise in stairwells as they descended, and withering AK-47 fire from below stalled their progress. Group Three of the commandos remained at the mouth of the facility, and Yaakov's group of twenty-five men brazenly took two of the huge elevators to the lowest level, eight stories below ground.

The first elevator door opened with an innocent 'Ding.'

One of the paratroopers, in a poor falsetto voice, said, "Eighth floor ... lingerie, adult toys, implants," while the door opened.

And then the second door opened. *Ding,* was repeated.

The Israelis poured out. The first six from each elevator arced their laser weapons in overlapping traces, and Iranian personnel not completely hidden by a steel structure were instantly cut down.

The paratroopers began to methodically expand their secure area and moved to help those pinned down in the stairwells.

Yaakov spoke into his headset. "We're coming," he said.

Revolutionary Guard soldiers at the bottom of the stairwells fired blindly and didn't notice Yaakov's group closing in on them. The Iranian soldiers were quickly cut down from behind.

"Clear," said Yaakov.

"Clear," repeated an Israeli from the other stairwell.

The other two groups of paratroopers burst onto the floor of the reactor-driven turbine room.

There was a short burst from an AK-47, and one of the Israelis sudden clutched at his neck as blood spurted from an arterial wound. He fell as others rushed to his aid.

"Quick, help me apply pressure to Danny's neck," demanded one of the Israelis who was also a medic, but to no avail.

The paratrooper's eyes promptly became a vacant stare, and he stopped clutching at his throat as his hands and arms became limp. He tried to speak, gurgled something that no one was able to understand, and then he was gone.

Two paratroopers moved in the direction of the AK-47 fire a moment earlier. One moved farther to the right and released a long salvo from his automatic weapon. The Iranian soldier backed away and to his right from the fusillade and became somewhat exposed to the second

Israeli. He arced his laser weapon up and then down and sliced the Iranian in half, from his head to his feet.

The Israelis methodically cleared all opposition.

Suddenly, the only sound in the seemingly fathomless room was a steady, high-pitched whirring from the four massive turbines powered by the nuclear reactors. All seemed normal.

Yaakov was amazed at the size of the facility.

As his men combed the massive rooms for other Revolutionary Guard survivors and killed those they found, Group Two found one room neatly set up with endless rows of centrifuges. Lights came on automatically as the Israelis entered the room, and they estimated there were easily thousands of centrifuges in twenty seemingly endless rows. They set dozens of explosive charges and withdrew.

Yaakov and Group Four quickly located the warhead construction room. It was reminiscent of a huge garage, and in the center were two apparently completed nuclear warheads. The overhead lights shined off the polished metal of the warheads gave them a surreal appearance. Off to one side of the room were two missiles with their rocket engines partially disassembled. They lay horizontally on huge devices similar to conveyor belts and appeared identical to those destroyed during Operation Cobra.

"Place explosive charges on the warheads as we did on Mount Damavand," ordered Yaakov. "The fuel tanks for the missiles are over there, so put charges on the tanks as well as the missiles," he added.

As his group left the enormous missile assembly room, one of the paratroopers asked a question. "What about the reactors, Yaakov? Do we set charges on them, as well? There is a risk of fallout."

"Yes," demanded Yaakov. "Tel Aviv has decided it's fine to have Iran deal with their own little Chernobyl, and any radiation should be confined to these rooms. We don't think the population of Bushehr will be in much danger."

"What about the Russians who may be exposed?"

"They may have to leave town," answered Yaakov.

The Israelis methodically set high explosive charges to each of the four nuclear reactors. They used their latest devices consisting of a semi-liquid core which, when activated by an electrical current, made C-4 look like an impotent Fourth of July sparkler.

The paratroopers raced unopposed up the stairways to discover their thirty comrades on the berm were engaged in a fierce battle with Revolutionary Guard troops.

Yaakov and six other commandos pressed the buttons on their remote-control devices, and the eruptions below ground were like an earthquake. The rumbling intensified as flames and smoke belched from the mouth of the facility. Spotters on the berm reported that armor was in the distance, moving toward them from the east, and Yaakov quickly summoned the helicopters.

Three Comanches arrived while the other helicopters hovered safely in reserve, nearly a mile offshore. They moved toward the Revolutionary Guard armored column and launched hellfire missiles at the first four Zulfiqar-4 Iranian tanks. A huge fireball consumed the tanks as their weapons and cannon shells exploded, and the advance of the remaining armored vehicles was stalled.

Yaakov's men joined the battle.

"Split into two groups," he said. "Micah, you take your group to the right, and I'll take my group left. We'll sweep both sides and open a path for the Comanches to come back for us. Berm, come in."

"Yes, Yaakov," said Micah.

"Concentrate your laser fire on the center of the Iranian position," said Yaakov. "Wait fifteen seconds after you see Micah's group and mine open fire, and as the Iranians react and move toward the middle of the road, mow them down. I want all thirty of you to activate your laser weapons simultaneously, and we'll catch them in a cross-fire."

"Twenty-seven, Yaakov. Three are gone, two more wounded," said Micah.

The smoke pouring from the entrance to the nuclear plant obscured their movements, and the two groups of Israelis assumed their positions.

"Micah, on my command, NOW," said Yaakov.

The coordinated laser fire was devastating. Revolutionary Guard troops hiding behind their motorized infantry transports were hit from both sides, and those moving away from the onslaught were caught by laser sweeps from the Israelis atop the berm. There had been nearly a hundred and sixty men in those transports and two officers, the first to arrive once the alarm was sounded. None lived through the Israeli counterattack.

Flames licked at the sky, and there was silence.

While the commander of the Revolutionary Guard support column awaited the roadway to be cleared, the other Comanche helicopters arrived.

With his men safely on board, Yaakov breathed a sigh of relief. An hour later, the Comanches settled onto the flight deck of the Reagan.

In their haste to retrieve their dead and exit the berm, however, the Israelis left something behind. Later, a soldier brought the object to the Revolutionary Guard Colonel

"They left this in their haste to flee, sir," said the soldier. "It's apparently one of their weapons, sir."

The Colonel hefted the laser weapon, and it seemed quite heavy and cumbersome to him.

"How does it work," he asked of no one in particular.

The Colonel realized the weapon had a trigger. He pulled it, and as he was intent on studying the weapon itself, he carelessly swung it a bit to the right.

The movement instantly decapitated two of his men. Startled, he swung it away from them, but he carelessly kept his finger on the trigger. He sliced three more soldiers cleanly in half before he dropped the weapon on the ground. He was terrified and surrounded by blood.

The airstrike at Natanz went flawlessly but inflicted little damage to the underground facility. The centrifuges there remained intact.

March 12, 2028 … Andrews Air Force Base, 1500 Hours

"Hello, Rahim. My name is Shannon Parks."

Rahim glanced for a second at the unbuttoned top portion of Shannon's pale blue silk blouse. He suddenly missed Nousha.

"Where is CIA guy?" he asked. "We were just starting to get along so well," commented Rahim bitterly.

"He's on vacation," she lied. He was seated in the adjacent room at the moment. He grunted, more than a little upset that someone way up the food chain had taken over the interrogation.

"So tell me, little CIA lady, what do you think of the University of Tehran? Is it a fine school, or not?"

"Yes, I do, Rahim. And it's amazing how many of your alumni now play in the NFL." Her disarming smile made him laugh.

He looked down at the handcuffs on his wrists and the chain between them wound through a half-moon metal ring embedded into the table top. Rahim thought there might just be a chance.

"Why the hell did Langley decide to send in Shannon Parks to interrogate this dude?" asked the senior interrogator of his colleague as they watched through the glass wall and listened.

"Not ours to reason why," said the other agent. "She creates the rules, Marcus. He did get Sassani's sister out of Iran, after all."

"This is bullshit," grumbled the surly, older agent.

Shannon slowly unbuttoned another button on her blouse,

"I noticed you looking, Rahim," she said, "so I thought I'd give you a better view. Do you like what you see?"

"What do you want, CIA bitch?" asked Rahim.

Shannon leaned forward.

"It seems really strange," she said, "that, in the course of just one day, you were able to pull off an elaborate escape from Tehran, pack a duffel with everything necessary for your trip except perhaps an assortment of DVDs for the road, arrange for the next guard on duty to come in later than usual, have a fully fueled fishing boat awaiting your arrival at the harbor at Ramsar, and then miraculously sail off undetected into international waters. Are you the new Iranian James Bond, Rahim?"

"Let me try to answer your questions, Ms. Parks," said Rahim. "And please button your blouse. I'm not at all interested. I'm in love with Nousha Sassani. First, I hastily threw a few things into a duffel, it's true. The more arduous task was jotting everything down in the notebooks I've provided you. That took quite some time."

"You've not given us anything we don't already know, Rahim," said Shannon.

"I told Nousha and her brother about my nation's two additional nuclear weapons at Bushehr, didn't I?" said Rahim. "So have you gone back to Iran and destroyed them yet?"

"We don't believe they exist, Rahim," said Shannon.

And in actuality, they no longer did.

"Then that's for those in Tel Aviv to judge, I guess," said Rahim. "Too bad you don't believe me. Now, Ms. Parks, let me please get back to your questions. The agent who was supposed to relieve me at midnight in the courtyard of the safe house in Tehran is newly married. He jumped at the chance to spend more time in bed with his bride, so that was easy to achieve. His absence until much later that evening gave us the time Nousha and I needed to escape. My neighbor is an official in the Ministry of the Interior, and he shouldn't have noticed his car missing until after dawn. That's precisely what occurred. And he's a pompous braggart, so very proud of his little fishing boat. I guessed the fuel tank would be full, and it was. The rest was up to Colonel Sassani. I don't know who he called in America, but those jets arrived just in time."

"He called *me*, Rahim," said Shannon.

"You?" asked Rahim.

"Yes, me. I am the Deputy Director of the CIA," said Shannon. "We owed Colonel Sassani a favor, and the only thing he asked for was that we save Nousha's life. It was relatively easy for us to do that, since you did everything else."

"Your aircraft blew those frigates out of the water with ease," said Rahim, "and I've never witnessed such fire power. If I'm part of some grand plot by Tehran, do you really believe that my government would construct a plan that necessarily included your aircraft attacking and sinking two of our warships? We lost nearly five hundred men when they went down."

"That was just simple target practice, Rahim," said Shannon, "and yes, I believe that your government cares nothing about the value of human life, even the lives of your own people. But getting back to you, are you asking me to believe that after a few sexual encounters with Nousha, you're madly in love with her ... so much so that you would risk the wrath of VEVAK and hideous interrogation at Evin Prison if you were captured?"

"Yes, I'm begging you to believe that, Ms. Parks," said Rahim. "It's true I've never had a woman before, and being with Nousha Sassani that way was dreamlike. But it's how I felt afterward with her in my arms that convinces me how much I love her."

Shannon looked incredulous, as the situation demanded. Her instincts told her this man was not telling the truth, even though he seemed sincere. She glanced at the one-way glass for a moment.

There was a single loud knock on the mirror, to indicate, yes, Rahim seemed to be telling the truth. Two knocks would have been another matter.

"And those warheads definitely exist, Ms. Parks, by the way," said Rahim.

Of course, Shannon knew that part of Rahim's story was accurate. The detailed report from Tel Aviv had given the CIA a complete account of their successful mission at Bushehr.

The remaining problem, she also knew, was the barely damaged nuclear plant at Natanz, but that was another matter.

Shannon stood and walked out of the room without any further comment. Two agents disengaged Rahim from the ring on the table and led him back to his cell.

March 12, 2028 ... Puerto Caballo, Venezuela, 1610 Hours

The *Righteous Hand* surfaced roughly a mile outside the mouth of the harbor and slowed to eight knots.

As she glided closer to the broad entrance of the naval base, Captain Ghorbani's preoccupation with several huge white, blue, and red flags of the Russian Federation atop the seawalls was suddenly interrupted. One of the submarine's diesel engines began to make a loud clank, loud enough for the Captain and XO to hear the noise from the bridge. The Chief Engineer, a man relatively new to his position, immediately looked into the situation and realized the problem was serious.

He phoned his Captain.

"Captain Ghorbani, this is not good. I suggest we immediately cut the starboard diesel engine and we'll investigate further once we're safely in our berth. We may need assistance from Russian naval engineers to clarify the situation."

Instead of making a glorious entrance as planned, the *Righteous Hand* limped into the harbor and needed assistance into her slip. His was the last of the four Iranian submarines to arrive, and Captain Ghorbani was highly embarrassed at this turn of events.

None of the other three captains said anything negative at dinner that evening, but Ghorbani could see it in their eyes. He was the most senior and experienced of the four, and the others seemed to be really enjoying his predicament.

He was furious, but the Captain maintained his composure.

His satisfaction, he decided, would be that his submarine would be the first to launch nuclear weapons at the Americans.

History would surely remember the name Jhanjir Ghorbani.

He smiled politely at the other three officers and sipped his tea.

March 14, 2028 … Puerto Caballo, Venezuela, 1100 Hours

The *Righteous Hand* was declared incapable of participating in "Operation Triumph." The decision was made by Tehran to outfit Captain Ghorbani's submarine with a towed array and missiles only after the other boats were armed and had set sail.

There seemed no great rush to arm a crippled submarine.

The piston cooling system inexplicably had failed in the boat's starboard engine and caused overheating. As a result, a piston failed. The proper action should have been to immediately slow down the engine dramatically and allow it to cool while still being lubricated, but absolutely not to shut it down abruptly.

That poor decision by the submarine's Chief Engineer caused additional thermal stresses in the affected cylinder. Russian naval engineers from a warship docked at Puerto Caballo were called upon to help resolve the issues, and the teardown of the damaged engine began. Parts were shipped by air from a military depot near Moscow that same day, and Captain Ghorbani was told that the estimated completion time for the engine repairs would be at most one week.

His rage was uncontrollable.

The boat's Chief Engineer was summoned and escorted outside into the bright sunshine by the XO. A breath of fresh air and the warmth of the sun was a welcome respite.

"Your incompetence has caused more issues in our starboard engine than were necessary," said the Captain.

"I am truly sorry, sir," said the engineer.

"I accept your apology," said the Captain politely.

He then withdrew a pistol from his shoulder holster and shot the man. The bullet entered his skull and blew an enormous cloud of brain tissue and blood upon exit.

"Call Tehran," Ghorbani said to his XO, "and tell them we're in need of a new engineer. I can only hope, *he* will have a full understanding of how to work on and repair diesel engines."

Killing the man made the Captain feel much better.

He took a deep breath of fresh salt air.

"I think I'll walk over to the main building now, XO, and have an early lunch before I have to put up with the other three captains. I'm in no mood to deal with their smug, patronizing comments."

He walked slowly and waved at a few seamen on the other submarines.

They smiled and waved back.

What a powerful nation we are, he thought.

CHAPTER 15

"Beware the Ides of March."
The Tragedy of Julius Caesar
Act I, Scene II
William Shakespeare

March 14, 2028 … Puerto Caballo, Venezuela, 1510 Hours

The *Yuriy Arshenevshiy* and her remaining escorts arrived shortly after 3:00 PM, eleven hours ahead of schedule after traveling at flank speed since the encounter with the USS *Missouri*. Her crew began unloading the freighter's deadly cargo immediately after sunset.

Assembly of three of the towed arrays went quickly. Russian and Iranian seamen first assembled the arrays on the freighter's deck, and then they were carefully lowered toward the water.

One submarine moved alongside the freighter to have an array completed and affixed to her modified stern, and then the next and the next. After a very brief sea trial, the submarines returned to the *Yuriy Arshenevshiy* for the more complex task of adding nuclear missiles to the arrays.

The huge cranes on the freighter strained awkwardly to balance the cumbersome missiles as they were lifted gingerly from the ship's cargo hold, but dozens of experienced Russian stevedores were up to the task. To them, these were simply cylindrical intermodal cargo containers.

The missiles were successfully loaded into the arrays.

Three submarines, three complex towed arrays, and six nuclear missiles. The work took seven hours, but it was done. Once again the submarines lined up, as patrons at some Quixotic buffet, and each of the missiles was fueled from storage tanks in the hold of the *Yuriy Arshenevshiy*.

Dawn was their deadline, and it was achieved with ample time to spare.

The *Righteous Hand* remained dormant in her berth.

Captain Ghorbani withdrew to his cabin and preferred not to see or talk to any of his crew. Being left behind was reprehensible, but he was confident that somehow, God would grant him a chance at redemption.

March 15, 2028 ... Puerto Caballo, Venezuela, 0430 Hours

The three submarines set sail on a starless night and moved very cautiously with such enormous weight secured to their sterns. The towed arrays, with their adjustable ballast tanks, were a tribute to Nazi engineering and stayed on an even keel with the submarines. The fear that the massive arrays and their weapons would become fateful anchors and immediately sink the submarines subsided, and the captains gained confidence in their mission. As the lights of the naval base faded into the night, the boats remained agile and responsive.

Nearly a mile outside the harbor, they each slid beneath the cold waters of the North Atlantic and disappeared. Their courses varied, but their destinations were the same, a point roughly a hundred miles due east of Atlantic City, New Jersey ... the launch position.

The next stage of Iran's "Operation Triumph" began flawlessly, as two of the Iranian submarines headed north-northeast in order to skirt the British Virgin Islands. They intended to part company and pursue separate courses at 0800. The third submarine turned at 0500 and immediately headed northwest. Her chartered course was to take her west of Cuba and then to run much closer to the American coastline than the other two submarines.

Awaiting them were the USS *California*, the USS *North Dakota*, the USS *Minnesota*, the USS *Washington*, and the USS *Colorado*, five Virginia Class nuclear attack submarines. Their defensive line began to the west and north of the Bahamas and spread to the east, well into the North Atlantic.

Three additional Virginia Class submarines maintained their vigil one hundred and thirty miles off the coast of Atlantic City, close to the reported position from which the Iranian submarines would launch their missiles. They were designated the last line of America's defense, should the Iranians somehow bypass the other submarines nearer the Bahamas.

On the surface off the coast of New Jersey, the three latest DDG 1000 Zumwalt Class destroyers prowled the turbulent sea, seeking target acquisition. Their equipment relentlessly probed the depths.

Contrary to the urgent recommendation of the Secretary of the Navy to sink the Iranian submarines the minute they entered international waters off the coast of Venezuela, the President insisted the Navy must wait until the Iranian submarines were clearly on a course to attack the United States. That meant the CIA and Naval Intelligence plan to go after the submarines south of Cuba and the Dominion Republic had to be scrapped.

Ray Mabus didn't like the President's edict, at all.

Allowing the Iranians to expand the playing field and enter a region of the North Atlantic nearest U.S. territorial waters from multiple directions seemed an unnecessary complication, but the Commander and Chief was firm in his decision.

The President had his reasons.

If this action escalated further and he approached Congress seeking a formal declaration of war with the Islamic Republic of Iran, there could be no possible misinterpretation of that hostile nation's intentions.

The chess game continued.

March 15, 2028 ... New London, Connecticut, 1030 Hours

Admiral Joseph E. Tofalo paced back and forth, and others in the room deliberately averted their eyes. Dozens of computer screens glowed in the darkened room and commanded their attention.

As COMSUBLANT, Commander, Submarine Force Atlantic, his probing questions were hurled through the air.

"So you're all telling me that we have no idea what technology the Russians have installed in those boats, correct?" he asked.

It was a rhetorical question and remained unanswered.

He turned to Ray Mabus, who had just arrived in New London to be at the naval command center for the duration of the operation to locate and destroy the Iranian submarines.

"Mr. Secretary, what about Langley?" asked Tofalo.

"Is there no one who knows anything around here?" added the Admiral in frustration.

"Let's go to your office, Joe," said Secretary Mabus.

The Secretary of the Navy closed the office door behind them a moment later and sat down across from Admiral Tofalo.

"The answer to your question is a simple 'no,' " he said. "The people at Langley have no information about Russian technology installed on those boats Moscow sold to Iran, other than it took nearly two years to install. And as you know, our intelligence communities at large have little information about the true level of advancement of any Russian equipment, whether it's in the air, on land, or on or in water. Of course, we have bits and pieces of information. In November of last year, two of Russia's Sukhoi T-50s, their most advanced fighters, apparently flipped on their stealth systems as they neared Finnish air space, and they simply disappeared. The move drove NATO nuts, especially since Finland was finally convinced to join NATO with the premise we're this strong big brother. The Russians seemed to be laughing at us by showing the world we can't track where they are or what they're doing, and there's murmuring now that the Finns may align themselves with Russia. It was embarrassing, to say the least.

"This is very much like boxing, Admiral, with far more serious and lethal consequences. We train, we prepare, we invent and perfect weapons, but until we step into that ring, we have no idea how strong the other guy really might be. Eight days ago, the President gave us the green light to find and destroy those four Iranian submarines before they reached the Russian naval base at Puerto Caballo. We surmised their course to be from somewhere south of Cape Town to a point east of Natal in Brazil, and they would have then paralleled the coast of South America until they reached port in Venezuela. This very office coordinated the mission to intercept those boats, Joe, and the three nuclear attack submarines stationed along that path came up completely empty. Miraculously, those four submarines slipped by all our sophisticated equipment and they sailed into Puerto Caballo as though our boats weren't anywhere in the vicinity. I know that knowledge disturbs you deeply, and I haven't slept for the past two nights. It seems that in our real-life boxing match with Moscow, they've already won round one."

"Or perhaps that was actually round two," said the Secretary of the Navy. "The tragic loss of the *Missouri* is also testimony to the strength of our opponent."

"Ray, what clearly troubles us here in New London," said Tofalo, "is that the technology in those boats, whatever the hell it is, will allow them to glide through our defenses again. Without the ability to detect those submarines, we can't stop them from launching."

"I know that, Admiral," said Mabus. "The one thing we do know is the speed at which those Iranian bastards will be traveling with those heavy arrays behind them. For a change, Langley and Naval Intelligence agree on something."

Admiral Tofalo asked a question with his facial expression.

"Eight knots, Admiral," said Mabus. "That gives us at most nine days before they'll be in range to launch their missiles at our cities."

"Nine days," reflected Admiral Tofalo. "Is the President aware of all this, and that we were unable to locate those subs prior to their arrival in Venezuela?"

"Yes, Admiral," said Mabus. "He's in the loop and we're briefing him twice a day. He's also aware of Langley's assessment that the three Iranian submarines will probably take separate courses toward our east coast. One of those subs is still in her berth at Puerto Caballo with some sort of mechanical issues. Our satellite photos show men at work on that boat, and she didn't sail with the others. So at least we have only three submarines with which to contend."

"How is the President handling all this, Ray?"

"He's scared shitless, Joe, just like you and me," said Mabus.

March 15, 2028 ... Langley, Virginia, 1100 Hours

"Shannon, why are you personally interviewing the Iranian who helped Nousha Sassani escape? There's some buzz about that," asked Paul.

"After I read the skeptical reports from the senior agent in charge of debriefing Rahim Tabataba'i," Shannon said, "I had to see for myself. I agree with the assessment by Marcus, and we both know he's usually dead on when it comes to interrogation and analysis. This Rahim comes off as some love-struck eagle scout, and while all our monitoring equipment says he's telling the truth, I don't buy it."

"We checked his shoes, Shannon," said Paul. "There's no thumb tack in one of them, so that his concentration might be on pain and he therefore can't react physiologically to questions. That trick to beat lie detector tests is ancient, anyway. I really don't see how he can fool equipment that's always been reliable on other interrogees. Why do you feel so strongly that he's lying, boss?"

"Maybe just years of experience, Paul, but Marcus senses it, too," said Shannon.

"Marcus is an obnoxious old man, to be quite blunt," said Paul.

"And he thinks you're an arrogant M.I.T. snob," said Shannon

"He's right about me," said Paul, "but he's still obnoxious. So what do you think is the story line with Rahim?"

"Rahim is too perfect," said Shannon. "He's a former soccer star, Olympic silver medalist in Rio at the 2016 games, and just the way he so quickly structured this entire process to get Nousha out of Iran. It went too well. And then there's the matter of my cleavage, Paul."

"What are you talking about?"

"When I went into the interrogation room, I unbuttoned two buttons on my blouse, and when he glanced, I unbuttoned another one. Every man who's ever faced me in that situation had a distinct hunger in his eyes, and to a woman it's unmistakable.

"But Rahim's glance at me was different, Paul. For lack of a better word, he was *controlled*, completely under control and unmoved by what I was doing to entice him. And that was not only strange, it was a warning to me that his testimony in all other areas of interrogation may be fiction."

"You think he can fool our instruments, Shannon?"

"Yes, yes I do."

"Well, at least he's locked up in a cell at Andrews," said Paul. "Do you intend to continue participating in his interrogation?"

"Absolutely," said Shannon.

"One other thing, my dear Ms. Parks," said Paul. "About your cleavage … are we still on for tonight?"

Shannon flashed a radiant smile.

"Absolutely," she said. "Just don't be an arrogant snob."

"With you in my arms, I am always humble and complete," said Paul.

Shannon knew it was a violation of protocol at the Agency, but it was too late. She already loved him fiercely.

"8:00 PM," she said.

Paul nodded, turned and went back to his desk to try and figure out how to detect seemingly invisible submarines.

March 15, 2028 … Moscow, Russia, 1350 Hours

Vladimir Putin was in exceedingly good spirits.

"The plan is so beautiful," he said to the two generals seated in his expansive office within the Kremlin complex. He stood at the windows, and admired the view of Alexander Gardens.

President Putin turned and continued.

"These Americans have no spine, and now they've shown us they also have no balls. Can you believe they didn't sink the freighter before it reached Puerto Caballo, and then they actually didn't attack the Iranian submarines while in their berths at our base? And then, they allowed the submarines to be armed, while the four of them were neatly lined up like sitting geese?

"This is becoming an epic tragedy worthy of Tolstoy at his best, but with the American President as the author. And their tragedy will become our most joyous moment, my friends. New York City and *Washington* will be vaporized by weapons fifty times as powerful as those they used against Japan, and justice will now prevail. It was the Americans who initiated the concept of nuclear war, and they will be paid back handsomely for that transgression.

"It is lovely to observe the imbeciles in Tehran moving forward as innocent pawns. On this elaborate chessboard of international intrigue, with our masterful technology assisting them, of course, they are unwittingly playing this game as Mother Russia escapes unscathed all actions of the Islamic fanatics.

"I understand that one of their submarines has experienced some sort of mechanical problems.

"Make certain it is repaired promptly and that it also sets sail for the American Eastern Seaboard. Perhaps they'll select other targets, Atlanta or Miami. I think our friends in Cuba might like Miami being vaporized … revenge for all those who fled our comrade Fidel's designs. In this deadly game we play, revenge is everything.

"Keep me informed about things as they progress."

"Yes, Mr. President," replied the generals in unison as they rose to leave. They turned to address an additional question.

"When will they be in position to launch?" asked the President of the Russian Federation.

"Nine days, at the most, sir," replied one of them.

March 15, 2028 … Tel Aviv, Israel, 1730 Hours

"Mr. Prime Minister, we've only achieved limited success," stated General Gadi Eisenkot.

Prime Minister Ben-Gurion sat back in his chair.

"So, Gadi, we're confident the Iranian nuclear facility at Bushehr has been neutralized, but we know little about damage to Natanz," he said.

"The heaviest weapons carried by American F-35s don't really have the explosive force to penetrate fifty or more feet of reinforced concrete and thirty feet of earth on top of that, I'm afraid," said General Eisenkot. "But we realized that before we sent in the aircraft," he added.

"So what was the purpose of the mission at Natanz?" asked Ben-Gurion.

"We did destroy whatever surface infrastructure that may have existed before our attack, but the underground nuclear weapons facility there has probably not been damaged at all." said Eisenkot.

"Then Iran still has nuclear weapons capabilities?" asked Joshua.

"Yes, Joshua, that's correct," said Eisenkot.

The Prime Minister turned to address the Director of Mossad.

"Zayde, we need to convince the Americans to use their B-21s against Iran's facility at Natanz. I frankly don't understand why the President of the United States won't agree to a pre-dawn bombing run by those warplanes in order to avoid heavy civilian casualties. In order to avoid killing many Russian 'advisors,' they could destroy that plant in the middle of the night, couldn't they? After all, that's when our air attack by the F-35s took place. Has Colonel Sassani given us detailed information about the capabilities of that facility?"

Director Mizrahi answered immediately.

"We've quizzed him about Bushehr and Natanz before our raid took place, and he's explained both nuclear facilities are structured basically along the same lines, except the one at Natanz is larger. He doesn't know exactly how many centrifuges are at Natanz, but his estimate is more than twelve thousand. And to answer your other questions, Mr. Prime Minister, first, our attack was structured to wipe out surface infrastructure, and Colonel Sassani assured us all Russian personnel would presumably be deep inside the complex.

"And second, about B-21s bombing that nuclear plant in the middle of the night to civilian avoid casualties, the Natanz nuclear plant is in operation twenty-four hours a day, with Russian scientists and engineers assigned to all shifts."

The Prime minister shook his head.

"Not good," he said. "And so it continues. Where is Colonel Sassani now?"

"When his sister and the Iranian VEVAK agent who helped her escape landed at the American Air Force in Baku, Colonel Sassani asked to be flown there to greet her," said Director Mizrahi. "They spent a day there together, and then we brought the two of them here. They're living temporarily at the IDF Ramat David Air Base, so we have immediate access to the Colonel if we need any additional information about Iran's nuclear capabilities. The Americans kept the former VEVAK agent and sent him to Washington for interrogation. He's currently at Andrews Air Force Base under CIA control, and Nousha Sassani asks about him every day, I'm told."

The Prime Minister turned to address the General.

"I know what you're thinking, Gadi."

"Yes, Joshua. We do not have the means to destroy the Iranian nuclear plant at Natanz, and it's just a matter of time before Iran creates more warheads. To make matters worse, Mossad has learned there is now a full brigade of Revolutionary Guards stationed at the immediate perimeter of that facility. That's roughly fifteen hundred men. They have armor, and a force of that size cannot be handled by our people dropping out of the sky."

Shlomo Mizrahi nodded in agreement.

"We could send back the F-35s on loan from the Americans," continued the General. "They could next be equipped with neutron weapons, Joshua. We'd wipe out the entire Revolutionary Guard brigade and all who work within the Natanz complex. But the centrifuges and all other equipment deep within the facility would remain intact.”

Director Mizrahi voiced his opinion.

“Gentlemen, we have just gone full circle back to the discussion we’ve had about releasing Plague Ten into Jordan, Iraq, and Iran.

“Our concern about other Arab States remains an ongoing issue, and if we elect to utilize any form of nuclear weapons against Iran, the backlash against us by those other nations will be significant. Our dilemma remains the same. First, our use of neutron weapons will allow Iran to staff Natanz with new people again and again, since the plant itself will remain unscathed. And second, I can assure you that if we use neutron weapons repeatedly against the Iranians at Natanz, the Arab world will quickly unite against us. I don’t want to wage war against the combined forces of Saudi Arabia, Egypt, and other nations who’ve decided to join the fight, especially since they’d have justification to begin to use nuclear weapons against Israel.

“No, this is not an acceptable path for us to venture upon. Gadi and I already agree on this. If the Americans will not assist us by destroying the plant at Natanz, our one option remains the release of Plague Ten. And our original assessment has validity, in spite of all our recently successful operations against Iran. We must attack all fourteen Arab nations at once, and kill them all.”

“I agree with Shlomo, Joshua,” added General Eisenkot. We are back to square one, and we must kill them all. If no one remains alive in an Arab nation, Israel will not face retribution.”

“Except from God,” said Prime Minister Ben-Gurion.

“Yes, except from God,” agreed Shlomo Mizrahi sadly.

“I would tell God we’ve simply done what He commanded us to do in a particular chapter of Deuteronomy,” added General Eisenkot with a shrug of indifference.

“He did instruct us to kill them all, did He not?” challenged the Israeli General.

CHAPTER 16

March 20, 2028 ... North of Bermuda, 1100 Hours

The emptiness of the vast ocean surrounding the USS *California* drove Captain Stanley Drummond insane.

Protocol dictated that he was to always maintain his composure, but his clipped sentences and abrupt orders were an indication of the frustration mounting within him.

Only a few days remained before the purported launch date by the enemy, and Stan Drummond knew those damned submarines were out there somewhere.

It had been seven days since the confirmed sailing of the three Iranian boats from Venezuela, and Captain Drummond was deeply concerned that the Russian technology onboard those boats would allow them to slip undetected past the American gauntlet. The first test of that technology had clearly been won by the Iranians, when they sailed toward Puerto Caballo from Iran and arrived cleanly without being detected by any of the Virginia Class boats in the area. But now, the Captain realized, the stakes were infinitely higher.

He leaned over the sailor's shoulder who currently manned the *California*'s passive sonar console.

"Nothing, Captain," said the sailor.

"Anything at all in the past few hours?" asked Drummond

"Just a whale or a huge shark about two hours ago," said the sailor.

"What was its heading, son?" asked Drummond

"015, sir," said the sailor.

The Captain addressed his Executive Officer.

"XO, I'll be in my cabin for an hour or so. Keep a sharp eye on everything and make sure we prowl to the outer edges of our assigned area. We cannot, and I repeat, *cannot* allow those Iranian submarines to get by us."

"Aye, aye, Captain," said his XO.

Nearly an hour later, sleep refused to arrive. While he stared at the ceiling, picturing the devastated expression on the face of Captain

Todd Alexander's wife Laurie, when she heard the USS *Missouri* was lost with all hands, he sensed there was something he was missing. It plagued him.

Captain Drummond left his cabin, intent on getting a cup of coffee. Perhaps caffeine might help him sort things out, he decided.

Midway down the narrow corridor, he knew.

Part of the gauntlet created and sustained by the U.S. Navy were three DDG 1000 Zumwalt Class destroyers, odd-shaped warships with highly sophisticated weaponry and stealth profiles. In briefings about these advanced surface ships, a comment had been made that their profiles appeared as small fishing boats on radar. And that was the link that Captain Drummond needed, the connection of all the dots on the massive display that swirled relentlessly in his head.

If a large surface warship like a Zumwalt Class destroyer can be made to appear as a small fishing boat to a radar display, what might an advanced stealth submarine look like to a passive sonar system, he asked himself. He knew the answer with absolute certainty as he headed rapidly for the bridge.

It might appear as a whale.

"Come to course 010," he ordered.

His XO gave him a curious look.

"We're going to sink a whale," added Stan Drummond.

March 20, 2028 … Andrews Air Force Base, 1220 Hours

"Rahim, I still don't believe anything you've told us," said Shannon Parks. "Your story and your credentials are all simply too neat and pretty for me to buy. That's not the way life is. I'm afraid you're going to end up in Guantanamo or some other high security facility, and you're destined to remain there indefinitely."

She motioned to the two men behind the one-way glass that the meeting was over, and she leaned back in her chair.

"Cuba awaits you, Rahim," she added.

The two-armed agents from the adjacent room came in.

One disengaged Rahim's handcuffs from the metal loop in the table, and in that split second of relative freedom, Rahim swung his clasped hands and struck the agent in the temple. The man went down, and as the older agent reached for his sidearm, Rahim grabbed one side of the metal table and hurled it in the man's direction.

The agent parried the blow from the table with his left hand, but the movement slowed the removal of his handgun.

Rahim was on the man instantly. He struck Marcus in the face and wrestled the Glock from his hand.

Rahim stood and shot him twice in the chest. He then turned and shot the other agent between the eyes. The noise was deafening within the insulated and soundproofed room.

Shannon had been knocked off her chair when Rahim picked up the metal table and threw it at Marcus. She turned and looked at the vacant stare that came over his eyes and watched him die.

"Do not move, or I will kill you, as well," said Rahim.

Shannon remained on the floor while Rahim quickly searched the dead agent's pockets for the key to his cuffs and shackles.

He found it.

He threw the handcuffs and chain that linked them together on the floor, removed the shackles from his ankles, and then removed the younger agent's clothes. He had to struggle a bit with the inert body, but the man had a build similar to Rahim's. He shed has orange overall prisoner's uniform and put on the dead man's trousers and shoes, then his shirt and ID badge.

"All right, Ms. Parks," said Rahim, "we're going to calmly walk out of here and head for your car. If you make any sudden movement or shout for help, you will be the next to die. Is that clear?"

Shannon nodded and slowly stood as Rahim reached down and retrieved the handcuffs. He stuffed them into his pants pocket.

They walked together, with Rahim's right hand and the handgun jammed hard into Shannon's back, just above her waist and beneath her business suit's jacket. Rahim glanced at the row of cells, but all were empty now.

They reached an elevator and entered it.

The door closed behind them, and Rahim leaned down and whispered demandingly in Shannon's ear.

"Enter your access code on the keypad, Ms. Parks, and take us to the parking level, or I will kill you here and now."

She had little choice and complied.

A moment later, they walked together down a brightly lit corridor of the Jacob Smart Conference Center. Signage verified that Shannon was leading them in the right direction.

He fished for the car keys in her purse, and also found her 9mm Beretta Px4 handgun.

"Two handguns are better than one," he said.

"You just killed two CIA agents, asshole," said Shannon. "And we're going to hunt you down and send your sorry ass to Guantanamo for months of 'special treatment.' I hope you like to play sports in addition to soccer, Rahim. We have a whole new one there for you to try … it's called water boarding."

"Get in the passenger seat," said Rahim.

He grabbed Shannon's right arm and handcuffed her wrist to the grab handle in the interior of her BMW, so that her arm was raised up and became pinned tightly against the window glass. He went to the driver's side, sat down, and started the car.

They left the parking area and signs directed them to the gates.

As the car gained speed and they headed toward I495, Rahim took Shannon's cell phone from her purse.

"Thank your highway commission for all these wonderful signs," he said. "I doubt you'd give me accurate directions."

He wasn't very good at driving and dialing a number, but the BMW miraculously avoided several potential disasters. As he turned onto I295 and sped toward the Capitol, his call was answered.

The other two agents scheduled to be on duty that afternoon in the interrogation area beneath the conference center arrived precisely on schedule at 12:55 PM.

"Marcus," began one of them as they entered the observation room, "we decided to stop at Charbar & Eli's deli on the way here and bring you two corned beef sandwiches for lunch. We …"

They though it odd the room was empty, and then they turned and looked through the one-way glass. They burst into the room and verified that Marcus Bernstein and Sam Morehouse were dead, and they realized Shannon Parks was missing.

Within minutes it was determined that her car was not in the parking lot. Calls to her cell phone were unanswered, and a call to Langley verified she had not yet returned to her office. It was then surmised that Shannon had become a hostage, and she and the VEVAK suspect had escaped in her car.

Alarms were sounded, and the FBI and State and local police were informed to locate her white BMW 555i.

Rahim spoke rapidly, and the man at the other end listened with few interruptions. The call lasted for more than ten minutes.

He then located an address on Shannon's cell phone with the assistance of Google and typed it into the BMW's NAV system.

"Where are you taking us?" she asked.

"To the embassy of the Russian Federation," he replied. "That's the only place where I might be protected here in Washington."

"We'll never make it there, Rahim. By now, other CIA agents have discovered the bodies of the men you killed, and the authorities have all been notified to look for my car."

"You're right, thank you," he replied as he moved into the right-hand lane and exited I295 at Suitland Parkway. A few blocks later he turned into the parking lot of the Anacostia Metro Station.

His search ended quickly, and he parked the BMW next to a newer model Ford Explorer at the far end of the parking lot.

Rahim used the Glock to shatter the driver's side rear window of the Explorer. He unlocked the door, sat down, and reached forward for the driver's switch to unlock the other doors. He reached under the steering column and tugged on wires nestled there, separated two from the bundle and touched their bared ends together.

The Explorer started immediately.

He roughly freed Shannon from the handcuffs, retrieved them, and attached her in the same manner to the grab handle on the passenger side of the Ford SUV. They sat for a moment while he entered their destination into the Explorer's NAV, again using Shannon's cell phone as his reference guide.

It took just a few minutes to exit the parking lot and get onto I695, and they crossed the bridge and headed toward the heart of Washington, D.C.

"Who were you talking to?" she asked.

"General Hassan Firouzabadi, Chief of Staff of Iran's Armed Forces," he replied. Rahim decided it was pointless to lie to her, since he intended to kill her in the next few minutes, anyway.

"I know who he is," she added.

After a brief silence as the Explorer sped toward their destination, Shannon turned to him.

"How did you learn the details of Israel's plan to release their Plague Ten virus and kill all the inhabitants of your country?" she asked.

He looked at her, clearly surprised.

"Rahim, I am fluent in Farsi," said Shannon.

Rahim shrugged and began to explain while he drove on.

"When Colonel Sassani flew to Azerbaijan to be reunited with his sister, the three of us were allowed to talk openly by your idiot associates in Baku. We stayed up half the night, and when I asked the Colonel why he agreed to help the Americans and the Jews destroy our nuclear weapons, he explained his decision was to avert a far greater catastrophe. That's when he told me about Israel's new weapon, Plague Ten, and it was at that moment that I decided I must escape to warn my nation. If not for that knowledge, I would have cooperated with you Americans and defected. I truly have deep feelings for Nousha, and it would have been acceptable, perhaps even magical, to live out my life with her in your Colorado. But because I know what the Jews were planning to do, loyalty to my country must necessarily come first. I had to do whatever was demanded in order to place that call to Tehran. Now that I've accomplished that, my hope is that the Russian Federation will protect me. If not, at least I've been able to warn General Firouzabadi that Israel has an enormously powerful weapon."

"What do you intend to do with me, Rahim?" asked Shannon.

"Colonel Sassani explained to me that it was immensely difficult for him to engage Republican Guard troops and participate in their slaughter, but he did that in the best interest of our Republic. We are at war now with America, Ms. Parks, and I must strike a blow for our nation, however great or small." said Rahim.

"So you intend to kill me?" asked Shannon.

"Yes," said Rahim.

They sat in silence as the woman's monotone voice in the NAV system directed them onward.

"Exit right onto Maine Avenue SW," said the voice.

As they passed the Washington Monument to Shannon's right, the voice said, "Continue straight onto Independence Ave SW at West Potomac Park."

"Independence Ave SW becomes Ohio Drive SW. Stay straight onto Ohio Drive SW."

They passed the Korean War Veteran's Memorial on their right and then the Lincoln Memorial.

"Ohio Drive SW becomes Ohio Drive NW."

The voice informed them that Ohio Drive becomes Rock Creek Parkway, and eight minutes went by.

"Bear slight left onto Cathedral Ave NW."

And then, "Turn right onto Connecticut Ave NW."

Shannon's mind was racing.

"Rahim," she said. "I have something for you to consider, please. I am also fluent in Russian and as a senior CIA officer, I'm sure they would very much appreciate you turning me over to them alive rather than dead. You have few bargaining chips in all this, and you're about to kill your most valuable asset."

Rahim reflected and realized she was right.

"Very well," he said. "I'll give the Russian Federation a pretty little present, and we'll let your associates at Langley think you've simply disappeared. That might actually cause more damage than your death."

"Turn left onto Van Ness St NW, and then make an immediate left turn onto International Drive NW."

"You have arrived at your destination, 3514 International Drive NW. It is on your right."

The two massive iron gates were open, and Rahim sped through them and into the courtyard. The open gates obscured the plaques on the exterior stone walls that stated the embassy's nation. He didn't think it odd that no flags were flying, to boldly proclaim this was Russian Federation soil, nor did he realize that all flags had been temporarily removed.

Six men with handguns drawn immediately encircled the car.

Four others wielded automatic weapons … Uzis.

"Get out of the car, and keep your hands up," one ordered.

"Welcome to the State of Israel," said another as Rahim slowly exited the car.

A third Mossad agent produced a large wire cutters with two-foot-long handles and promptly snapped off the interior grab handle to which Shannon had been pinned.

Rahim was stunned and confused. He submitted without any resistance, and his wrists were tied securely behind his back with a zip tie by the Israelis.

After Shannon's handcuff was removed, she and Rahim were escorted into a small office to the immediate right of the main hallway of the embassy. A man awaited them.

"Sit," he commanded, and they obeyed. Two other agents stood silently behind them, to their left and right.

"Ms. Parks, are you all right?" he asked gently.

Shannon breathed a sigh of relief.

"Yes, thank you," she said.

"Glad to see it works," she added.

"I don't understand what just happened," said Rahim. "Your car's NAV system was supposed to take us to the Russian embassy."

"It's a program one of my closest associates at CIA has recently developed, you asshole," said Shannon. Her fury at witnessing the murders of two good men returned in a wave of outrage.

"It's called 'Google Confuse'," she added, "and it's been installed in many of our cell phones and in our personal car NAV systems. The reasoning behind it is simple. If a 'bad guy' gets to one of us and seeks a safe haven here in Washington, it will most likely be at the embassy of the Russian Federation. When Google is accessed on any of our phones, the address of the State of Israel's embassy pops up instead and the staff here is instantly alerted. Today was the first test of that software, and I'm glad to say it worked flawlessly."

"Yes, it did," said the Mossad senior agent. "Per our willingness to cooperate with your CIA's 'Google Confuse' project, I should remind you that our agreement is that if a captive is of interest to the State of Israel, he is ours to interrogate for seventy-two hours. After that, he is yours to have and to cherish."

"Just make sure he's capable of standing trial after you're done with him, Mr. Blue," said Shannon.

"Of course, Ms. Parks. A car has been sent for you and should be here shortly, by the way," said the Israeli, code named "Blue." His actual name was Dahan.

"Thank you," said Shannon. "My car keys are in this asshole's pocket. I'll have someone pick it up later … I'm a bit too shaky to drive."

The agent came around his desk, and as he reached forward to retrieve Shannon's keys, Rahim kicked him viciously between the legs before the other two Mossad agents could react.

Remarkably, the man maintained his composure.

"Thank you, Rahim, that decision by you will make our next three days simply delicious, I assure you," said Dahan.

He retrieved the keys and handed them to Shannon.

Another man entered the room.

"A car is here for Ms. Parks," he said and closed the door.

She rose and shook Agent Dahan's hand warmly.

"Thank you, again," she said.

"You're quite welcome. And my compliments to your associate, Paul Vander Vere, for the success of his brilliant software," said the Mossad's Station Chief.

"I'll thank him properly tonight," she assured the Israeli.

He understood and nodded.

At the doorway, Shannon turned for a moment.

"Farewell, Rahim," she said with a disarmingly radiant smile.

The door closed behind her, and the Israeli looked at Rahim.

"And now, my friend, you are mine," said Meyer Dahan with fire and venom as his fist slammed downward onto Rahim's face and knocked him to the floor.

March 20, 2028 … North Atlantic Ocean, 1340 Hours

About three hundred and fifty miles due east of Miami, the sailor who manned the passive sonar system onboard the USS *California* spoke up to his Captain.

"Contact, sir! Bearing oh-eight-five," said the sailor

"The signature is that whale again, Skipper," added the XO.

"What is her course, XO?" asked Captain Drummond.

"340, sir," said the sailor.

"Range?" asked Captain Drummond.

"Twenty-eight thousand yards, sir," said the sailor

"Battle Stations, XO," said the Captain.

"Battle Stations," repeated Lt Cmdr. Carter into his microphone for the entire crew to hear.

"This is not a drill. Repeat, this is not a drill."

"I have a theory," said Captain Drummond as his crew prepared for battle.

"It's obvious that the Russian Navy has developed technology superior to ours, Carter." said the Captain. "That's why those Iranian boats were able to slink past our line of submarines and enter Puerto Caballo completely undetected. But my theory is that the Russian technology was never designed to hide a care package towed behind one of their boats. So the small signature we've detected doesn't emanate from the submarine herself, but rather from the towed array behind. And if that's true, our CBASS torpedoes will zero in on the towed array, rather than on the Iranian sub. So we'll fire three torpedoes soon, XO, and allow one to track and destroy its target. That contact should be the towed array carrying missiles. But when the second CBASS is a thousand yards from its target, which will also be the towed array, you'll switch it to manual control and concentrate on a point of impact two hundred feet to port of our first torpedo's impact point. And we'll aim our third CBASS two hundred yards to starboard of the first torpedo's impact point and guide it, also with manual controls. That way, whichever way the Iranian turns, we'll have a present for her, whether she's to port or starboard of the towed array. If I'm correct, the second or the third torpedo will find the hostile boat herself."

"Aye, aye, Skipper," said the XO.

Twenty minutes went by, and to the crew in the Control Room of the *California*, every second seemed an eternity.

"Range?" asked Captain Drummond.

"Eight thousand, five hundred yards, sir," said the sailor

"FIRE ONE," said the captain.

"One fired, sir," said the Fire Control Technician.

"FIRE TWO," said Drummond..

"Two fired, sir," said the technician.

"FIRE THREE," said Drummond.

"Three fired, sir. CBASS all running straight and true, sir," said the technician.

The Mark 50 Mod 8 torpedoes streaked through the ocean at nearly seventy miles an hour and locked onto the small signature of the Iranian submarine's towed array of weapons.

"Sir, target is diving and turning hard to starboard, sir!"

"So whales don't like CBASS torpedoes," commented Captain Drummond. He and the XO exchanged a glance.

"Gotcha," commented the XO.

Five miles were traversed quickly, in less than ten minutes, and the CBASS torpedoes changed course four times as they followed the desperate measures of the Iranian submarine.

At a thousand yards from their target, Lt Cmdr. Carter took over control of the second and third torpedoes. He noted the depth and course of the towed array and positioned the impact point of his torpedoes two hundred feet to port and starboard of that target.

The first explosion was massive as the two missiles and their fuel supply erupted when the first CBASS found its target. The torpedo's seven hundred pounds of high explosive hit the center of the array, and it only took a few seconds for the impact wave to be felt by the crew of the *California*, miles away.

The Iranian submarine, instantly crippled by the force of the explosion immediately to her stern, was swept around violently by the force of the explosion, but not enough to appreciably change her course. The *California*'s XO remained focused on his task, and the third Mark 50 also found its target.

The second violent explosion was confirmation that Captain Drummond's theory was correct.

"That's for the *Missouri* and her crew, gentlemen," he said into his microphone for all to hear.

He turned to the ET-Comm.

"Send a high-priority message to New London, son," he said. "Tell them our other subs need to look for a small sonar signature that is easily interpreted as a whale. But that's actually emanating from the towed array behind an Iranian Submarine. Three torpedoes should be released, one at the 'whale' and the second and third at a manually controlled point roughly two hundred feet to port and starboard of the array's position. One of those other CBASS should strike and destroy the submarine herself."

"Aye, aye, sir," replied the Communications Technician.

"Continue our scheduled patrol, XO," said Drummond. "It's always possible we'll encounter another one of these bastards, but at least now we know what to look for."

"Great job, Captain," said Lt Cmdr. Carter.

Less than three hours later, the USS *North Dakota* reported a similar sonar track and promptly sunk the second Iranian submarine.

The specific location of the third Iranian sub remained a mystery, however, for an additional fourteen hours until the USS *Washington*, the Virginia Class submarine on patrol closest to U.S. coastal waters, detected a whale heading due north just fifty miles off the coast of St. Augustine.

The whale was promptly terminated with extreme prejudice.

CHAPTER 17

March 21, 2028 … Washington, D.C. 1000 Hours

"Well done," said the President.

"Thank you, sir," said Secretary of the Navy Mabus.

"Yes, Ray," echoed the Chairman of the Joint Chiefs and the Secretary of Defense.

"Shannon," said the President, "I'm truly sorry about the loss of two of your colleagues at Andrews when the Iranian escaped, and I'm certainly glad you emerged unscathed. As it was described to me late yesterday, your fellow who created that misguidance software is quite brilliant. Please extend my congratulations to him, as well."

"Thank you, Mr. President," said the Director of the CIA, "and yes, we'll pass your comments on to Paul Vander Vere, sir."

"Mr. President," said the Secretary of the Navy, "we still have the matter of that fourth Iranian submarine. Satellite photos have suggested she is undergoing major repairs, and we've captured photographs of heavy crates with Russian markings on them on the dock adjacent to the submarine. We tracked backward and noted that a Russian transport plane flew from one of their air bases south of Moscow and landed at the base in Venezuela the other day. Then, crates suddenly showed up on the dock, so there's no question that the Russian Federation and Vladimir Putin are deeply involved in the plot to attack the United States, sir. Their involvement is significantly more than merely supplying slips for one of their allies' submarines. It now includes transporting towed arrays and nuclear missiles on the *Yuriy Arshenevshiy* and most recently, rushing heavy equipment by air to repair one of the Iranian boats."

"Mr. President, if I may interject something sir," said Shannon.

"Yes, Ms. Parks, please do so," said the President.

"The Russians are enamored with the game of chess, and that's what this is to them. Yes, we have incontrovertible proof that towed arrays were attached to Iranian submarines, and that those boats had sophisticated Russian technology installed in them at the Admiralty Shipyards in Saint Petersburg before delivery to the Islamic Republic of

Iran. But we do not have absolute proof that those arrays were actually delivered to Puerto Caballo by the Russian freighter *Yuriy Arshenevshiy.* That's conjecture. We also don't have video evidence of engine parts and heavy equipment being off-loaded from the Russian Transport plane that arrived in Puerto Caballo the other day. That's also conjecture.

"So if there is about to be a thought process in this room to call the Russians on their insidious involvement to nuke our cities, we do not have hard evidence to back up that claim.

"Mr. President, Vladimir Putin will laugh at us if we confront the Russian Federation with accusations without substantive evidence to support our claims. Everything they do has a foundation in plausible deniability."

"What do you folks at Langley suggest we do?" asked General Dunford in obvious frustration.

Shannon stood for emphasis.

"Gentlemen, when Rahim Tabataba'i held me captive," she said, "he made it quite clear he intended to kill me. He considered any blow to he could strike at this nation, however trivial, was mandatory. He was quite open with me, since he assumed anything he confided to me would be preserved by my death.

"Among other things Rahim mentioned, he revealed that when Colonel Arshad Sassani was reunited with his sister Nousha in Baku, Colonel Sassani seemed compelled to justify his actions and decisions to a fellow Iranian. The Colonel revealed Israel's plans to use Plague Ten against Iran on eleven April and explained his decision to help Israel destroy Iran's nuclear arsenal was in the name of a greater concern ... the imminent deaths of all who live in Iran.

"Rahim Tabataba'i placated the Colonel in that conversation, but at that moment he realized he must warn those in Tehran of Israel's latest weapon. His escape from the CIA detention area at Andrews was to enable him to call General Firouzabadi, and he accomplished that goal. I was in the car with him when he made the call.

"Iran is now aware of Israel's plan to release Plague Ten by or on their Passover, and our feeling at Langley is that the Iranians will intensify their efforts to produce additional nuclear weapons at Natanz.

"Iran's nuclear arsenal, to the best of our knowledge, has been temporarily eliminated. Their plant at Bushehr has been greatly damaged, but their nuclear plant at Natanz is intact. Colonel Sassani told us there are at least twelve thousand centrifuges installed and active at Natanz, perhaps as many as twenty thousand.

"Tehran is at a crossroads, Mr. President.

"They have witnessed incredible capabilities from both the Israeli military and our own. Now, they will either cease this quest to arm themselves with nuclear weapons and sit at a peace conference, or their resolve to arm and retaliate will be strengthened. We will easily be able to monitor which path they've chosen, sir. If they choose the path we pray they do, there will be no appreciable activity at Natanz. But if they choose the latter path as Colonel Sassani and I fear they may, activity at Natanz will escalate significantly, and flights from the Russian Federation will increase accordingly."

"Then what?" asked the President.

"Israel cannot eliminate the threat posed by the plant at Natanz," said Director Brennan of the CIA, so either we have to do that for them or in a few months Iran will launch against Tel Aviv. And I can assure you that the Israelis won't wait for that to happen, not when they have Plague Ten in their arsenal."

"And, of course, we're still on Iran's target map, as well," said Secretary Mabus.

"So you want me to authorize B-21s to take out the plant at Natanz," concluded the President. "Is that what you suggest, even though we'd kill a lot of Russians in the process?

"Not yet, Mr. President," suggested Director Brennan. "Maybe Iran will stand down and abandon their nuclear weapons program."

"All right then, and thank you," said the President. "Keep me informed."

The President stood and left the room.

On the way to their cars, General Dunford approached Shannon.

"So, Ms. Parks," he said, "what do you think the odds are that the Iranians will finally give up their continuing quest for nuclear weapons?"

"Zero, General," said Shannon, "but I hope I'm wrong. If I'm right, our President will have an increasingly difficult dilemma in front of him. That plant at Natanz will become more and more productive in one way and in one way only ... with the assistance of many Russian nuclear specialists, many more than are currently on staff there.

"I have great respect for the office of the presidency and for our President personally, but if he's hesitant now with the current level of Russian 'advisors' working at Natanz, what will he decide to do if there are five or perhaps ten times the number of Russians there in a few months? Vladimir Putin is unafraid to make incredibly bold moves on this chessboard, General, and I feel that we must play with the same sort of reckless abandon. In chess, you cannot merely play defense and win.

It is that and a combination of bold, aggressive moves that yields victory."

"So you advocate bombing the shit out of the nuclear plant at Natanz, regardless of how many Russians we kill?" asked Dunford.

"Yes, that's correct sir. And one aspect of those bombing runs should also include the use of neutron weapons, to make damned sure we kill them all, General."

He looked at the slight young woman, and her intensity amazed him. The rumors about her were quite apparently true. As they exchanged a handshake, Shannon stopped.

"More than three hundred years ago, General, an English poet and essayist named Joseph Addison, in his play entitled, *Cato*, coined the phrase, 'He who hesitates is lost.'

"That is how I run my life, and that is how I run my Agency, General Dunford, and I can only hope and pray that the President of the United States understands the need for that philosophy. If Iran starts to beef up that plant at Natanz, Israel will prepare to release Plague Ten, I'm sure of it, since that will be their one remaining option. They are no longer people who will shuffle quietly to their deaths, as they did in the 1940s. If our President hesitates and Plague Ten is released, there is no reliability in that action. That virus can kill all life on Earth."

March 21, 2028 ... Puerto Caballo, Venezuela, 2100 Hours

"This is a truly sad day in our Republic's history," began Captain Ghorbani. He then explained to his assembled crew that information from Moscow and Tehran indicated the other three submarines had been destroyed by the Americans, with all hands lost.

"It is the sacred task of the *Righteous Hand* to strike at these Americans, not only for the glory of our Republic, but now to avenge the deaths of our fellow seamen."

Work on their submarine intensified and was ahead of schedule. In two days, the *Righteous Hand* would once again be seaworthy. Orders from Moscow had been crystal clear and came directly from Vladimir Putin. Give the Iranians whatever they need.

It was 0930 Hours the following morning.

Vice Admiral Dimitri Bespalov immediately agreed to a request by Captain Ghorbani for a meeting aboard the *Pyotr Velikiy*, a Kirov Class heavy missile cruiser. She was in port as a show of Russian strength and prowess on the high seas, but the Admiral and his crew had been drained by recent developments. They mourned the loss of their fellow seamen when the *Chabanenko* and the *Kharlamov* went down with all on board, and their desire for revenge was high. Many on the cruiser had known those on the two ships lost at the hands of an unidentified submarine, but they knew in their hearts she belonged to the American navy.

"Sit down, please," said the Admiral cordially.

Ghorbani accepted the chair.

"Thank you, sir," he said.

"I have never seen such an enormous and powerful warship as yours, Admiral Bespalov," he said.

"Thank you," replied the Admiral, but he refrained from stating his initial thought, that the *Pyotr Velikiy* was quite a lot larger than a camel. He reminded himself that these despicable Iranians were allies of the Russian Federation.

Strange bedfellows we are, he thought.

"How may we assist you, Captain?" asked Bespalov. "And, by the way, would you like tea?"

The Iranian politely indicated that he would not.

"I have a theory, Admiral," said Ghorbani. "It is my belief that the Americans were in the area surrounding this base, and anticipated our arrival here. Yet, all four of my nation's submarines were able to sail into this harbor safely and without challenge. That is testimony to the skill of your naval architects and to the sophistication of the equipment your people have installed in all four of our submarines. We were simply invisible to the Americans, and your technology is vastly superior to theirs."

"Thank you, Captain, you are most kind," said Bespalov

"Tragically, however," continued Captain Ghorbani, "it is quite apparent that the Americans somehow were able to detect our boats as they sailed toward U.S. territorial waters, and as you know, all three of our submarines have been lost."

"A tragedy, I agree," commented the Admiral.

"There is but one irrefutable conclusion, sir," said Ghorbani. "If the Americans were unable to detect our boats on their way to Puerto Caballo and they then were then able to detect our submarines once they left port here, the difference must have been the towed arrays behind them. Your technology was clearly never designed to hide what a submarine might tow behind it, and that's what allowed the Americans to detect us."

"Your logic impresses me, Captain," said the Admiral. "Go on, please."

"It is foolhardy, in my opinion, Admiral Bespalov," said Ghorbani, "to complete the repairs on the *Righteous Hand* and then arm her in the same manner we employed when arming the other three submarines. The Americans will detect and sink my boat, as well, I'm afraid."

"What do you suggest?" asked Bespalov.

"That the *Yuriy Arshenevshiy* set sail today, alone and without her escorts. She will head to and dock at Havana, in Cuba. Without an array towed behind the *Righteous Hand*, when we set sail we will once again be invisible to the Americans, and we will rendezvous with the *Yuriy Arshenevshiy* a few miles out to sea, directly north of the Cuban city of Matanzas.

"To the Americans, the lazy and unescorted sailing of the *Yuriy Arshenevshiy* from Venezuela will verify her mission is over, and a Russian freighter heading into Havana should draw little scrutiny. And when she sails from Havana and steams east, the American Navy will correctly assume she is returning to Mother Russia. Her little stop in the middle of the night to arm my submarine with a towed array and nuclear weapons will go unnoticed, and as the freighter continues to steam east, the *Righteous Hand* will hug the American coastline and launch missiles at New York and Washington. It's true we may be detectable at that point because our towed array will no longer allow us to be invisible, but if the Americans are not as vigilant as before, perhaps several months from now, we'll be able to slip through. With God's grace, we will have our revenge for your nation's sailors and for mine, as well."

Admiral Bespalov was astonished at the logic and complexity of Captain Ghorbani's plan. It only took ninety minutes to put it into effect. Moscow agreed that it was brilliantly conceived, and when Vladimir Putin was advised, he clapped his hands in delight.

"Perhaps we should sell them more submarines," he commented gleefully to his senior commanders.

At 1400 Hours, the *Yuriy Arshenevshiy* set sail for Havana.

March 24, 2028 ... Tyson's Corner, Virginia, 2230 Hours
She was on her left side, curled into the warmth of his body.

Paul caressed her delicately, and when she didn't react, he knew enough to stop. He realized her mind was elsewhere.

"I'm going to shower and get dressed," decided Shannon.

Ninety minutes later, he brought her a cup of coffee. She was all business by then, as she skimmed reports and emails. Once again her subordinate and seated in her office at Langley, Paul was mesmerized by her efficiency and relentless beauty.

"Thanks for the coffee, Paul. Where's yours?" asked Shannon.

"On my desk. I don't expect I'll be in your office very long," said Paul.

"Thanks again for the coffee," said Shannon. "I counted about twenty of our colleagues at their desks out there. Did they stay late or come in early?"

Paul smiled.

"Does it matter?" he asked.

"Guess not," said Shannon. "Paul...."

"Six days," he said.

Shannon looked at him quizzically.

"It'll take that freighter six days from the date she sailed to get to Havana," said Paul, "assuming that's where she's heading. So at twelve knots, the *Yuriy Arshenevshiy* should arrive in Cuba three days from now."

"How did you know that was my question?" asked Shannon.

"Intimacy has its rewards," said Paul.

For a moment she was sorry she didn't respond to his touch while curled in his arms. But there would soon be another time, she decided.

"What's your opinion?" asked Shannon.

"The *Yuriy Arshenevshiy* set sail without her destroyer escorts in order to make us believe she no longer contains a deadly cargo," said Paul. "The Iranians and Russians are smart enough to realize we only were able to pinpoint those three submarines because our sonar found the arrays being towed, rather than the subs themselves.

"The fourth submarine has set sail after repairs were performed, and we've not yet detected her because that boat is not towing an array yet. As you know, to do the same thing the same way over and over again and expect a different result is one definition of madness. Besides, our adversaries realize that once that fourth boat is equipped with a towed array of missiles, we'll be able to find her, especially now that we understand what to look for. So they're being clever, and they've decided to have their last submarine that was docked at Puerto Caballo leave there without an array. That's why our navy is in panic mode right now ... because whatever technology that's been installed by the Russians is superior to our detection equipment, and that boat is invisible. She will rendezvous somewhere with the *Yuriy Arshenevshiy*, and that's when that submarine will be armed."

"The President is not going to like this, at all," said Shannon.

"Our subs need to look for whales north of Cuba," said Paul Vander Vere. "And we need to pray they locate one."

"That's it, we must 'pray'?" asked Shannon.

"Sometimes it works," said Paul.

Shannon rose to leave.

"I presume you've noticed this Agency, to which we've dedicated our lives, is hardly a church," she said.

"Yes," said Paul, "but even though this is certainly not a church, my dear and lovely Ms. Parks, I did pray here fairly often that one day you'd notice me. And now, you quite apparently have."

With that, Paul left her office.

Shannon thought for a fleeting moment to start attending church again. She dimly recalled enjoying it in her formative years. But her church was now Arlington National Cemetery, its pews filled with endless white headstones, and there was little time in her life for another.

CHAPTER 18

March 27, 2028 ... Washington, D.C. 1100 Hours

"Where is that damn fourth submarine?" asked the President.

"We haven't been able to locate her yet," said Ray Mabus. His hand shook a bit as he raised a coffee cup to his lips, and the three other men seated in the Oval Office noticed. The Secretary of the Navy continued after he carefully placed the cup and saucer on the table before him.

"Mr. President, the Russians have apparently developed some sort of technology that's superior to ours and, when activated, the submarines they furnished Iran, and probably their own submarines, cannot be detected by our SOSUS network or the passive sonar systems on our boats.

"Compared to the size of a submarine, those towed arrays are relatively small, and that's why their signatures were initially thought to be whales and ignored. The captain of the *California* was brilliant to have figured all this out. Our best guess is that fourth submarine does not yet have its towed array attached, and that's why she is invisible. But once that connection is accomplished, we're confident that we'll be able to locate and destroy her."

"When and where will that Iranian submarine be equipped with an array?" asked the Chairman of the Joint Chiefs.

The Director of the CIA joined the conversation.

"Our best people feel that the array and additional missiles are on the *Yuriy Arshenevshiy*, and that the freighter will rendezvous with the submarine once she leaves Havana and perhaps begins to head toward a Russian Federation port. That simply can't happen while the freighter is docked in Havana. You don't just park a submarine next to a freighter in a busy port and offload nuclear tipped missiles onto the sub without instantly becoming the talk of the town.

"But to answer your question, General Dunford, we don't know when and where the transfer of weapons from the freighter to that submarine may occur. It's still distinctly possible the fourth Iranian sub is already towing an array, and we simply haven't located her yet."

"So it's possible that the remaining Iranian submarine is armed, we haven't at this time pinpointed her location, and she's heading our way," stated the President.

He looked up from his clasped hands.

"Gentlemen, I do believe it is time for me to have a little chat with Vladimir Putin. This game we're playing is about to spiral out of control, and I'm going to remind that flaky son of a bitch that he's playing with fire. Assemble my full Cabinet tomorrow morning here at 9:00 AM. General, I want you to place our forces at DEFCON 2 immediately, so the Russians will know we're serious about all this. I've had quite enough.

"First, it still rankles me that Israel has blackmailed us into this Plague Ten crap, and we've committed to shoot down defenseless civilian aircraft if they release that virus. And these rabid Iranians and their relentless plots to target us, with great assistance by Putin, are really irritating the hell out of me. Perhaps we should let Israel end all this madness, once and for all. From a puritanical point of view, I am opposed to wiping a nation off the face of the Earth, but from an expeditious standpoint, I honestly am beginning to love the logic behind that decision. As President of a nation sworn to value human life and decency, I will continue to pursue a course of action that will save lives, rather than sacrifice them. But my buttons are now being pushed, and pushed hard by Putin. Tomorrow morning I intend to remind him about a few things. I'll see all of you tomorrow, at 0830 Hours."

The President stood, the others shook his hand and departed.

"Evelyn," said the President into the telephone on the Resolute Desk, "please arrange for a call to Vladimir Putin at 0900 Hours our time tomorrow. I'll take it in the conference room."

"Yes, Mr. President," replied his personal secretary.

He leaned back in his chair. Whenever he referred to a time of day in military time, it somehow made him feel important. He looked around the most powerful office on earth and chuckled.

"That is truly silly," he said out loud.

The President thought about the escalation of events and about the recent visit by Israel's Ambassador to the United States.

When they were alone in the Oval Office, the Ambassador opened his wallet and gave the President a small sealed plastic bag. It contained fifty small yellow pills, the antidote to Plague Ten ... a small gift, as it was explained, from Prime Minister Ben-Gurion.

He reached into the top right-hand drawer of his desk, opened the small package, and took out two of the pills.

The President poured himself a glass of water and swallowed one of them, took the stairs to the second floor residence wing of the White House, and instructed his wife to take the other pill.

With no assurance as to what the future held, it was prudent to take precautions, he felt. But there was no little yellow pill to help them withstand the perils of nuclear war, and it was imperative for the President to now make Vladimir Putin clearly understand the path both nations were on.

March 28, 2028 ... Washington, D.C. 0900 Hours

President Robert Jones Portman glanced around the conference table at the faces of more than twenty somber men.

"Show time," he said without humor.

He picked up the phone on the second ring and switched on the speaker to allow others to hear the Russian president..

"Good morning, Vladimir. I hope this call finds you well," he said.

"Yes, thank you, President Portman. And I hope you are also well," said Putin.

There began a brief lag in the conversation after each man spoke to allow the translators to perform their tasks.

"Yes, thank you. Vladimir, let me get right to the point," said the President. "I have my full Cabinet with me here this morning, as well as the Chairman of the Joint Chiefs of Staff, General Joseph Dunford. His full staff is also present. As you are most certainly aware, The United States military has been put on a full alert, at DEFCON 2, per my directive yesterday. That means that my country has been pushed and prodded into this most serious position, as a prelude to war."

The President paused for a moment to allow the translator to catch up. A nod from the U.S. translator indicated that the Russian on the other end was being accurate and thorough.

"With all due respect, Mr. President," said Putin, "perhaps your advisors are being somewhat confused. "Should you not call Tehran rather than Moscow?"

The smug reply by Putin so infuriated the American President that he stood and leaned forward, as if to bully the inanimate telephone on the desk before him.

"Now you listen to me, Mr. Putin," he said. "These are the irrefutable facts in this matter. You sold the Iran diesel-electric submarines and then your government proceeded to equip them with stealth technology which has but one purpose ... to give those boats offensive capabilities. You have been giving Iran nuclear assistance for years, both in engineering and scientific in nature, as well as other technology to produce fissionable material. A freighter, the *Yuriy Arshenevshiy*, flying under the flag of the Russian Federation and protected by four warships of your nation's navy, left the Iranian port of Bandar Abbas and docked at your naval base at Puerto Caballo in Venezuela. She carried arrays to be towed behind the four Iranian submarines docked there, as well as eight missiles armed with nuclear warheads. Your nation is intimately involved in attacks now being mounted against the United States, and these, sir, are acts of war."

"Mr. President," said Vladimir Putin, "the Russian Federation is in the export and import business, as is the United States on a much larger scale, I might add. First and foremost, we have strict controls over the types of weapons we sell to other nations, and I can assure you that we have never, nor will we ever, sell nuclear weapons to Iran or any other nation.

"Specifically, let me address your concerns about the cargo carried by one of our freighters, the *Yuriy Arshenevshiy*. Her manifests indicate she carried 'machine tools' and nothing more. These crated materials were the documented property of a reputable company with headquarters in Tehran, and we merely transported them to our base in Venezuela, where they were turned over to the Iranian Navy. What the Iranians might have had in those crates, and what they did with that cargo once it arrived safely in Puerto Caballo, is not of our concern. It is truly regrettable that your navy elected to harass our warships while they were en route to Venezuela, and you provoked one of our naval vessels into responding to those provocations. Great loss of life on both sides was the pitiful result of what you've denounced as an action by a 'rogue' submarine captain. In our navy, for what it's worth, we select our captains much more carefully. The wounds you have inflicted on our navy and nation are deep, Mr. President, I can assure you."

"I agree that the loss of one of our submarines and two of your warships is tragic," said the American President, "but why did your nation elect to escort the *Yuriy Arshenevshiy* to Venezuela with warships, Vladimir?"

"Simply because your nation is currently engaged in conflict with Iran, and we feel it prudent to protect any of our vessels leaving that nation's ports. That opinion seems definitely accurate, does it not? Why else did you have at least two nuclear submarines chasing the *Yuriy Arshenevshiy*, if not to sink her?" asked President Putin.

"Because that freighter contained towed arrays and nuclear missiles, Vladimir. We both know that's the case," said the President.

"No, I'm afraid that is a figment of the imagination of one of your CIA … what is the word in American slang? … 'spooks,' as you call them," said Putin. A fabrication. If you have proof of that accusation, please send it to me, and I will deal harshly with those here who have misled me, Mr. President."

The American President recalled Shannon Parks' warnings about Vladimir Putin and how adept he is at playing chess.

"Mr. President, I have a question for you," said Putin.

"What is it?" asked the American President.

"As I've stated, your nation and mine are in the import/export business, and we both export various technologies and weapons to many nations around the world," said Putin. One of your arms manufacturers is a company called Smith and Wesson, is that not correct?"

"Yes, what about it?" asked the American President.

"As part of you nation's massive weapons sales worldwide, if a terrorist, for example, uses a Smith and Wesson weapon to kill the innocent, who is to blame? Is it the man wielding the weapon, the manufacturer of the weapon, or the nation that exported the firearm? I doubt you'd condemn Smith and Wesson if and when one of their products is used for evil purposes, any more than you would blame the manufacturer of a frying pan if a housewife uses it to bludgeon her husband to death."

There was muted laughter in the background in Moscow. They seemed to be enjoying the show.

"Mr. Putin," replied the American President coldly, "the one fundamental difference between your nation and mine is that we don't provide weapons or technology to terrorists or terroristic states, while your nation willingly and eagerly does so. And while we cannot hold your Tula Arms Plant, for example, responsible for production of the Kalashnikov AK-47 assault rifle whenever it falls into the wrong hands, we can and will hold your government accountable for selling those weapons to terroristic governments. You will not be allowed to hide under a vague and ambiguous claim of innocence, Vladimir, and my nation has had enough of Russian Federation involvement in plots against the United States.

"I hereby warn you, Mr. Putin, that there are about to be more serious repercussions due to the ongoing actions of your nation, and I remind you of something stated in hindsight by Admiral Yamamoto after Japan elected to attack our naval forces at Pearl Harbor, an act which led to the onset of World War II. Admiral Yamamoto said, 'I fear we have awakened a sleeping giant,' and he was correct in that analysis. Good day, President Putin."

The President hit a button to terminate the call without allowing the Russian the courtesy to respond.

He then looked up at the Director of the Central Intelligence Agency.

"John, what's the latest report about the Iranian nuclear plant at Natanz? And where is the *Yuriy Arshenevshiy* right now?"

Director Brennan spoke slowly and deliberately.

"Mr. President, first, the *Yuriy Arshenevshiy* has already docked in Havana. We don't know how long she'll be there, sir."

"We have four Virginia Class submarines in international waters just to the north of Cuba," interjected the Secretary of the Navy, and they're watching and waiting for that fourth submarine to appear."

The President nodded in approval. "John, continue, please."

"The Iranians have concluded a massive cleanup of the surface damage at Natanz after the F-35s borrowed by Israel flew from Baku and dropped their ordinance," said Brennan, "and there's been a significant increase in activity there. We've also been monitoring flights from Moscow, and there's no question the Russian Federation is increasing their technical assistance to Iran. There is a clear and distinct indication that Iran has not learned the lesson we'd hoped they would, and they seem determined to produce more nuclear weapons, Mr. President."

"So more and more Russians are arriving every day at Natanz, is that the gist of your analysis, John?"

"Yes, that's correct, sir," said Brennan.

The President glanced at his watch. "I've come full circle on this, gentlemen," he said. "As you know, I was concerned that a strike by our Air Force at Natanz would kill many Russians, since that plant runs twenty-four hours a day. Now, I've adopted the opposite mentality. Let's wait three days and allow more and more Russians to arrive in Natanz.

"At 1200 Hours on the thirty-first, I want two waves of our B-21s to bomb the hell out of that facility. If Putin wants to play chess with me, I'll express shock that the Russian Federation had so many 'specialists' in place there, but that will be after they are already dead. Utilize neutron weapons to kill everyone in that plant, gentlemen, and pulverize it into dust. I want the Russians to recognize that the sleeping giant is fully awakened, and he is really pissed off. And call Tel Aviv to let them know our revised intentions at Natanz, so they don't release that damned Plague Ten virus."

"Yes, Mr. President," said the Secretary of State.

March 31, 2028 ... Matazanas, Cuba, 0230 Hours

The *Righteous Hand* surfaced on the starboard side of the *Yuriy Arshenevshiy* and quickly slowed to ten knots, so both vessels could move in tandem. They were well within Cuban territorial waters, and it was correctly assumed that the Americans lurked in the depths to the north somewhere.

The freighter had been traveling with its deck lights ablaze since her departure from Havana, and her course was due east. The array was assembled prior to the submarine's arrival, and it was quickly lowered into the water without either vessel slowing down.

Fortunately, the sea was dead calm, and the two nuclear missiles were carefully lowered into the array without difficulty. Once they were fueled, the submarine turned to the southwest and submerged.

The *Yuriy Arshenevshiy* immediately set a course for home.

March 31, 2028 ... over Athens, Greece, 0900 Hours in Tehran

"Three hours to our target, Colonel. We're right on schedule."

The six B-21 stealth bombers had been refueled over England and now flew at six hundred miles per hour at sixty-four thousand feet as they bisected Greece en route to their target at Natanz. Their flight plan called for roughly forty-eight continuous hours in the air and appeared as a huge teardrop on a map, originating and ending at Whiteman Air Force Base near Knob Noster, Missouri.

Well above the ceiling or challenge by fighter aircraft and with their stealth systems activated, the aircraft passed over friendly and unfriendly nations without a wisp of discovery.

Each B-21 had a two-man crew, and the lead plane was commanded by Colonel Bradford "Brick" McAllister. He turned and glanced at the officer seated next to him, the aircraft's Mission Commander, Major Nicholas Scoletti.

"Nick," he said, "what's the estimated casualty count at Natanz after all six aircraft release our weapons?"

"Just a minute, Brick," said Major Scoletti.

He leafed through the huge briefing report and analysis prepared by U.S. Air Force Intelligence and Langley for a moment.

"During a typical day," said Brick "at the height of operations, there can be as many as fourteen hundred people there, plus an unknown number of Russian scientists, advisors, and technicians. According to these comments by the staff at Langley, the Russian involvement there is increasing every day. There seems to be no question that Tehran is determined to weaponize more plutonium and plots further attacks against us and Israel. This is getting ugly, Brick."

Colonel McAllister turned to look at the Major.

His shock of thick reddish-brown hair stuck out in all directions from underneath his headset, and despite his age, rank, and achievements, he had the appearance of a kid playing a video game.

But this was no game.

The B-21s each carried a payload of more than thirty tons of deadly high explosive ordinance.

Four of the aircraft were equipped with a pair of huge "MOP-2" conventional weapons, the U.S. Air Force's latest version of the Massive Ordinance Penetrator, a thirty-four-thousand-pound bomb capable of penetrating deep into underground facilities. The original MOP design could blast through two hundred feet of reinforced concrete and then deliver nearly seven thousand pounds of high explosives, but the new MOP-2 could penetrate nearly double that thickness of walled protection and deliver ten thousand pounds.

In addition to carrying one MOP-2, the other two B-21s in the formation were also armed with twenty-four one-thousand-pound red mercury-based neutron bombs, which were to be rained on the plant at Natanz after all six aircraft released their complement of MOP-2 weapons.

By authorizing this violent action, the President of the United States sent a clear message to those in Tehran and Moscow:

We can do this to you anywhere and at any time. You may believe mountains and caves may shield you, but they cannot, and this is what happens when diplomacy fails and you push and prod at the most powerful nation on the face of the Earth.

Elsewhere, around the globe and at precisely 1100 Hours, the U.S. military was placed at DEFCON 1 by order of the President. It was a show of defiance, daring those about to be targeted to respond.

Colonel McAllister voiced his concern as his bomber streaked toward Natanz.

"Nick, I know exactly how General Tibbets felt when he piloted the Enola Gay toward Hiroshima in 1945," said McAllister. "There won't be as many casualties from our mission today as there were in Hiroshima, but while we're honing in on personnel intimately involved in a war effort against our country, there is a huge fundamental difference between Tibbets' mission and ours. His was to end a war, and ours may very well kick start the next one.

"I'm really concerned about how all this is going to play out," said Nick.

"Not, me, Brick," said McAllister. "As you know, I grew up in Brooklyn, and my entire family still lives there. So this is personal for me. Screw the politicians. As far as I'm concerned, I'm doing this to protect my mother and the millions of others who live in New York City."

They flew determinedly on.

The process is termed "Network-Centric Warfare", and at its heart is the doctrine of "observe, orient, decide, and act," as first described by Colonel John Boyd of the U.S. Air Force in the 1990s. In the twenty-first century, however, the highly refined concept of networking sensors, commanders, and those who directly control weapons to enhance accuracy and precision was now an art form.

It was precisely 1200 Hours in Tehran.

Three satellites more than twenty-four miles above the Earth and traveling at nearly seventeen thousand miles an hour triangulated the position of the thick berm above the nuclear plant at Natanz and locked on those coordinates as ground zero for the attack. A laser zeroed in on the gaping open blast doors to the facility and the flow of continuous information was transmitted in real time to each of the six B-21 bombers.

Major Scoletti opened the bomb bay doors of the lead B-21, and five other Mission Commanders followed his lead.

Buttons were depressed and ordinance was released from each aircraft as the line of B-21s swept silently over their target.

The wave of MOP-2s descended at speeds approaching Mach-2 and streaked toward the ground below, guided by the satellites above.

The sixteen hundred and twenty-eight people within the Natanz nuclear plant at that moment all died within a few seconds, their bodies either pulverized by collapsing structure, burned within the inferno created as high explosives detonated, or as a result of the neutron weapons irradiating everyone within the facility. The B-21s of the 510th Bomb Wing lazily banked to the left, came to a new course which would allow them to briefly refuel over Turkey, and then they set an adjusted course to their home at Whiteman Air Force Base. Colonel McAllister decided it was time to take a nap.

"Nick, take over for a while, please," he said.

On the ground below, nothing of substance remained.

An enormous crater was testimony to the carnage, but there was no one left alive to conceivably inspect it.

Occasional swirls of dust within the barren landscape and the newly formed crater became silent headstones for those who had just perished. Several hours passed before Tehran understood what had happened. Moscow was then informed.

March 31, 2028 ... Washington, D.C., 1030 Hours

"Evelyn, put through the call, please," said the President.

"Yes, Mr. President," said his personal assistant

The President was seated at the Resolute Desk in the Oval Office. When the call came through, he picked up the handset on the second ring. There was no opportunity for niceties.

"Mr. President," began Vladimir Putin angrily, "this unprovoked attack by the United States Air Force on a nuclear plant designed to provide vital electrical service to hundreds of thousands of citizens of the Islamic Republic of Iran is an outrage. I demand that...."

"Vladimir, the facility at Natanz, like the facility at Bushehr, produced nuclear weapons to be used against the United States and Israel. So let's cut the crap. You can stand on your soapbox all day long and play games, you can express outrage and describe the lack of adequate electrical service in villages and perhaps even send me photographs of you holding and kissing Iranian children, and you will not move me, sir. There is neither time for bullshit, nor for assuming we do not comprehend what your nation is doing. You are hiding behind Iran and assisting them in every possible manner, in order to orchestrate attacks against my nation. We have destroyed the Iranian nuclear facility at Natanz, and we will continue to perform similar actions as long as the Iran attempts to build more weapons of mass destruction. If you want to do your nation a service, convince the Iranians to stand down. If not, we will methodically bomb them back into the stone age."

It took a while for the interpreter to catch up.

"Mr. President," said Putin, "your bombs at Natanz killed two hundred and eighty-two highly skilled Russian scientists and technicians."

"I am truly shocked by that news, and I am truly sorry for your nation's loss," said the American President. "But what were they doing there, Vladimir?"

"Assisting the Iranians, so that they might perfect nuclear technology. They have hired us to assist them. In my opinion, Mr. Putin, you've just admitted that you were assisting Iran in their Jihad, and that makes the Russian Federation guilty of collaborating with the Iranians to wage war on the United States. As I'm sure you're aware, my nation's military is currently at a DEFCON 1 alert status. That means we have hands on the triggers of our weapons. Do not test my resolve, Vladimir. Further assistance to Iran will be considered by this office as an act of war."

There was a click as the connection ended.

In the elaborate game of chess being played, it appeared that the Russian had just surrendered his Queen.

"Vladimir, please be reasonable," begged one of the fourteen generals seated around him.

President Putin glared at the man for his insolence.

The General continued, nonetheless.

"We cannot launch nuclear missiles at the Americans. Even if we did that in a week or two when they are no longer at a DEFCON 1 status, their retaliation would be devastating."

"General," said Putin, "you are the one who has assured me that the nuclear defense systems we've elaborately deployed around our Capitol are capable of withstanding an attack, and the Americans have no such system in place around any of their cities."

"Yes, that's true, President Putin," responded another soldier. "But what of the rest of our nation? And if the Americans are clever and detonate only one nuclear weapon upwind of Moscow, the residual fallout will bypass our defense systems and still kill us all. A nuclear initiative against the Americans is out of the question, sir."

Vladimir Putin was livid, but he did not proceed with a nuclear response against the United States. That meeting in his office within the Kremlin was one of the most pivotal moments in history, as the world narrowly escaped a path toward nuclear devastation.

Now that he'd lost his Queen, the Russian might next have tipped over his King. But Vladimir Putin was not a man to admit defeat.

He decided instead to move a pawn forward.

"Send Tehran our latest air defense systems," he said.

The delivery of multiple 55R6M Triumfator-M mobile surface to air defense systems was scheduled later that year. If the American bombers returned, the Islamic Republic of Iran would be prepared.

Other decisions were made in Moscow, as well.

CHAPTER 19

April 1, 2028 … north of Havana, Cuba, 0600 Hours

The *Righteous Hand* had been traveling parallel to the northern coast of Cuba until she turned due north briefly and then northwest to a revised course of three-five-zero. Captain Ghorbani's plan was to follow the American coastline at a relatively shallow depth for a submarine, and he hoped the concentration of the U.S. Navy would be into deeper waters. His plan remained to position his submarine roughly one hundred miles offshore and flood the towed array in order to launch his missiles.

The millions who would subsequently die in New York City and Washington would be ample blood on the mighty sword of God he commanded. He was the tip of the spear of his great Republic, and he would not fail this test. The name "Ghorbani" would be spoken with reverence by schoolchildren in his nation for generations.

For a moment, he considered launching immediately at the busy metropolis of Miami, but he followed orders and the *Righteous Hand* came to a new course of 010 as she crossed through the waters between West Palm Beach and Freeport in the Bahamas. Later that morning and due east of Charleston, she turned to 040 and continued to parallel the American coastline.

It was 1250 Hours.

"Captain, I have a contact bearing 160," said the sonar operator of the USS *North Dakota*. She was the westernmost of the defensive line of Virginia Class submarines prowling the Atlantic.

"What do you have, Brett?" asked her Captain immediately.

"It's really faint," said Brett, "but it sounds just like the same kind of whale noises we detected from one of the first three Iranian boats, sir."

"Distance?" asked the Captain.

"Eighteen thousand yards, sir."

"All right. XO," said the Captain, "set a course to intercept that contact."

"Aye, aye, Skipper," said the XO.

The *North Dakota* began to turn.

"Full speed," ordered her Captain.

"Battle stations!" said the XO.

Forty seconds passed.

"The American Virginia Class submarine has turned toward the Iranians, Captain. They have found the *Righteous Hand*!"

"Огонь Один!"

"Fire One!"

"Огонь Два!"

"Fire Two!"

Straight and true they ran.

"Captain, torpedoes in the water," screamed the sonar operator of the *North Dakota*. "High speed screws and closing fast. Distance nineteen hundred yards. They've acquired us, sir."

"Come to course 280 and release countermeasures!" shouted the Captain of the *North Dakota*. "Dive, dive!"

His well-trained crew responded immediately, but the two RPK-7 Vyuga Starfish torpedoes were not deterred by the *North Dakota*'s countermeasures. They reacquired the submarine and raced toward her at more than sixty miles an hour.

"Eight hundred yards and closing, sir!" said the sonar operator.

"Come to 170, release more countermeasures!" shouted the Captain of the *North Dakota*, but too late.

"Five hundred yards, sir," said his subordinate. "Impact in six seconds, sir!"

The first Vyuga Starfish struck the *North Dakota* amidships just aft of her conning tower, and the second torpedo wasn't necessary.

It struck exploding debris and detonated needlessly.

The K-335 Russian submarine named "Gepard," a lethal Akula III Class nuclear predator, turned gracefully to starboard, in search of deeper waters.

"Good shooting, Captain," said her XO.

"Thank you, Gennady," said the Captain. "We all participated in this victory."

Captain Mikhail Andropov smiled, immensely satisfied.

The Akula III had passed her battle test admirably.

"The American submarine never had a chance, Gennady," he said. "Our Akula is invisible, a credit to the genius of our stealth technology and the brilliance of Russian engineering."

Captain Andropov sat for a moment with pen and paper.

"Send this message to Fleet Command," he ordered and handed his Executive Officer a carefully written outline of the encounter.

"Let the foolish Americans believe that pathetic little Iranian submarine has fangs," said Captain Andropov as he slapped his XO on the shoulder. "The beauty in all this is that the Iranians are also armed with our Starfish torpedoes, so the American Navy will never know we've been here and played a role. In the future, they will now be more cautious when they encounter an Iranian submarine, which can only help our cause."

"Time to track our next target," said the XO.

"Yes," agreed the Captain. "Gennady, take us down to two hundred meters and increase to flank speed, immediately."

"Aye, aye, sir!" said Gennady firmly, for all present to hear.

"Flank speed, set down degree angle at fifteen percent, and level off at two hundred meters. Course Oh-three-oh," barked the Executive Officer.

The submarine *Righteous Hand* continued north, unchallenged, and the Akula lurked not too far behind, at four thousand yards. The young Iranian sonar operator dutifully reported a distant and violent underwater explosion to Captain Ghorbani, but had no explanation as to the cause.

"Gepard" is the Russian word for "Cheetah", and the Akula was that, in every way ... a skilled and deadly hunter, carefully stalking her prey.

April 2, 2028 ... Langley, Virginia, 1600 Hours

Neither of them had left CIA headquarters in four days.

Shannon called Paul Vander Vere into her office as she refused to allow herself to yawn. They were both on edge, as was the entire military of the United States.

"We have to assume the *North Dakota* is lost, Paul," said Shannon.

"I've been in constant contact with Secretary Mabus and the Naval Warfare Department in Maryland," said Paul, "and they refuse to believe that Iranian submarine could have taken out the *North Dakota*."

"Perhaps she went down due to an internal failure, or maybe her reactor blew up, and maybe we'll never know," replied Shannon.

"But her Skipper reported that she had a contact, and he was about to pursue it to determine if it was that phantom submarine," said Paul. "And then the *North Dakota* simply disappeared. I can't accept it's simply coincidence that at that precise moment in time, our submarine had a fatal failure of some internal system and went down without a sound."

"Perhaps the Iranian sub got the best of her," said Shannon.

"Nope. Not a chance in hell," said Paul. "The *North Dakota* would have stalked that Iranian sub from behind or from an angle astern to port or starboard, but not from head on ... which means the Iranian could only have shot at our submarine from her stern torpedo tubes."

"Then perhaps that's exactly what happened," said Shannon.

"Shannon, the initial contact reported by the *North Dakota* indicated a profile similar to what was reported by them and our other subs," said Paul. "when they discovered and destroyed the original three Iranian boats. We now have come to the frightening realization that without towed arrays, those Iranian subs are somehow invisible to our naval sonar equipment, and the only way we can detect them is when they're towing arrays. So that fourth Iranian submarine must have been also towing an array, when the *North Dakota* found her."

"Where are you going with this, Paul?" asked Shannon.

"A submarine towing a large array armed with nuclear weapons cannot use her stern tubes in combat, Shannon," said Paul. "They are blocked by the array and are useless."

"So what's your conclusion?" asked Shannon.

"No captain in our navy would ever stalk an enemy submarine and engage in a frontal attack unless absolutely mandatory," said Paul, "especially if he knew the enemy's stern tubes are necessarily obstructed. We can first assume there was not an untimely and sudden failure in the *North Dakota*'s systems that caused a catastrophic failure at the exact moment she turned to follow that contact. The probability of that occurrence is virtually zero. And we can also assume that if the Russian naval engineers were able to install stealth equipment in Iranian submarines that makes them invisible, submarines of the Russian Federation's navy are also equipped with that technology. There is, therefore, only one possibility remaining."

"And that is?" asked Shannon.

"There was a third submarine involved," said Paul, "a silent Russian killer that sank the *North Dakota* without warning ... probably one of their latest Akula Class boats. We now know that Russia has developed stealth technology superior to our ability to detect their submarines, so I believe an Akula was silently trailing along, watching our every move. And when the *North Dakota* discovered the Iranian sub and turned into an attack position, the Russian boat promptly reacted."

"My God, do you seriously believe Russia would have the balls to do that?" asked Shannon.

"We've both read the briefing report about how the President pistol-whipped Vladimir Putin two days ago," said Paul, "and we both know that Putin is a megalomaniac. It'll take a couple of months or more to verify what I'm about to say, but I'm confident that when naval salvage people locate and inspect what's left of the *North Dakota*, they'll discover she went down as a result of a torpedo strike to her stern or sides, and not from the front. The Iranian submarine, if she actually was able to sink the *North Dakota*, would have necessarily fired torpedoes that struck our sub in the bow area."

"We need to prepare a report about this for the Secretary of the Navy and the President," said Shannon.

"It's already done." said Paul.

"Do you really believe Putin is crazy enough to come out from his position of hiding behind Iran and is now directing his navy to confront and attack ours?" asked Shannon.

"Yes, I do," said Paul, "and for one primary reason. He still believes they have plausible deniability. I'm sure the Iranian submarine is armed with Starfish torpedoes, as are Akulas. So he'll maintain that the Iranian submarine sank the *North Dakota*. Putin will also maintain his subs were nowhere near our coastline, and since Russian Federation submarines are currently invisible, we have no proof that's not the case … except for logic, of course."

Shannon rubbed her exhausted eyes.

"Where is this all going?" she asked.

"We are already at war, but no one dares admit it yet," said Paul. "We still have to locate that Iranian submarine now, and two other Virginia Class subs are heading north of the Iranian's last reported position at flank speed."

April 3, 2028 … North Atlantic Ocean, 0500 Hours

She slowed to two knots and maintained a depth of fifty-five meters as the *Righteous Hand* began to flood her towed array.

The process took twenty minutes, and finally the two nuclear missiles were in a vertical position. Captain Ghorbani felt as though the preparation process was another lifetime as he gave the command to ignite the rocket engines.

She was on a line south southeast of Atlantic City, New Jersey at that moment, eighty miles from American soil.

"Are our divers clear?" asked Captain Ghorbani.

"Yes, Captain," replied his XO.

"Fuel pressure adequate?" asked Ghorbani

Systems were verified and fuel pressures were confirmed.

"Yes, Captain," said the XO.

"Ignite both rockets!" said Captain Ghorbani.

"Ignition confirmed, Captain," said the Fire Control Officer.

It was 5:26:04 AM, EST.

"Launch Number One!"

The *Righteous Hand* shuddered as the first rocket streaked away from the array in which it had been tethered. It shot upward through the thin veil of ocean and burst into the crisp early morning air as its onboard computer immediately took command.

Its ground zero coordinates were set as Latitude 40.712784 and Longitude -74.005941 ... New York City.

It was 5:26:17 AM, EST.

"Launch Number Two!"

A second violent shudder was felt by the entire crew of the submarine as the second nuclear missile was released.

Locked into the rocket's computer were Latitude 38.907192 and Longitude -77.036871 ... Washington, D.C.

"Have the divers release the towed array immediately!" said the Captain. "We must free ourselves from the albatross."

The command was executed immediately, but ultimately needed nearly fifteen precious minutes to complete. While the *Righteous Hand* waited to retrieve her two divers and expected to immediately turn to a course plotted toward the depths of the Hudson Canyon and extremely deep water, other events occurred simultaneously.

It was 5:26:12 AM, EST.

"XO," said one of the crewmen, "we just had a missile launch from a position farther out to sea and roughly forty-six miles from here, bearing 115, sir."

"Track it," was the instantaneously barked command, "and call the Captain to the bridge ASAP!"

It was 5:26:22 AM, EST.

"NORAD just picked it up, as well, sir," said the warship's Mass Communications Officer. "They've issued a message that a nuclear attack is imminent to every branch of service."

The young seaman looked up at the XO pleadingly.

"Please tell me this is all a drill, sir," he said.

"Sorry, son, it is not," said the XO. "PEOPLE, this is real. Weapons status?"

"All on line and available," was the immediate response.

The XO prayed for the Captain of their warship to appear on the bridge, but that hadn't happened yet.

It was 5:26:26 AM, EST.

"Sir, a second missile launch has just occurred, same bearing."

"Another warning from NORAD, sir ..."

"It states, 'This is not a drill, repeat this not a drill!' "

"My God," muttered the XO of the Zumwalt Class Destroyer DDG-1001 USS *Michael Monsoor*.

She was unlike any other warships designed and constructed before her, with the exception of the two other DDG Series ships of that same class. DDG-1001 contained a deadly assortment of high-tech and futuristic weapons in order to combat surface ships, aircraft, and threats from below. Her angular profile made radar detection difficult, and she was designed to be fast and soundless.

This particular Zumwalt Destroyer possessed one newly installed experimental weapon, straight from the drawing boards of dreamers at General Dynamics at their Bath Iron Works facility.

It was bulky in appearance and covered with a huge shroud on the foredeck, and its scheduled testing had been scrapped in order to have the *Michael Monsoor* participate in the current urgent mission in the North Atlantic.

It was 5:27:03 AM, EST.

Captain Raymond Cummings burst onto the bridge. He wasn't wearing his normally perfect uniform shirt, nor his shoes.

"Take the shroud off the GENDYN weapon," he screamed at anyone and everyone, "and get someone who's passed the instruction tests on that weapon down there, in the booth and on that console within the next sixty seconds!"

Captain Cummings quickly consulted a radar screen.

"Turn to course 280 and give me flank speed," he demanded. "How far are we from landfall?"

"About thirty-five miles, sir," replied the XO.

"We need to get closer, and fast," said the Captain.

The destroyer flew through the water at thirty-plus knots.

"Has anyone plotted the trajectory and impact points of those two missiles yet?" asked the Captain.

"Yes, sir," said a seaman at one of the many consoles. "One is heading for New York City, sir, and the other is heading toward our Capitol."

"Our Capitol?" barked the Captain. "Son, you and I happen to be both from the lovely God-given State of North Carolina, our cherished home. So do you mean to tell me that goddamned missile is en route to Raleigh, or do you wish to convey some other information to me?"

"Sir, I meant Washington, D.C., our *nation's* Capital, sir."

"Then say what you damned mean, son," said the Captain. "I don't have time for guessing games like Twenty Questions on my bridge."

"Sorry, sir," said the seaman.

The Captain glared at his Executive Officer.

"If we live through all this, Tom," he said, "I'm going to make United States Navy seamen out of these young kids if it's the last thing I do."

It was 5:28:12 AM, EST.

"Tell me about the trajectories, son," asked the Captain of the *Michael Monsour*.

"Sir, from the launch position data and angles of trajectory, it's clear that both missiles will head well into the ionosphere and then peak at one hundred and twenty-eight miles before they begin their descent."

"What will be their rate of descent?"

"Approaching Mach 5, sir."

"Approaching? What do you mean by *approaching*, son?"

"Three thousand seven hundred and twelve miles per hour, sir."

"Time to impact?"

"The first missile, designated as Vampire One, will impact in five minutes, thirty-four seconds and counting, sir. Target designated as Vampire Two in six minutes and fifty-two seconds, Captain. Both of the missiles are running straight and true, sir."

"Sir, the GENDYN One is manned and ready," said a voice.

"Who's at the console?" asked the XO.

"Petty Officer 3rd Class Jerome J. Jerome, sir," replied the Mass Communications Officer.

The XO turned quietly toward Captain Cummings.

"What's his qualification on this weapon?" he asked.

"None, whatsoever, Tom," said Cummings. "I chose him to learn that weapons system because I read his profile in our data base. Other of these kids do all sorts of things while on leave, as you'd expect, but this kid is just content sitting and playing video games. The name he uses online is always the same … 'J-Cubed,' and he's proud that no one can beat him on any of the games he elects to play. Just a hunch, Tom, when I selected him … just a hunch."

"This is one helluva video game he's about to play, sir," said the XO.

Captain Cummings nodded.

For nearly four years prior to February of 2028, Raytheon had tried and failed to meet performance standards required by the U.S. Navy for an advanced "Close-In Weapon System", or CIWS, which could deal with threats to a warship and also address intercontinental ballistic missiles on their downward path toward a target. Raytheon's design attempts were accurate enough, and even impressive, when it came to addressing threats to a U.S. warship posed by enemy aircraft, submarines, or incoming missiles traveling at Mach 2.

But a trajectory from the ionosphere and speeds approaching Mach 5 and beyond were beyond the abilities of Raytheon's weapons designers. General Dynamics eventually won the award for a laser-based weapon that was essentially point and shoot at this stage of its development. Later, it was scheduled to be automated.

Aside from the slight curvature of a laser beam due to the Earth's gravitational pull at a distance of up to a current maximum of two hundred miles from shooter to target, it was not necessary for the laser weapon's operator to particularly care about muzzle velocity, windage and other normal firing considerations when shooting from great distances. Because the GENDYN's laser burst "bullets" traveled at the speed of light, when it sighted and shot at a Mach 5 target, it was as if the target were tacked onto a wall and motionless. Still, there was great skill involved, and the fate of millions was being placed in the hands of a twenty-four-year-old sailor from a small town near Birmingham, Alabama nicknamed J-Cubed.

"Mr. Jerome, this is the Captain," said Cummings. "Are you tracking Vampire One and Vampire Two, son?"

"Aye, aye, sir," said the young sailor.

The XO leaned over a seaman, and stared at his console.

"Sir, if we shoot when Vampire Two is fifty miles above ground zero for that weapon," he said, "that's a distance of one hundred and forty-three miles from our current position. That's well within the range of the GENDYN weapon, sir."

"What about Vampire One?" asked Cummings.

"Much less, sir," said the XO. "New York is closer to us than Washington."

"Mr. Jerome, engage both targets when they are on a downward path and have reentered the stratosphere," said Cummings. "Engage when they are at fifty miles from their respective points of impact."

"Aye, aye, sir," said Jerome.

"Anything you need from this end, son?" Cummings asked.

"You may want to slow this bad boy down just a bit, Captain," said Jerome. "Bein' bounced around ain't gonna help me none, sir. And if it's not too much trouble, sir, could someone bring me a Coke?"

"XO, slow to fifteen knots," said the Captain. "Someone bring that kid a goddamned Coke. And someone go to my cabin and bring me my shirt and shoes. I don't particularly care for commanding this four-billion-dollar pride of the U.S. Navy in my skivvies."

It was at that moment he considered retirement, once this entire drama had been played out.

"Aye, aye, sir," two crew members called out, as they scrambled to comply.

It was 5:30:01 AM, EST.

"Gennady, the *Righteous Hand* has just launched both of her nuclear weapons, and she is in the process of removing herself from the array that brought them here," said Captain Andropov. "Plot a course to intercept once she turns, and open torpedo doors one and three. Close to one thousand yards."

"Yes, Captain Andropov," said Gennady

The *Cheetah* moved forward silently in the darkened waters of the North Atlantic and prepared to attack.

It was 5:31:07 AM, EST.

Target Vampire One streaked downward at Mach 5.

As it approached a position fifty-one miles above the Financial District of Manhattan, J-Cubed fired the weapon.

"Missed, sir," he said casually, as though Captain Cummings sat at the console near him. "Laser went high and to the left. A bit less influence by gravity than I anticipated."

It was 5:31:15 AM, EST.

Vampire One was now less than forty-two miles above its detonation point.

"Sorry, missed again, sir," said Jerome. "Low and to the right. Overcompensated a hair too much."

"Son, that missile is descending at a rate of one mile per second," said Cummings. "That means every time you take a sip of that goddamned Coke, we lose a mile or more in which to conduct this mission. Hit the fucking target!"

The Captain of the *Monsoor* as he looked at the ceiling and shook his head. He had never felt as helpless in his entire career. He waited for only nine more seconds.

It was 5:31:24 AM, EST.

"BOOM!" yelled Jerome, just as he did when he downed alien spacecraft in his small bedroom in Alabama.

"Mr. Jerome …," said the Captain.

"Vampire One is toast, sir. Locking onto Vampire Two now."

It was 5:32:09 AM, EST.

"BOOM!" yelled the seaman again. "Captain, I'm happy to report that I destroyed Vampire Two with the first shot, sir. This equipment is really cool, by the way, sir. Any time you need me to do this again, just give me a call."

"Thank you, I'll keep that in mind," said the Captain. "Great job, son."

"Thank you Captain," said Jerome. "Can I call my mom and tell her I saved the world, sir?"

"No, you may not," said the Captain. "This exercise is classified."

"Understood, sir," said Jerome.

"XO, I want you to notify the Naval Warfare Department about what's just happened here," said the Captain, "and make sure we tell them the launch position of that submarine. Reverse course and take us back to the launch point ASAP. This won't be over until we locate and destroy that Iranian sub, and I really want to sink our teeth into her."

"Aye, aye, sir," said the XO.

"And I intend to write a detailed report, Tom," said the Captain, "about that new weapon designed by General Dynamics, along with my strongest possible recommendation that that kid of ours become an instructor as the weapon is deployed."

The *Michael Monsoor* turned abruptly to starboard and a new course as she increased to flank speed.

Time to find and kill the Iranian sub.

Captain Cummings sat down and let out a sigh. He looked at his XO appreciatively.

"You and I are dinosaurs, my friend," he said..

The XO nodded.

"Pretty damned big and dangerous ones, though," he said.

"BOOM", added the XO, and they both laughed.

It was 5:40 AM.

As the remnants of the towed array hit the ocean floor beneath her keel, the *Righteous Hand* accelerated and turned to her new planned course of 050. The depths of the huge Hudson Canyon would mark their exodus from these dangerous waters.

Captain Jhanjir Ghorbani was ecstatic.

Their mission was a success, and the mighty sword of Allah was about to lay waste two populous American cities. Striking at the head of the ugly beast, the American President in his cushy Oval Office and having him perish in an inferno, was to be the glorious reward for his crew's hard work and dedication.

In a few minutes, he would turn on the intercom and address them. Back home, he personally would present each of them medals.

"Take her down to three hundred meters, Asad," said the Captain. "Flank speed."

"Flank speed, set down degree angle at twenty percent, and level off at three hundred meters," said the XO.

It was 5:45 AM.

"Attention, crew of the *Righteous Hand*," he began, "this is your Captain speaking. Gentlemen, we have struck a mighty blow against the Americans, and a great victory is ours today. By now, their cities of New York and Washington are vast wastelands, and millions of these evil demons have perished. We now return home to Bandar Abbas and you will all be treated as heroes, I can assure you. Let us all …"

"Captain, torpedoes bearing 195, close contacts, range eight hundred yards and closing. They've acquired us, sir."

The *Righteous Hand* attempted to change course, but to no avail, nor were its countermeasures useful. Both Vyuga Starfish torpedoes found their mark, and the submarine erupted and broke apart.

As he drowned, Captain Ghorbani had no idea his role in this complex game was but of a pawn, easily sacrificed.

The *Cheetah* turned to port.

"Once again, good shooting, Captain."

"Thank you, Gennady." said the Captain. "Now we head for Sevastopol."

In the privacy of his cabin thirty minutes later, the Captain decided to speak candidly to his XO as he placed two small glasses on his desk and poured them each a Stolichnaya.

"Gennady, do you understand what's going on here?" he asked.

"Not completely, Captain," said Gennady.

The Captain downed his drink in one quick, fluid motion and poured himself another.

"Gennady, we've just meticulously followed our orders from Moscow and destroyed a submarine operated by one of the Russian Federation's allies," he said "Do you not think that strange?"

"Yes, Captain, I do," said Gennady.

"That dead Iranian submarine and her crew will remain our nation's escape hatch, Gennady," said the Captain. "They all had to die, and just as importantly, that sub's full complement of Starfish torpedoes had to erupt in the firestorm we created. There must be no proof and no survivors to argue with Moscow's contention that the Iranians sank the American Virginia Class submarine we destroyed. President Putin wants to make sure there is no one left alive to dispute that contention.

"I have an idea, Gennady. The Iranians are dead, but there is no way the Americans know that. I'm confident that they spotted the launch point when the *Righteous Hand* launched her missiles, and I'm equally sure that American submarines and surface craft are streaking toward that X on a map of the North Atlantic right now.

"We are sitting in an invisible Akula Class submarine, my friend, and we are armed with Starfish torpedoes, as was the Iranian boat. There is no logical reason I can imagine why we cannot, therefore, destroy additional American ships as they arrive. If Putin is to blame Iran for launching missiles at the United States and sinking whichever submarine we, in fact, sent to the bottom, why cannot he also explain away the loss of a few more American ships with the same logic?"

"Sir, our orders are to head immediately at flank speed back to our home base at Sevastopol," said Gennady.

"Screw the orders, Gennady," said the Captain. "We have this ripe plum on the tree in front of us, begging to be plucked. When we set sail in a few days and Vladimir Putin sees what we've done here, we will receive medals for our ingenuity and resourcefulness."

"But Captain Andropov, our orders are...." said Gennady.

"Enough," said the Captain with conviction. "Have our *Cheetah* maintain a position fifteen thousand meters north northeast of the *Righteous Hand*'s reported missile launch point, at a depth of two hundred meters."

"And then what, Captain?" asked Gennady.

"We wait," said the Captain.

It was 6:12 AM.

"Sir, we have a contact," said Captain Andropov's XO excitedly. "Looks like a probable American warship moving at high speed, at more than thirty knots. She's heading for the last reported position of the *Righteous Hand*, sir."

"Any signs of additional surface ships or submarines yet? They should be flocking to that dot on the map like sharks in a sea of blood by now," said Captain Andropov.

"No, sir. Just the one contact for now," said the XO.

"Plot us an intercept course, " said Andropov.

"195, sir," said the XO.

"Come to 195, full speed," said Andropov.

"Set new course to 195, full speed, set the boat at periscope depth," said the XO.

"Distance to target?" asked Andropov.

"About forty thousand meters, sir," said the sonar operator, "but I'm having a lot of difficulty maintaining contact. Since the American is traveling at thirty-three knots, her profile should be lighting up my console, but that's not what's happening, sir. Her profile is sometimes a ship, sometimes she is only the size of a small fishing boat. I don't understand what I'm looking at here."

"Is it our equipment?" asked the XO of their sonar operator.

"I don't know, sir," said the sonar operator.

"Run a systems check, now!" said the Captain.

It was 06:15 AM.
Shannon hung up the phone.

"Paul, get in here," she yelled.

Paul Van de Vere raced into her office.

"What is it?" he asked.

"I just received a call from Secretary Mabus," said Shannon. "He's been sitting on his people over at the Naval Warfare Department, and they just received a message from Ray Cummings, the Captain of the new Zumwalt destroyer *Michael Monsoor*. That damned Iranian sub slipped by everything we had and actually launched her two nuclear missiles. We were too late to stop them, Paul. But the *Monsoor* had a new developmental laser weapon on her deck that was scheduled for testing, and the seaman trained on it used it to blow those missiles out of the sky as they were just coming out of the ionosphere and were heading toward their targets."

"Laser weapon intercepts descending missiles? Sounds a lot like a video game to me, Shannon," said Paul. "At what, Mach 4 or Mach 5?"

"Five." said Shannon.

She was looking at him strangely.

"Why did you liken the use of this weapon to a video game?" she asked.

"Because it sounds like one, that's all," said Paul.

"The Captain of that Zumwalt destroyer, in selecting a seaman best suited to learn and operate the new equipment, did so because the kid was apparently extremely adept at video games," said Shannon.

"My God, I know that kid, Shannon," said Paul. "Not directly, but I'm also a Gamer and whenever his scores are posted on a game, no one can come close to what he's achieved. He's a legend."

"He's also now a hero, Paul," said Shannon. "SECNAV wants to bring him to the Oval Office and have the President give him a medal."

"Wow," said Paul. "So where is the *Michael Monsoor* now?"

"She's heading toward the launch point to search for the Iranian submarine," said Shannon. "and we have a couple of Virginia Class boats en route, as well. Don't know about any other resources. Secretary Mabus didn't elaborate about that, but I'll clarify later this morning."

Paul was silent. His focus remained on the nameplate perched toward the front of Shannon's desk.

"What is it, Paul?" asked Shannon.

"Let's assume I'm right about all this for a moment," said Paul, "and that it'll be determined in several weeks that the *North Dakota* was destroyed and sunk as a result of torpedo strikes to her stern area. That information should support my thesis that the Iranian sub did not sink the *North Dakota*, because had that been the case, torpedo hits to our submarine would have been toward her bow."

"Okay, go on," said Shannon.

"So that means there is a hunter-killer Akula in the area," said Paul, "and she actually torpedoed the *North Dakota*, not the Iranians.

"So now, the Iranian submarine is free to escape and will probably return to Venezuela for refueling. And when that happens and we see that sub once again in a berth at Puerto Caballo, I'm going to argue that we need to go in there and at least have our SEALs do a snatch and grab. We need to kidnap that Iranian Captain and perhaps a few other of his officers and bring them back for questioning. Our President will demand proof of any Russian involvement, and he'll want to know if that Iranian boat was the one that torpedoed the *North Dakota*. We can only do that through interrogation and a quick inspection of the Iranian submarine."

"Sounds like a plan," said Shannon. "But it needs to be on hold until the Iranian sub is reported back in Venezuela."

"It will never return, and that's the problem," said Paul. "By now, the Akula has probably sent that Iranian submarine to the bottom."

"What? Why?" asked Shannon.

"Because Putin doesn't like loose ends," said Paul. "If he ordered one of the Russian Federation submarines to sink the *North Dakota*, he'll want no possible proof to verify what they've done. Russia can ill afford us to parade that Iranian Captain into an interrogation cell and to have our SEALs verify his submarine has a full complement of unused Starfish torpedoes. Nope, the Akula has orders to sink the Iranian boat now, and it's probably already been done. And if that's true, that Russian silent killer will either be headed back to her home base at flank speed, or the other possibility exists that concerns me greatly."

"What's that, Paul?" asked Shannon.

"The Russians operate under the assumption they can blame the loss of the USS *North Dakota* and the launch of nuclear missiles completely on that Iranian submarine," said Paul. "With that in mind, why can't an Akula, completely invisible to our sonar, stick around and sink a few more of our warships and submarines, Shannon? They can so easily blame that action on the Iranians, too."

"So you think the *Michael Monsoor* and our Virginias might be in danger, and that an Akula waits to ambush them?" asked Shannon.

"Absolutely," said Paul. "That's exactly my concern."

"We'd better contact SECNAV now," added Shannon.

"When you contact him," said Paul, "ask Secretary Mabus if any of our sonar operators in the area picked up sounds that could be a ship or submarine breaking up and sinking, especially near the coordinates of the reported launch position. They may have to backtrack over their saved data, so ask them to concentrate on the first thirty minutes immediately following the missile launch times. If I'm correct, the Iranian made lots of noises in her death throes, Shannon."

As she picked up the phone, Paul said. "Tell Secretary Mabus and Naval Warfare there may very well be a highly unfriendly Akula in the area, Shannon."

She nodded as she dialed.

CHAPTER 20

April 3, 2028 … The North Atlantic Ocean, 0700 Hours

The Zumwalt Class Destroyer *Michael Monsoor* was to go it alone.

A copy of the message sent by Naval Warfare to the *California* and the other Virginia Class submarines heading toward the war zone had also been sent to Captain Cummings.

"Tom, read this," requested the Captain.

"An Akula may be out there?" asked the XO.

"Yup," said the Captain. "Apparently one of the whiz kids at Langley has this all figured out, and when the *California* confirmed her sonar operator heard sounds like a submarine exploding and breaking apart from a great distance, that was enough to confirm Langley's suspicions. At first, the sonar operator on the *California* thought those sounds might have come from an oil rig or more offshore drilling, but upon further review, it was decided it was more likely that noise was the Iranian submarine going down with all hands."

"And the conclusion at Naval Warfare is that an Akula did that to a submarine operated by Iran? This is nuts," said his XO.

"Actually, I see the logic in all this," said the Captain. "The *North Dakota* has been lost, and the original thought was that the Iranian sub sank our boat, which I doubt. It makes no sense to me that an older Iranian submarine, plodding slowly through the water, could somehow properly defend herself and sink the *North Dakota* coming at her from astern. And I agree with Langley on that point. It also makes sense that if they thought they could get away with it, the Russians would sink the *North Dakota* in order to enable the Iranian boat to launch her missiles."

The XO shook his head.

"So what's waiting out there for us is an invisible Akula," said the XO, "prepared to sink any and all U.S. Navy ships coming into this area?"

"That's the concern at Langley," said the Captain, "because the Russians can blame more attacks on us as having been initiated by that Iranian submarine, and that opinion apparently has enough weight with SECNAV to keep our Virginia Class boats from joining in the fight."

"Secretary Mabus made this call, Skipper?" asked the XO.

"Yes, this decision comes from the top," said the Captain. "So let's show them all what we can do best, XO."

"Aye, aye, sir," said the XO.

"Battle Stations," said the Captain.

A claxon began to sound as the *Monsoor* prepared for war.

The ancient game of death, between "mongoose" and "cobra," was about to begin. Snakelike and lethal, the Akula Class submarine Gepard was the cobra. It lurked quietly or moved gracefully in order to obtain the advantage and always prepared to strike in an instant. And on the surface, the highly maneuverable destroyer *Michael Monsoor*, with her powerful gas turbine engines was the mongoose, capable of lightning moves and well-prepared to join the battle.

"Sir, we're now ten thousand yards from the launch coordinates we recorded earlier," said a seaman.

"Sonar, do we have any contacts?" asked the Captain.

"Negative, sir," said the seaman.

"Slow to one-third, turn slowly to starboard, and continue that until we've gone full circle," said Captain Cummings.

"Captain, …" began the XO. He knew the inherent dangers in the Captain's orders. Their ship was being made an easy target.

The Captain raised up one hand to silence his XO.

"We need to determine the position of the Akula, Tom," he said. "And the only way to do that is to become a target."

Their lazy arc continued without incident.

"Set a course for the exact reported position of the Iranian sub when she launched those missiles," said the Captain, "and we'll do this circle again."

The XO gave his Captain a look of concern at their ship becoming a target, but he complied.

It was 0730 Hours.

The *Michael Monsoor* was midway through her second slow circle, with the center as the precise coordinates of the Iranian sub's missile launch position.

"Sir, torpedoes in the water," yelled the sonar operator. "Distance twenty-three hundred meters, sir. And they've acquired."

"Do you have the position locked from where they were fired?" asked Cummings.

"Affirmative, Captain, and they're those super- Starfish, sir," said the sonar operator.

"Time to impact?" asked the Captain.

"Sixty-eight seconds, sir," said the seaman.

"XO, launch the ASROC in pattern 'Tango,' now!" the Captain shouted.

The pattern had already been mapped into the Anti-Submarine Rocket control panel, and the Fire Control Technician on the bridge of the *Monsoor* hit a red button.

The young seaman hit the ASROC launch button, and he made a humorless comment under his breath.

"This Bud's for you," he muttered.

"And for the *Missouri* and the *North Dakota*" added the XO.

"Let's show those Starfish torpedoes our stern!" said the Captain. "Left full rudder, come to course 320, flank speed!"

The XO repeated the order, and the destroyer responded with quickness and extraordinary agility.

The RUM-139D version of the ASROC drops a torpedo into the water, which then acquires a hostile submarine and sinks it. That version of the weapon requires the torpedo's sonar system to locate and lock onto the target. Captain Cummings elected not to use that weapon, however, since he reasoned the torpedo's sonar would fail to locate the submarine, as was the case with the more sophisticated sonar system on the *Monsoor*.

Instead, the *Michael Monsoor* launched an ASROC Rum-139E, which is armed with a nuclear warhead.

Upon impact, the weapon descended to a depth of one hundred feet, somewhat below normal periscope depth for an Akula, and the ASROC then erupted. The weapon had been guided to an ocean impact point one hundred yards directly in front of the Akula's reported position, which allowed the submarine to glide directly into the path of nuclear detonation.

Immediately after she launched torpedoes at the destroyer, the Akula quickly turned to port and increased her speed to twenty knots.

The nuclear explosion less than three hundred yards away from her position crushed the starboard side of the submarine's hull, and the destruction was so massive that she immediately began to take on water and sink. Her hull gave way at a crush depth of five hundred meters, and she went down with all hands.

Captain Andropov's last words were to his XO.

"Gennady, the Americans have killed us. I didn't expect them to react to our presence with a nuclear weapon. Let us hope and pray that our Starfish provide us ample vengeance."

As the destroyer headed away at nearly thirty-five knots, the sea behind her suddenly exploded violently. A water plume at least four hundred yards high filled the morning sky, and a moment later, the shock wave from the underwater nuclear blast caught up to her and tossed the stern of the *Monsoor* up and out of the water briefly.

She recovered her course quickly.

The massive shock wave disabled one of the pursuing torpedoes. Its motor was silenced, and it gradually sank into the depths. But the other Starfish reacquired the destroyer and pressed on at nearly double the top speed of the destroyer.

"Only one torpedo tracking us now, sir," said the sonar operator. "The second appears to be out of commission."

"Good," added the XO.

"Time to impact?" asked Captain Cummings.

"Forty-nine seconds, sir," said the seaman.

"How much distance has that Starfish traveled from its initial launch position, sailor?" asked the Captain.

"Right at six miles, Captain," said the seaman.

The XO glanced at Captain Cummings. His face told the story they both knew … a modern Starfish has a range of just over thirty miles, and it was going to be impossible to outrun it.

"Release countermeasures, come to course 015," said the Captain. The crew of the *Monsoor* responded instantly. "Tom, we need to try something, pronto."

"What are your orders, sir?" asked his XO.

"That new Tomahawk we have onboard is designed to intercept enemy warheads," said Cummings," so let's see if one can figure out the warhead coming at us is underwater, closing at seventy miles an hour."

"Sailor, put in the coordinates of that Starfish and its course and speed into the Tomahawk computer," demanded the XO.

"Done, sir," said his subordinate.

"Launch Tomahawk, now!" said the Captain

The seaman pressed a button.

"Tomahawk away, sir," he said.

"Time to the Starfish impact with us?" asked the Captain.

"Thirty-seven seconds, sir," said this seaman.

"Turn to course 355," said the Captain.

"Sir," said the XO quietly, "that will put the incoming torpedo directly astern of us."

"That's right, XO," said the Captain. "If that Tomahawk misses, I want our stern laser cannons in a perfect shooting position to blow that damned torpedo out of the water. Make sure those two seamen are ready. They'll be our last line of defense"

"Laser cannons armed, manned, and ready, sir," assured the Fire Control Technician a moment later.

The Captain and XO left the bridge and went outside into the crisp morning air.

"Let's pray that Tomahawk doesn't decide we're a nicer target than that damned torpedo, Tom," said the Captain.

"My thought exactly, Skipper," said the XO.

They watched the missile arc and begin its return path. For one tedious moment they both thought it would continue to turn and return home to the destroyer with a vengeance, but the Tomahawk immediately located the Starfish and angled toward a computer-guided intercept point.

The explosion directly astern of the destroyer was massive.

As the Captain and XO returned to their stations, their sonar operator turned to look at them. A broad smile was on his face.

"BOOM!" he yelled loudly as he removed his headphones and tossed them in the air in triumph.

In this battle to the death, the mongoose had prevailed.

April 3, 2028 ... Over Wichita, Kansas, 0800 Hours

"Ms. Parks, I'm proud of you and your staff, and your extraordinary skills are clearly well-beyond your years. Not only did all of you at Langley, and in particular, this Paul Vander Vere you've mentioned on several occasions, sort this entire business out, but you remained at your posts, knowing that a nuclear missile was headed your way. You all have my sincere and deepest admiration."

"Thank you, Mr. President," said Shannon. She was seated in her office at Langley, and she had the call on speaker phone. "Good day, sir."

Air Force One continued to streak west. Its intended destination: Vandenberg Air Force Base near Lompoc, *California.* An eleventh-hour decision by insistent Secret Service personnel and the Secretary of Defense had been made to remove the Vice President and the President from harm's way.

The Vice President's plane had already landed in Chicago.

At Langley, once the call ended, Shannon looked up at Paul. He seemed unimpressed by the President's words of praise.

"Shannon, this entire mess is far from over," he said "Yes, it's true we destroyed two nuclear missiles launched by the Iranian submarine, but the mere fact they were able to actually launch them is a sign of success and will buoy their future attempts against us. They still have two more submarines in their navy, and Vladimir Putin can easily sell them additional ones. Any new submarine that Iran acquires can also be outfitted with stealth technology. I fear it's only a matter of time until we're doing a redo of what just occurred.

"Our navy can't track those submarines yet, at least until we're able to improve our technology, and we certainly can't see an Akula lurking in the depths somewhere, either. The Russians have a huge stealth advantage over us, and worst of all, they know it."

"You're right about that," said Shannon. "Our entire naval establishment is really unnerved about a complete inability to locate and track Russian Federation submarines, from SECNAV on down. The other thing you should know is this. Before I put the call from the President on speaker phone, he mentioned that when Air Force One returns to Washington, the day after tomorrow, he's going to ask the Congress to declare a State of War between the United States and Iran. Perhaps that will dissuade other nations, including Russia, from assisting them."

"It won't, Shannon," said Paul, "and we both know that. But at least we now have an established course of action if Iran continues to build nuclear weapons facilities."

"Right," said Shannon. "It'll be the Sunday morning B-21 show, starring MOP-2s and friends, again and again and again."

"If it's going to be that simple," said Paul, "I wouldn't be worried. It's an incensed Vladimir Putin who concerns me. If he decides to provide Iran with nuclear warheads directly, they can arm again very quickly, wipe out Israel, and perhaps their next wave of submarines may just get through. We were very lucky the *Michael Monsoor* was on station where she was, and we may not be as fortunate next time."

"So what do you suggest, my incredible MIT hotshot?" asked Shannon.

"It's funny you addressed me like that, Shannon. Remember how you were annoyed when that character Rahim kept referring to you as 'CIA Chick' or worse?"

"Of course, I remember every word that little worm said to me in that interrogation room," said Shannon. "And I also vividly remember how that piece of shit killed two of our colleagues, including Marcus. He was like a father to me, even though you couldn't stand the man."

"I didn't particularly care for his crudeness," said Paul, "but I did have great respect for his knowledge and abilities."

"So why are you bringing up that scumbag, Rahim again?" asked Shannon.

"Where is our friend Rahim now?" asked Paul.

"Now that the Israelis were done with him, we're tossing him into a dark cell at Guantanamo," said Shannon. "Why are you so interested in him, anyway?"

"It occurs to me that the loose cannon in all of this is the guy named Putin in the Kremlin," said Paul. "I think we should brainstorm over the next few weeks about how to take him out. Sorry, in the vernacular of this building, we should send him a job termination notice, with 'extreme prejudice.' " Paul chuckled and shook his head.

"Your cynicism is out of line, mister," said Shannon. "There is protocol and tradition here, and those traditions are to be respected."

"Sorry … really," said Paul. "Getting back to our buddy, Rahim … perhaps we can turn him and send him to Moscow. If he can get near Putin, perhaps meet him personally …"

"You're thinking of mounting an operation to assassinate Putin?" asked Shannon.

"No," said Paul "But I *am* thinking about an operation to have someone terminate his employment in the Kremlin with 'extreme prejudice.' "

Paul grinned broadly. Shannon frowned, but Paul continued, unintimidated.

"With Putin out of the picture," said Paul, "I think the Russian Federation would cease their clandestine antics in Iran. And Rahim, or someone like him, needs to be the one to carry out that mission. Plausible deniability is what it's all about, as you very well know."

"Paul, I've had entirely enough of this for the day," said Shannon, "or for the past several days, I should say. And as far as Rahim Husayn Tabataba'i is concerned, there is no damned way that slug is ever going to be put on the street again and have a chance to bolt, at least not while it's my foot on the gas pedal around here."

"Speaking of him, by the way," asked Paul, "whatever happened to Colonel Sassani and his sister, Nousha? The last I heard they were being kept in Tel Aviv through all this turmoil."

"They've been given asylum here," said Shannon, "and I'm not at liberty to say more about their location. But they're off the grid someplace out west, living simply and at peace. The Colonel did us all a great service by revealing Iran's nuclear agenda, and we owe him a great deal. Word is he and his sister are very happy."

"Hope you're as happy as they are someday," said Paul. "You give everything within yourself to this nation every day, and you certainly deserve tranquility one fine day."

"Maybe when I retire," said Shannon, "in another thirty years, bud."

She looked at the clock on the wall.

"I'm leaving for the day at 1600 Hours," she said. "I'm going home, I'm going to take a long hot bath, and when that's over I expect to walk into the bedroom and see you lying there awaiting me."

"Is that an order, boss?" asked Paul.

"Yes, it is," said Shannon.

"Always at your service, ma'am," said Paul.

As he stood and was leaving her office, Shannon said something that stopped Paul in his tracks.

"Hey, MIT guy," she said, "I love you fiercely, you know, and thank you for putting up with me."

He turned.

"I don't merely tolerate you, Ms. Parks," said Paul. "I want to someday learn how to paint, so that I might replicate your beauty and memorialize your perfect face for generations upon generations to admire. And I hang on your every word, for I am unaccustomed to being in the presence of a goddess. I love you fiercely, as well, Shannon, and I am honored that you have feelings for one as insignificant as I."

Paul turned again and left her office.

He's a genius AND a poet, thought Shannon.

"And you're also damned good in the sack," she said out loud, but very softly. "Well, just wait until tonight, buddy."

Shannon now turned her attention to the ton of papers scattered across her desk.

"Candles, wine, cheese and thou," she muttered.

April 3, 2028 ... Tel Aviv, Israel, 1830 Hours

Prime Minister Ben-Gurion was the first to speak.

"It appears that Vladimir Putin has awakened the sleeping giant, gentlemen, at least that's the reference the President of the United States used three times in our conversation earlier this afternoon. He was referring, of course, to the famous comment made by Admiral Yamamoto after Japan's attack on Pearl Harbor. I would describe my current mood as 'cautiously optimistic.' With the Islamic Republic of

Iran's nuclear weapons destroyed, their nuclear weapons plants in ruins, and a hard-nosed ally in the Oval Office prepared to rain down bombs on any further construction attempts by Iran, there is a ray of sunshine in this room."

Joshua Ben-Gurion looked at the other men seated on either side of him, men he trusted implicitly, and he smiled. He loved these men.

"Whatever your part in this might have been," he said, "I'm proud of your efforts on behalf of this nation," he added.

"I agree with your cautious optimism, Joshua," added General Eisenkot. He actually sounded to be in somewhat of a good mood to the astonishment of the others at the conference table. "With the American commitment to use their B-21 long range bombers to destroy any and all future Iranian nuclear facilities long before they become operational, it seems that Iran will no longer be able to mount a nuclear offensive against our nation. And if the United States moves ahead with a Declaration of War against Iran, the maniacs in Tehran may actually tread lightly in the future."

Shlomo Mizrahi looked concerned.

"As always, I keep in close contact with Shannon Parks of the CIA," he said. "Her concern is not of Iran's capabilities, for we all seem to agree those capabilities are now highly limited, but she expressed grave concerns about an unpredictable Vladimir Putin in our conversation earlier today.

"The Russian Federation has lost two large warships and an Akula Class nuclear submarine in recent engagements with the U.S. Navy, and an additional three hundred scientists and engineers during the bombings at Natanz. Shannon and I agree that it is neither in Putin's demeanor nor DNA to limp quietly into a corner and lick his wounds. Langley fears he may decide to ship nuclear weapons directly to the Iranians and bypass the need to build more nuclear weapons plants there. But at least for the moment, I agree, we have a great victory to celebrate, and we no longer have to utilize Plague Ten as our last desperate weapon of choice."

Joshua Ben-Gurion sighed.

"I concur, Shlomo," he said. "Dr. Bachman, you are hereby directed to lock our canisters of Plague Ten in your laboratory's underground vaults, and General Eisenkot, the plan to launch a biological attack on the Arab States no longer needs to be executed."

"At this time …," added Shlomo Mizrahi rather ominously.

"Sadly, the Americans are highly unpredictable," said Ben-Gurion, "and every four or eight years their focus and policies shift like the winds blowing around the sands of the Negev. One minute they will be with us, and as their priorities change, so may their dedication to our alliance. What if the next American President is unwilling to continue B-21 strikes in Iran? These are questions that keep me awake at night, gentlemen."

"But if they formally declare war on Iran…" said the General.

The Director of Mossad cast a weary glance from face to face.

"Tensions may continue, but actions may not," he said.

The Prime Minister gave the Director a questioning glance.

"As you know," he said "I've spent many sleepless nights wrestling with the dilemma of having to save the State of Israel by perpetuating another holocaust, and I thank God that the decision to necessarily move forward with the release of Plague Ten has been averted."

The General rolled his eyes.

"And just in time," he said.

"Mr. Prime Minister," said Dr. Bachman, "your instructions to lock up the Plague Ten virus — forever, we hope — will be followed precisely. That process will take my staff perhaps a week. And as an additional measure of security, once Plague Ten is under lock and key, the keys to our vaults will be turned over to Director Mizrahi at Mossad for safekeeping."

"Thank you, Dr. Bachman," said Joshua. "And Doctor, I'd like to give you a personal apology about something. In a highly impassioned moment, I referred to us as the 'New Nazis because we were about to embark on a mission that was genocidal in nature. It was a rash statement directed at a man who has given decades of his life in a laboratory with but one thought in mind, to preserve the State of Israel through whatever means may be necessary. I would like to personally applaud your efforts on behalf of this nation and for your patriotism. I also hope I did not offend you by that caustic remark."

"Thank you, Mr. Prime Minister," said Dr. Bachman.

He was embarrassed by the attention, and knew his dedication was no greater than that of the others seated around him.

The remainder of their meeting went well, and the four most powerful men in the State of Israel joked and laughed as only old, dear friends can do.

April 4, 2028 … Tehran, Iran, 1130 Hours

As he spoke, beads of sweat formed on his balding head, and one droplet slowly descended toward his right eye. It lingered for a moment on an eyelash and then fell to the floor. General Firouzabadi did not expect to survive this meeting, and every word he uttered sounded like a hollow excuse.

The Minister of the Iranian Intelligence Directorate, Mahmoud Alavi, listened to the General with growing impatience.

"General, may I remind you that we have lost four of our fleet of six submarines," he said, "lost with all hands I might add, two coastal defense frigates in the futile pursuit of Arshad Sassani's sister, four sophisticated fighter aircraft, and our two most modern and expensive nuclear facilities have also been destroyed, presumably beyond salvage or repair. Even a novice, armed with those facts, would deduce that your efforts to damage the will of the Americans and to kill Jews are a complete failure."

"Yes, Minister, we have suffered great loss of life," said Firouzabadi

"You sound as though you mourn our dead, General!," said Alavi "Do not do that! These brave men who died in pursuit of a most noble cause are martyrs. MARTYRS, do you not understand? There has been no loss of life here … only glory."

The General stared at the floor.

"Yes, Minister," he said. .

"General, look at me," said Alavi.

Firouzabadi raised his head and looked into Minister Alavi's eyes. They were on fire with an all-consuming passion.

"General Firouzabadi, inform the Russians we are unafraid of America's bombs or their other weapons," said Alavii. "Inform the Russians that we are unafraid of Israel's biological weapons, as well. Inform the Russians that to the very last martyr in our Holy Republic, we will carry the sword against the Jew and the infidel, until their blood is up to our knees. And you, my dear and loyal General, you are to convince our Russian Federation loyal allies to support us, through these most trying times. Create and this time properly execute a plan. We must, at all costs, kill our enemies and lay waste to Israel."

"Yes, Minister," said the terrified General.

A moment later, he was dismissed.

General Firouzabadi walked hastily to an exit, and he dared not breathe until his limousine was moving and surrounded by other vehicles on the busy thoroughfare.

During the short drive to his headquarters, the General thought of ways to please Minister Alavi, and he began to map out a plan.

CHAPTER 21

"Haste me to know't that I, with wings as swift as meditation or the
thought of love, may sweep to my revenge."
Act I, Scene V
The Tragedy of Hamlet
William Shakespeare

April 5, 2028 … Tel Aviv, Israel, 1830 Hours

There was a knock on their door.

The man shrugged as if to ask of his wife, "Are you expecting anyone?" Her look indicated that she was not. He rose from the dinner table and opened the front door.

"Dr. Yoachim Bachman?" said one of the two men in uniform.

"Yes," he whispered. He knew what their presence meant, and his heart nearly burst in anguish.

"May we please come in, sir?" said one of the uniforms.

"Yes, of course," said Yoachim. "Esther, we have company, dear."

The two IDF officers were ushered into the home's small living room and they sat together on a well-worn sofa bursting with fading burgundy and white flowers.

They remained at attention, although now seated.

Esther Bachman walked into the room, and when she saw the two officers seated there, she had to reach for and grasp the arm of a Queen Anne chair to prevent from collapsing. Her husband gently urged her to sit, as he then did in the other matching chair.

"Doctor and Mrs. Bachman," began one of the officers gently, my name is Colonel Ariel Schreiber, and this gentleman is Major Eli Cohen, your son's Brigade commanding officer in the IDF. There was an encounter earlier today near Gaza on the outskirts of Sderot, and three members of your son's platoon were casualties. We're here to inform you with our deepest regrets that Lieutenant Daniel J. Bachman was among those killed."

Esther Bachman clasped her hands together tightly on her chest as she began sobbing uncontrollably. Her husband began blinking rapidly to suppress his tears as he choked out a question.

"How did our son die?"

"Hezbollah was apparently involved," the Major explained, "and after our platoon had them pinned down and we were moving in, they suddenly counterattacked with Nasir self-propelled grenades. At that time, our people had inadequate cover, and three of our men perished. I am truly so very sorry, sir."

The two officers declined a cup of tea and soon left Dr. Bachman and his wife to mourn their son.

Well past midnight, he was awakened from a fitful sleep. Esther gasped and clutched at her chest.

"Yoachim, I need my nitro. It's in my purse," she added.

Yoachim hurried to the bathroom and then their closet. He searched in vain for her purse and the medication. It occurred to him that her purse might be in her car, and it was.

"Here, Esther, I found it," he said, desperately.

She didn't respond. He called 101 for an ambulance, and with roaring sirens it arrived a few minutes later.

The two young paramedics tried in vain to revive her.

A weakening heart and the loss of her son had taken their toll.

An hour later, Dr. Bachman carefully made himself a cup of tea. In the course of one evening, he'd lost his only son and his wife of thirty-seven years.

"For what?" he asked himself repeatedly.

He despised terror tactics and terrorists, but Hezbollah was not his focus that night. It was their weaponry that plagued him.

It was a Nasir self-propelled grenade launcher that had taken his precious son Daniel. And it was produced and furnished to terrorists by Iran.

The funeral of his son and later that same day, his wife, were attended by many, including members of his staff, his colleagues at Technion, and also the Prime Minister of Israel, who gave moving addresses to those gathered at both ceremonies. Shlomo Mizrahi, Yaakov Rafaeli and several others of Mossad were also there, as were friends and Dr. Bachman's two older daughters and their families. He didn't hear a single word, however sincere. His mind was pacing, quite patiently, until the hideous day ended and he was once again finally alone.

It surprised everyone that Dr. Bachman was back at work in his laboratory the very next day, and his ability to concentrate astounded them all. Unknown to them, however, his focus had changed.

Two tedious days went by.

April 9, 2028 … Tel Aviv, Israel, 1030 Hours

He dialed a number at Israel's embassy in Bern, Switzerland.

After two transfers, the call was connected to his cousin, Reuven.

"Yoachim, is that you?" asked Reuven. "I heard the terrible news about Daniel and Esther, and I'm so very sorry, cousin."

"Yes, yes, and thank you for the sincere expression of sympathy," said Yoachim. "I know your thoughts and prayers are with us here. I want to send you something, but I must tell you in confidence that it's not for you. I ask that you just act as an intermediary in this and follow my instructions precisely to forward the package on. Can you do that, please? You must trust me."

"Of course," said Reuven. "Anything for you, Yoachim."

Yoachim sent the package via FedEx next day air that afternoon, went home earlier than usual, and later opened a bottle of wine he'd been saving for a special occasion. Dr. Bachman settled into one of the Queen Anne chairs, set his glass of wine and the bottle on a small table beside it, and opened his well-worn copy of the Torah.

It took him a moment to find the passage he sought.

With the Torah opened to Deuteronomy 32:41, he raised his glass and read the brief passage aloud in defiant Hebrew. The words were spoken as sharpened spears defiantly thrown at the setting sun.

The ancient passage stated, "I will render vengeance to Mine enemies and reward them that hate Me."

"For the Sons and Daughters of Israel," he added as he drained the glass and poured himself another.

April 10, 2028 … Bern, Switzerland, 1100 Hours

The small package arrived precisely on schedule at the Israeli embassy at Alpenstarre 32. Reuven followed instructions and removed the contents from the original meticulous wrapping. Inside was another box, labeled quite professionally. It had official Rolex SA markings all over it and was strangely addressed to someone in Iran … General Hassan Firouzabadi at his headquarters in Tehran.

He hesitated, thought he should take this box to the Mossad station chief in Bern, but he ultimately decided to follow his cousin's directions and ignore his better judgment.

He brought the package to a FedEx office on his lunch hour and paid to have it shipped to arrive the next morning.

"It is done," he reported later in a brief phone call to Tel Aviv.

"Thank you, Reuven. Enjoy your Passover meal with your family tomorrow, my dear cousin." As they said their farewells, Reuven sensed that Dr. Bachman seemed in good spirits.

"Where will you be tomorrow evening, Yoachim?" asked Reuven.

"I've been invited to my elder daughter's home, thank you," said Yoachim. "What's left of our family will gather there and thank God for sparing us and allowing Moses to lead us into the Promised Land."

Yoachim Bachman slept fitfully that night, because he knew full well his role should not be the one he now played. He prayed his actions were not misguided as the wheels now set in motion could no longer be reversed.

Somewhere, in the recesses of his mind, he recalled bits and pieces of a quotation about absolute power. He hoped he was to somehow be an instrument, rather than merely a victim of his own personal demand for justice.

Near dawn, Yoachim pictured Moses, leading those around him to safety.

April 10, 2028 ... Washington, D.C., 1100 Hours

The Yoshino cherry trees were in full bloom, quite abnormal for that late in the season, but they were spectacular nonetheless.

Their car entered Arlington National Cemetery, turned a few times, and slowed to a stop along Roosevelt Drive.

Captain Peter James Donoghue exited the front passenger seat of the dark blue sedan and opened the rear door on his side of the car. He was in full dress uniform, as was their driver. Ray Mabus, Secretary of the Navy, exited the vehicle and walked around to the other side of the car. He opened the other rear door, and Shannon Parks stepped out as he offered her his hand.

"Thank you, sir," she said.

Captain Donoghue took a step forward.

"May I assist you and carry the wreath, ma'am?" he asked.

"Thank you, but no," she insisted. "This is to be my journey."

It had been a simple task to allow them to park there for a few minutes. A call from the President to the right person accomplished that with ease. After her meeting in the Oval Office, she had been given the option of taking a few weeks off, or longer if she preferred, but Shannon respectfully declined the kindness.

Instead, she asked permission to simply do this.

They walked.

A delicate metal easel had been set up in front of the Tomb of the Unknown Soldier, and Shannon took the last few steps forward alone. Ever so gently, she placed the wreath on the easel and stood there for quite some time. When she turned to face her two patient companions, her tears flowed without pause.

Later, when she attempted to describe that moment to Paul Vander Vere, she could not be sure if she had been standing there to thank the thousands upon thousands of silent dead for their heroism or if she was praying that they might forgive her.

That evening, in each other's arms, they were at peace. And for the moment, a holocaust of epic proportions had been narrowly averted. A simpler world seemed within their grasp.

It was 6:11 AM. Shannon was already awake with her head on Paul's chest and a leg draped over his torso. Shannon listened to his quiet breathing for a while, and as she was about to reach down and playfully awaken him, her cellphone began to buzz. She reached for it as she sat up.

Paul stirred as she said, "Shannon Parks here."

She listened for a few seconds and spat out, "Son of a bitch!" as she tossed the phone over her shoulder in complete disgust. It landed on the bed a few inches from Paul's face.

"What?" he asked.

"Goddamit!" She shouted and hit the nightstand with an open palm.

"Get dressed," she said.

As Shannon stormed toward the bathroom, her words trailed behind her.

"Rahim was transported to a plane that was to take him to Guantanamo," she said.

Paul stood and followed her.

"What happened?" he called out..

"He escaped," yelled Shannon through the hissing noise of the shower.

April 11, 2028 … Tel Aviv, Israel, 0630 Hours

Dr. Yoachim Bachman was already awake, showered, and dressed. He sat in silence, and stared into the cup of tea on the table in front of him.

His wife Esther's face seemed to form in the milky fluid, and their three decades as husband and wife flashed through his mind, a kaleidoscope of enchanting and beautifully vivid memories.

The image of her face suddenly faded and was replaced instead by fleeting images of his precious son.

Yoachim began to cry. His tears dampened his tea as if they were the drops of wine that symbolize the plagues of Egypt in the traditional Passover ritual.

It was 0900 Hours.

Dr. Bachman sat through a well-attended Passover service but didn't hear the words or incantations. Later, he sat until darkness slowly began to envelop his silent home.

As the afternoon hours continued to pass, he remained in a dream-like state, and he prayed repeatedly for forgiveness with his eyes tightly closed and wet. He suddenly recalled something and looked up the entire quotation by Lord Dahlberg-Acton:

> *"Power tends to corrupt, and absolute power corrupts absolutely. Great men are almost always bad men, even when they exercise influence and not authority."*

The words rang true.

Yoachim Bachman felt they had been written specifically for him.

April 11, 2028 … Tehran, Iran, 1130 Hours

While those in Israel recalled a historic time and the ten plagues set upon their enemies by God, there was also this.

The FedEx driver dutifully delivered the package to the offices of the General Staff of the Revolutionary Guard on Dabestan Street in the heart of the Abbas Abad District of Tehran. He obtained the required signature and departed.

The man seated at the desk didn't quite know what to do, even though the package was innocently postmarked from a division of Rolex in Bern, Switzerland. Packages, any packages, were always of immediate concern, but to open something, perhaps a gift directed personally to the General, might infuriate him. Two other men were called in, and they decided to X-ray the package.

It was, indeed, apparently a gift or perhaps an item the General had ordered, and the security personnel finally relaxed and placed the package on General Firouzabadi's desk. Upon his return, he eyed it suspiciously, but his people assured him its contents were harmless.

He glanced at his watch.

In fifteen minutes others would arrive for their meeting, but his curiosity had been aroused. The General reached into a desk drawer and withdrew an ornate eight-inch blade. He sliced open the Rolex packaging and withdrew the carefully sealed clear plastic case.

Attached was a note in Farsi that said, "From your loyal friends at Hezbollah." He looked at the gold and silver watch on its pedestal within the case admiringly, and decided to try it on.

He slit open the case and placed the watch on his wrist.

It fit perfectly. Just in time, he placed the packaging materials in a trash container beneath his desk as the two Russian Federation nuclear scientists were ushered into his office.

"We have no nuclear weapons remaining, and our two weapons facilities and Bushehr and Natanz have been destroyed with great loss of life by the Americans and the Israelis, as you are both aware," said the General.

"Please remember that the Russian Federation has suffered great losses as well, General," said one of the scientists.

"I want you to go back to Moscow and ask President Putin to immediately supply us with nuclear warheads, gentlemen. This concept of building nuclear plants and weaponizing plutonium takes far too long, and as we've painfully discovered, our plants become bullseyes for American bombers. This path seems quite pointless. Send us the weapons we need, and we will uncrate them and launch against Israel the very next day."

"What of your plans to have submarines attack the United States homeland, General?" asked the scientist.

"The plan conceived by Captain Ghorbani is the most logical," said the General, "and we do have two more submarines in our fleet. Your nation can ship two more arrays and nuclear tipped missiles to Cuba in a few months and our submarines, we already know, can arrive in Cuban territorial waters undetected.

"The Americans will not field a gauntlet of Virginia Class submarines and surface vessels forever, so I'm confident the next round in this fight will easily go our way. I know President Putin will be thrilled with our ultimate success. Go now. You don't want to miss your flight."

The General glanced proudly at his beautiful new Rolex watch.

"We are scheduled to meet with President Putin late tomorrow," said the other scientist. "Someone from the General Staff will get back to you later this week, sir."

The three men shook hands and the scientists departed.

Later that afternoon, General Firouzabadi developed a fever. It escalated into the night.

The Aeroflot flight from Tehran to Moscow went smoothly, and as the two Russian scientists were at the baggage claim carousel in the crowded terminal, one turned away and said, "Excuse me, Sergei."

He felt a bit light-headed, and he began to cough.

THE END
of
THE TENTH PLAGUE

AUTHOR'S NOTE

Soothsayers, that's what we authors sometimes are.

Novelists who write fiction primarily dwell in the world of fantasy and write purely to entertain you. But this novel is a departure from the world of fantasy in that its basis is a single event, a pivotal and gravely dangerous moment in history. I truly pray that what I've written never occurs, but I fear that on November 24, 2013, a countdown began. On that date, the P5 + 1 entered into an agreement with the Islamic Republic of Iran which released billions in assets to that nation in return for an assurance that Iran would curtail nuclear development activities for a period of ten years. Under the terms of the "Joint Comprehensive Plan of Action" agreed to on that fateful day in 2013, the government of Iran will later have free rein to expand its nuclear development program after the ten-year term expires.

The novel is set in the year 2028, and Iran possesses nuclear weapons.

Finally, if you enjoyed my story, remember that Chickadee Prince Books, the publisher who brought this to you, is a small independent author-run press devoted only to quality work, and it needs your word of mouth to survive. Please tell a friend and write a review on Amazon and Goodreads of this book or other CPB books.

Alan N. Levy
December 2018